FRESHMAN WITCH

Supernatural Academy Book 1

INGRID SEYMOUR

KATIE FRENCH

SUPERNATURAL ACADEMY MAP

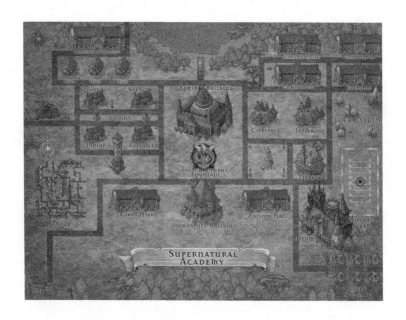

CHAPTER ONE

FALL SEMESTER
EARLY SEPTEMBER

I WAS NO DENTIST, but I was sure Trey's tooth was a goner.

It would really affect his ego, losing a front not-so-pearly white, but that was just the shitty life we lived, a life where teeth were a luxury.

Trey was telling everyone that the guy who punched him was so strong he must have been an actual werewolf, but that was also his ego talking. I'd seen the guy who decked Trey, and he'd seemed pretty normal to me—not that I was an expert at identifying Supernaturals—but I didn't imagine they stole hamburgers out of people's hands. Some of them probably could magically make juicy filet mignons appear out of thin air.

Besides, the only real Supernaturals I'd ever seen—a couple of registered warlocks in black cloaks despite the heat—had seemed pretty well-fed to me. Supers weren't all that common since only certain people had the required DNA to be one *or* become one, or some such nonsense. Not that I knew much about that. I was just a *Regular*, according to their terms.

The Supernaturals kept to themselves for the most part since their coming-out, so to speak, ten years ago. Sure, it took people a long while to actually believe it and by then, the hysteria had mostly settled down. So, there were witches and warlocks, vampires, werewolves, and more lurking among us. They were regulated, though, registered and under control. At least, that's what we were told on the news. And, I'd never seen anything to the contrary.

Plus, we didn't exactly get the news pumped into the abandoned warehouse Trey and I called home. We were too busy trying to survive to worry about who might be riding brooms or howling at the moon. Normal humans were way more dangerous, thus Trey's tooth predicament and my mission to save the day.

As I rode on my skateboard, tall buildings surrounded me, their thousands of glass windows sparkling under the scorching sun. Office workers rushed around like ants on their lunch break, suffering the heat that radiated from all the concrete that surrounded us. Summer in *Hotlanta* had to be as close to Hell as one could get this side of eternity.

The wheels of my board *clacked* against the concrete sidewalk as I swerved around one of the suits who worked at the Georgia Pacific Tower. Like usual, I got a dirty look from the man, a stodgy middle-aged dude with a watch so big and fancy it could probably feed Trey and me for six months. Suit types didn't take well to a homeless teenage girl on a skateboard. Go figure.

Ignoring him, I pushed with my right leg, speeding up, and turned toward the convenience store. When I got there, I hopped off, flipped the skateboard into my hands, and tucked it under my arm.

Head down, I walked into the store and stopped in front of the aisle with the small section of over-the-counter medicine. The smell of stale hot dogs from the roller grill saturated the air, reminding me I hadn't eaten lunch... or breakfast.

Ignoring my rumbling stomach, I perused through the medicine, searching for something to help Trey with his toothache.

The big bottle of ibuprofen was twelve bucks, so I picked a small one that looked like a tube of Chapstick. It only had ten pills in it, but maybe they would hold off the pain until he came to terms with his *loss* and decided to go to the Good Samaritan Health Center where dental students pulled teeth out for free. Also, the ten pills only cost three dollars, which the five-dollar bill in my pocket could actually afford.

A box of toothache gel caught my eye. I picked it up and checked the price. Five ninety-nine. *Damn.* Why was medicine so expensive?

My gaze darted toward the door, then the cashier. He was staring straight at me. *Crap.* My attention snapped back to the medicine boxes in front of me.

Out of nowhere, there was a twist in my gut, and I felt like throwing up. I winced, swallowing and rubbing my stomach. *Great.* All I needed was to get sick, too. But what did I expect from eating street tacos for dinner last night?

Another wave of nausea hit me, and a *whooshing* sound filled my ears. My chest tingled. I blinked, head swimming. The entire store started spinning.

I squeezed my eyes shut and took deep breaths, willing the vertigo away. It disappeared. Suddenly, I was fine.

What the hell? Was I having a panic attack? A seizure?

The electronic *ding-dong* on the door sounded as someone else entered the store. My eyes sprang open as I heard their steps in the aisle behind me. The new customer pushed all the way to the back, where the cold drinks were kept in glass-door refrigerators.

I glanced back and saw an old lady browsing for something to drink, her back to me. She wore a muumuu dress in a red, funky pattern that suggested a flower garden had thrown up on it. It stopped mid-calf and hung loose around her bent-over shape, looking more like an old curtain than any sort of clothing. Gray, wiry hair hung in thin strips down to her shoulders, and a pair of massive orange Crocs capped her feet.

As she stood there, she juggled a walking stick from one hand to another, her movements not bad for someone her age. I smiled. I bet she could fend of any pickpocket who tried to slip his hand into her double-wide sized purse. I was enthralled by her confident attitude despite her misplaced fashion sense and extreme age. That was what I wanted to be like at eighty, a badass old lady in orange crocs.

After a moment of pondering, she opened the fridge and pulled out a bottle of prune juice. I almost gagged. Nevermind. I definitely didn't want a future with prune juice in it.

Drink in hand, the lady turned on her heel and headed for the register. This time, she took the aisle in front of me. Her profile was all edges: hook nose, sharp jaw, jutting chin. A huge wart like a ready-to-burst tick clung to the end of her eyebrow.

Sensing my attention, she turned her two-toned eyes on me and bared a smile with a missing front tooth. I hunched over, lowering my head and wondering why one of her eyes had been so cloudy. Cataracts, maybe? The good feeling drained out of me completely.

Was that how Trey and I would look after a lifetime of homelessness? Half blind and toothless? Trey wasn't even twenty, and he was about to lose his first tooth. Would we end up drinking our food and buying prune juice to unclog our pipes? I shook myself out of my stupid thoughts. I tended to get carried away with my imagination at the worst times. Trey needed his medicine, and I was here daydreaming about how our pathetic lives would play out.

At the register, the old woman dug in her purse, her arm practically disappearing inside its folds. A minute later, she pulled out a zip bag full of coins and dropped it on the counter. The cashier stared at the bag, looking as if he was about to burst a blood vessel. He sneered at the old woman, clearly annoyed.

"It's money, ain't it?" the woman asked in a voice that seemed to rustle like dry leaves. "Ain't it?" she repeated in a louder tone, her head thrusting toward the man with insistence.

The cashier jumped back, eyes widening. "Get...get the hell out of here," he barked. "We don't serve your kind here."

The a-hole! Why was he being so rude?

The poor lady was constipated, and she had to put up with this guy's ignorant ass because she was homeless, like me. All the signs were there. I'd been living on the streets long enough to spot one of us.

Unsure of what made me do it—I seriously despised confrontations—I stepped out of the aisle and let the cashier have it.

"What the hell's the matter with you? No one taught you to be nice to your elders, you jack wad? Give her some respect." I gestured toward the old lady, my hand tightening around the ibuprofen as anger roiled in my chest. It was one thing to push around a teenage kid, quite another to disrespect a poor grandma.

He glanced at me, looking pissed. "You're... with her, aren't you? I knew you were no good!" He leaned forward, a hand reaching under the counter.

Uh-oh. Just the reason I'd learned to mind my own business.

Defensive instincts kicking in, I took two strides toward the lady and put a hand on her shoulder.

"Let's get out of here," I said.

At the touch, a crawling sensation traveled up my arm, feeling like the hairy legs of many spiders marching toward a trapped fly. I shivered as my ears started thudding with the beating of my own heart.

I jerked my hand away, unsure of what was happening to me.

The old lady's head swiveled in my direction as if in slow motion. Her good eye focused on me, while the other one stood blank. By degrees, her wrinkled skin turned gray, while her nose widened and flattened, warts sprouting all around it. Her lips blackened and doubled in size. Her thin hair grew fuller and longer until it resembled a lion's mane in shape and color. Small leaf-tipped branches sprang around her ears, and metal claws replaced her fingertips. She lifted her walking stick—now a gnarled, rotting branch—and shook it in my face.

Either I really was having a seizure or she was really a... a Supernatural.

I took a step back, my insides trembling like gelatin. What the hell was she?

"Oh, shit!" the cashier exclaimed, jumping as far away from the counter as he could, pressing his back to a glass display of cigarette cartons.

"I have holy water," he spat, reaching a trembling hand into his pocket. "I command you to go back to the pits of hell, evil spirit."

"I'm not a spirit, you ignorant human. I'm Yama-uba, and I'm hungry." She looked at me as if I were a medium-rare steak with a side of mashed potatoes.

Fear cracked across my body like a whip, and something inside me seemed to splinter. The nausea returned, and I felt physically ill again as if a flu virus from hell were threatening to fracture me in two. What was wrong with me?

Something like electricity sparked and crackled inside my chest as if I'd turned into a human taser gun, and I felt surrounded by an aura that was not my own.

The hag's face morphed from hungry to terrified. "Witch!" she cried out, pointing a knobby finger in my direction. Her mouth opened wide, sharp, filth-encrusted teeth forming an terrifying maw. She hissed.

She was afraid of *me*?

The cashier screamed.

I screamed.

Then I ran.

Ran like my ass was on fire. I pushed out the door, threw my skateboard to the ground, and jumped on top of it, my heart hammering out of control.

Like a horror movie, the old woman's face played on repeat inside my head, the image of her gaping mouth imprinted in my brain. Why had she yelled witch at me? And what was happening to my body? Forget Trey's tooth, I need a psychiatrist, an electrician or both.

"Stop right there!" a hesitant, trembling voice shouted.

I had no idea who was screaming or exactly what was happening until someone shoved me from behind, and I went rolling on the ground, my knees and elbow hitting the sidewalk as I spun two or three times. Pain blared from multiple scrapes and cuts, but the constant thrum of fear and nausea blotted everything else out. I was being attacked.

I sprang to my feet on my last tumble and found the cashier bearing down on me like a madman.

"It was all a trick," he said in a trembling voice, "so you could steal from me."

My eyes darted behind him, searching for the old woman. No one was there, not even inside the store. But what the hell? Why was this doucheface out here accusing me of stealing, instead of cowering inside?

I pulled my hands behind my back, desperately trying to figure out how to get rid of the medicine I'd accidentally taken with me.

As my luck would have it, the commotion attracted the attention of a Path Force police officer who was riding his bicycle in the opposite direction and, on a dime, turned and started pedaling toward us instead.

People stopped to gawk. Sweat trickled down my back as I clenched my teeth and tried to decide whether or not to run for it. I glanced around looking for my skateboard, but it had rolled under a parked car. My body ached and my ankle felt tweaked, if not sprained. Running wouldn't really work.

My throat closed off, panic climbing up from my chest. There was no way I could outrun a cop on a bike even in tip-top shape. I was screwed.

Too fast, the cop was there, hopping off his bicycle and demanding what was happening.

"She's a thief," the cashier said. "She stole from me, pulling some con with one of those Supernatural *freaks*." He pointed toward the store as he said the last word like a nasty slur.

"I'm not a thief," I said. I'd never stolen anything in my life, despite needing to many times over. This was all just a big misunderstanding.

"Young lady, did you steal something from this man's store?" the cop asked, glaring down at me from under his stupid bike helmet.

No, I didn't.

I knew I hadn't, but the proof was in my hand, behind my back. If only... if only I could get rid of it.

"I... didn't," I croaked. My chest tingled with that same energy from before, a sort of crackling burst of electricity that didn't hurt so much as light up every neuron in my body.

"Yeah, right. All you freaks are the same," the cashier said, crossing his arms over his sunken chest.

"Can you please show me your hands?" the cop asked, gesturing to them with one gloved hand.

Aware that there was no other alternative, I extended my hands forward, palms up.

To my surprise, they were empty.

CHAPTER TWO

FALL SEMESTER
EARLY SEPTEMBER

NEVER IN MY life had I been so happy to see the abandoned building where Trey and I lived. It was rat infested, leaky, and dangerous, but at least it wasn't the inside of a prison cell.

My mind reeled as I skated around raised sidewalk sections toward the cut in the fence that would let me in.

Where had the ibuprofen gone? I was still racking my brain about it. It was in my hand one second and gone the next. Had I dropped it in the commotion? That was the most likely scenario in a day gone completely crazy town.

But what the hell had been up with that hag and the strange sensation in my chest. I felt okay now, a little shaken up and achy from my fall, but my heart wasn't pounding, and I certainly wasn't feeling like my insides were wired directly into the mainframe.

The hag had called me a witch. Why?

I shook the thought away, willing myself not to dwell on the insanity I'd experienced. Maybe the ancient crack cocaine Trey and I had found downstairs a few weeks ago had gotten into my system even though I'd only touched it to throw it away.

Nope, that didn't make any sense. That was three weeks ago. But there was no logical explanation for anything that had happened today.

The only thing that *did* make sense was that I'd failed Trey. No medicine for his tooth. No pain relief. I was going to need to convince him to go to the clinic with me.

Good luck with that, my inner critic chimed in.

Trey was my best friend. Okay, my *only* friend since I left home two years ago. My mom had died in a car accident when I was thirteen and dear old dad had taken up drinking after that. He was never a peach before the alcoholism, but he became increasingly worse as the years wore on. Mom had been the glue of our family. She went to work, cleaned, cooked, took me to school, read to me at night, helped me with homework, and a million other things. Without her, our home fell apart, as well as my heart.

Dad stopped working and spent his days in his bedroom with the door shut, coming out only to grunt at me or stare into our nearly empty fridge. Then one day, he was just gone. I'd lived alone for three months until someone tipped off Child Protective Services. There was no way I was going into a foster home—I'd heard enough horror stories—so I took off before they came for me.

Trey had also run away from abusive parents at seventeen and had been on the streets since. Thank God we'd found each other in a shelter not too long into my new life as a homeless teen. Trey was tough and funny and great at scaring away creepy meth heads. Though he often took risks he shouldn't, putting his personal safety and wellbeing to the bottom of his priority list. He could be stubborn, bullheaded, and self-destructive when it came down to it, making me wonder if he had a bit of a death wish.

Thus, the punch in the mouth that put his front tooth in its current precarious position.

If he'd only reigned in his temper, for once, he wouldn't be facing the possibility of a gapped-tooth smile. He was meticulous about his appearance, even though we both had to bathe in public restrooms and the occasional shelter—fulltime shelter living would separate us, so it wasn't a long term option. Going tooth-less would really hurt Trey's self-esteem. How could he get an upscale beauty salon job, his lifelong dream, with a smile like that?

I sighed.

We both need a spa day, I thought wryly as I hopped off my board, gripped it, and lifted up the cut chain link, entering our humble abode.

Our abandoned building was pretty standard as far as build-ings like it went. It was five stories of boarded-up windows, *graffi-tied* walls and tumbling brick. Near the center of Atlanta, the crime was pretty bad, but our corner was relatively quiet, thanks to the string of empty buildings and the lack of any tourism, employment, or anything particularly interesting to steal.

And yet, we did have one thing going for us. Our buildings hosted many famous drawings, elaborate graffiti art paintings created in the early 2000s before the city put a stop to it. Some-times, artists and brave tourists drove by, marveling at the multi-colored drawings and tagged brick sections before speeding out, the stench of poverty sticking in their air vents.

Our building's claim to fame was one drawing by a semi-famous artist known as Gin Minister. His clever name accompa-nied his clever art. I walked past his now-fading painting of a trippy, psychedelic owl, the word "Never" spreading out on either side like wings.

Everything in my world lately was freaky and psychedelic, and I didn't even use drugs. Lucky me, not living up to the homeless stereotype.

I gave our Never Owl a pat as I walked along the side of the building, dodging Styrofoam take-out containers, a soggy pillow, and an empty ten-gallon bucket with the stench of human waste wafting from inside.

I definitely did not want to know what that bucket had most recently been used for.

Entering the side door where the particle board had been pried away, I called up so Trey knew it was me and not Homeless Randy who sometimes stopped by to harass us for cash.

"Trey, it's your favorite person!"

There was a shuffling down the hall and a head peered around the corner.

"Angelina Jolie? Is that you, here to adopt me? All my dreams have come true!" He pantomimed running toward me and then stopped, putting his hand to his chest in exasperation. "Oh, it's you, Charlie. Dream shattered." He flopped against the wall dramatically.

I chuckled despite myself. Trey was hilarious. Seriously, he was the reason I didn't spend my nights crying myself to sleep. He always had a joke or a biting quip that made me forget how damn depressing life was.

"Angelina has enough trouble on her hands without the likes of you," I said. "She and Brad broke up. Or was that a rumor?"

"Angelina can handle anything. Did you see her red carpet look at the 2009 SAG awards? If she can pull off a blue potato sack, and own it, she can parent the likes of me. What'd you get at the store?"

I set my skateboard down, my stomach churning with the knowledge that I had to tell Trey I'd failed him. I could already deduce from his muffled speech that his tooth was still hurting. I hated letting him down. Absolutely hated it.

"So here's the thing..." I dug my toe into a clump of paper trash, scattering loose pieces and hoping not to expose any pink rat babies like I had last week. "Something happened at the store."

"What? A sale on Flamin' Hot Cheetos? What could have possibly happened at the store?" His eyes narrowed. He could read me like a book.

How could I say this? That I ran into a hag that transformed into some weird tree person and she'd called *me* a witch? That I almost got arrested and made the evidence disappear just in time to save my ass?

Nope.

"The cops..." I started.

"Cops? Harassing you? I swear to God, the cops in Atlanta can kiss my—"

"Trey, it wasn't that. They thought I stole something. I guess I did. Accidentally. There was a lot going on. I just... walked out holding it. But then..."

He strode over and put his hand on my shoulder. "Babe, you don't need to steal for me. If you went to jail, who would stop the rats from taking over this place?"

I gave a sad smile. "Rat exterminator is not my only life skill," I murmured.

"But, love, it definitely isn't your fashion sense." He gestured jokingly to my ripped jeans, dirty Vans and thrift store T-shirt, then patted my arm. "It's okay if you didn't get it. It's fine. The tooth doesn't even hurt anymore. I think it's fixing itself. Like I'm an X-man or something. Or one of those warlocks." He twiddled his fingers as if casting a spell. "*Tootho repairo.*"

I froze. It was too unnerving to joke about magic after what happened. "That's not funny. Those Supernaturals are creeps." I thought about the hag and the way she'd reeled back from me.

"Okay, Miss Sensitive," he said lightly. "Now, come on. I panhandled enough at the college to buy us a Hot-and-Ready and a two-liter of Mountain Dew."

"I think Mountain Dew's slogan is 'The best thing for a busted tooth.'" I rolled my eyes. "Did you get water too at least?"

"Yes, yes, *mother*. Don't ruin my pizza party vibe. Can we do hairdos tonight? That would cheer me up at the disappointment of my dreams deferred as Ralph Waldo Emerson would say."

"It was Langston Hughes who said that, and sure. Hairdos it is."

Trey was an amateur hairstylist and, frankly, my tattered pony-tail could use the attention. Whatever it took to cheer him up after I'd failed him so badly, all as long as he didn't burn a hunk of my hair off like that time he used that curling iron he found in the trash.

He took my arm, strolling with me down the debris-filled hallway like we were a royal couple at the ball. We lived on the third floor, farthest away from the aforementioned rats, and high up enough to flee if anyone broke in. The fourth and fifth floors were waterlogged from the non-existent roof. Mildew and mold ran rampant. Not good for respiration.

Still, our situation wasn't particularly safe. A handful of times we'd been woken by people rifling through our stuff, the last one a few months ago where we literally had to punch our way out. Once, someone had set fire to trash on the first floor, nearly burning down the south half of the building before the fire department put it out. We spent a few weeks in shelters and church basements until we couldn't stand to be apart anymore and made our way back here.

Be it ever so abandoned, there's no place like home.

Up the creaky stairs we climbed. At the third floor, he pulled me down a hallway and into the open space we used as our apart-ment. When I rounded the corner, I could see the set-up he'd concocted.

A few candles flickered in the center of the room, creating a welcoming ambiance. On a blanket on the floor, he'd placed the pizza box and the soft drinks to make it appear like an outdoor picnic. Quiet, acoustic guitar music played from an old boombox that had been recently out of batteries. Newspaper garlands hung in loops from the rafters, reminding me of old

Christmas streamers my fourth-grade teacher used to hang as we counted down to the big day. He'd even cut paper hearts and butterflies and taped them to the walls to cover up the peeling drywall.

The effect was magical. Transformative.

"Oh, wow," I whispered, gaping. "How did you do all this?"

He smiled, proud of himself. "What can I say? I'm a god with paper crafts. And, really, I have a lot of free time on my hands. I'd been storing it for a few weeks, waiting for the perfect opportunity. And it seems like today is that day."

I strode in, feeling the weight drop off my shoulders. The windows glittered with candlelight. The mood was jolly and festive even though it was only September.

"Trey, this is really amazing."

He led me over to the blanket and popped open the pizza box, the gooey cheese and spicy pepperoni making my mouth water. It had been nearly a full day since my last meal and that pizza smelled to-die-for.

I sat beside my best friend, grabbing a slice. He poured me some Mountain Dew into my favorite Harry Potter mug, then filled his metal tumbler.

"A toast," he said, sitting cross-legged, and tossing his dark blond hair out of his eyes. "To the best friend a guy could have."

I held up my mug. "To the best interior decorator a girl could ask for. Thanks for making our night magical."

He winked at me and clinked his glass into mine.

"About that tooth," I said, but he held a hand up.

"I don't want you to worry about it anymore," he said dismissively. "It's going to be fine. I haven't been to a dentist in ten years and I haven't died yet."

"Trey," I whined, sounding very much like the mother figure he'd complained I was trying to be. Maybe it was because my mother died when I was so young that I was always throwing myself in her role. Or maybe I thought others should have the benefit of some mothering since it had been tragically ripped from me.

"Char, honestly. It's fine. I'd rather talk about something else. Oh!" He waved his free hand excitedly in the air. "I saw that guy I want to set you up with on the quad today. The one who looks like a young Heath Ledger."

I rolled my eyes. "Right. I'm sure he'd be super interested in all this." I gestured to my dirt clothes and waggled my shoulders in mock seduction.

"You're a babe, little sister. If he can't see beyond the superficial, he doesn't deserve you." His eyes glowed in the candlelight as he smiled at me. It wasn't just flattery, Trey meant every word.

There was nothing romantic between us. He always called me his little sister, and he sure felt like the big brother I never had. Both of us had such a great need for a family that we didn't want to mess up what we had with a stupid boy/girl relationship. As brother and sister, we could always count on each other no matter what, and we would never have to be alone again.

"The only person I need in my life right now is you." I leaned toward him, letting my head rest on his shoulder.

Suddenly, the building around us shook. The floor rattled, knocking the Mountain Dew over the picnic. The sound of breaking glass echoed up each floor until the windows around us exploded in sharp shards that pelted our bodies. Bricks tumbled and boards clattered as they snapped off wobbling foundations.

I grabbed Trey's hand, staring up at the swaying paper garlands. What was happening? An earthquake? In *Atlanta*?

Trey's terrified eyes locked into mine. This building couldn't withstand an earthquake. It was already structurally unsound. If we didn't get out of here, we'd die under a pile of rubble.

We didn't need words. Standing up, we tore toward the staircase.

Just as a group of people was running up toward us.

Trey and I skidded to a halt, clutching each other as we took in the invaders crowding the stairwell. Our only exit. But that wasn't the shocking thing.

They were Supers.

The first man wore a black trench coat to cover his body, but there was also something disguising his face, though he wore no mask. As I stared, I realized his features were shifting and blurring as if I was viewing him through a camera lens that could not find focus. What the hell was wrong with him? His nose and eyes were nothing but a blur.

The next person coming up the stairs didn't make me feel any saner. Beside Mr. Smudge Face was a *freaking werewolf*, though, at the moment, he was walking erect like a man. He was eight feet of muscle and fur, a snarling wolf snout and glaring red eyes. Large ears tilted toward me as his eyes narrowed. The growl that pushed between canine teeth sealed the deal.

We were going to die.

Behind him, a shimmering shape hovered, made entirely out of darkness, as if a human's shadow had separated from its body and was now hovering in my stairwell. But that was the least of our worries.

My heart pounded in my ears. I wanted to scream, to run, but I was frozen.

What the fuck? More Supernaturals.

I'd only ever seen two warlocks in my lifetime, but never a werewolf, nor hag, nor whatever else the other two were.

All looking like they were about to rip us limb from limb.

The man with the blurry face stepped forward, legs akimbo and arms out as if to snatch us up if we made one false move. Three of his fingers were missing on his right hand, letting me know this was not his first fight. I wanted to scream at him or give him a punch in the mouth, but I couldn't really pinpoint his features since they oscillated faster than a hummingbird's wings.

"Who..." he growled, his nasally voice vibrating as if it too were out of focus, "Who used magic?"

My mouth fell open. What were they talking about?

I tried to speak, to tell them it was all a big mistake, but then Trey attacked.

He ran toward them, his fists raised, a battle cry tearing out of his throat.

He was going to fight them just as he had done with that meth head. Only this group was not one strung-out, old man. These were three freaks of nature. They had magic.

"Trey, no!"

I reached for him just as the werewolf stepped forward and raked his paw through the air.

Claws hit Trey in the chest, two quick slashes. The sound of ripping fabric and flesh rent the air. Blood splattered the wall, hitting one of his precious paper butterflies. Staining it red.

Then Trey crumpled to the ground and didn't get up.

CHAPTER THREE

FALL SEMESTER
EARLY SEPTEMBER

I WAS ON MY KNEES, my hands on Trey's chest, blood seeping through my fingers. His eyes were open. Blank.

He's not dead. Not dead.

It was all a nightmare. I just had to wake up, and he would be humming a Janet Jackson song, folding his bedroll to keep the rats out of it.

"It was her," the man in the trench coat said, walking closer.

I kicked back, trying to pull Trey with me but he was too heavy, and I fell on my butt barely moving him an inch. The creature loomed over me, growing blurrier the closer he got.

"Yeah," he said with satisfaction, his voice vibrating as if he were talking through a running fan. "It was her." He extended a hand in my direction. "I can feel it now that she's truly spooked."

The werewolf growled deep in its chest, its red eyes growing brighter as it dropped its forepaws to the floor. It began walking on all fours, claws clicking as it advanced.

Feet scrambling desperately, I slid back, putting a few yards between me and the creatures. Trey. My gaze lingered on him for a moment. The freaks were after me, not him, so he was safer back there. I would come back to help him as soon as I could.

I rolled to one side, jumped to my feet, and ran. I hadn't gotten far when a sheet of darkness spread before me, shimmering like an oil spill. My heart leaped in my chest, almost jamming itself into my throat. A strange coldness slithered over my skin, worse than taking cold showers at the shelters. I clawed at my arms, trying to get rid of the awful sensation that now seemed to be filtering all the way into my bones.

"Don't struggle, girl," the rattling voice said from behind me. "It's useless."

Teeth clenched, I fought against the numbness that was spreading over me, but despite my efforts, it seeped into every corner of my body, like water soaking into dry soil.

The werewolf padded into my field of vision, leering at me with its evil eyes. I tried to take a step back, but my legs remained nailed to the spot. I tried again to no effect.

I was paralyzed.

What the hell was going on? Why couldn't I move?

A throaty laugh sounded to my left as the blurry guy appeared behind the werewolf, his face a smudge. "I told you it was useless."

He gestured down toward my feet. I followed his gaze to my shadow on the torn floor. It was dark with a well-defined shape, even though there was no proper light to help cast it. The shadow lifted a hand and waved at me. A gasp caught in my throat, my eyes darting to my raised hand. I hadn't moved it. Yet, my fingers were up in the air, wiggling as if saying *toodle-oo*.

It's just a hallucination, Charlie. A bad dream.

"I told you there was no reason to come," Smudge Face told

the werewolf. "Easy as walking through a ghost." He leaned into me, laughing. "The noobs always are. She doesn't even know how to use magic yet."

Repelled by his undetermined face, I tried to move away from him, but my muscles didn't respond.

"Probably never heard of a Shadow Puppet," he said, just as my arms and legs started moving out of control as if some master puppeteer were pulling on invisible strings. The movements felt real, even if *I* hadn't controlled them.

Maybe this wasn't a hallucination, after all.

Shit, I'm in trouble.

I tried to scream for help but no sounds escaped my throat.

He laughed again and so did the werewolf, if the convulsive semi-growls could be called laughter.

Suddenly, the werewolf went still, his ears perking up and tilting in the direction of the stairs.

"What is it?" Smudge Face asked.

The two supernaturals exchanged a glance and, as if they could read each other's thoughts, they sprung into action. The werewolf took off down the staircase, jumping over Trey. At the same time, Smudge Face turned down a side corridor and took off running. Against my will, my legs pumped, following. I fought to stop, but my body wasn't my own.

Oh god. Was I possessed? Was a Shadow Puppet some kind of demon? If it was, then I would need an exorcism, preferably before my head started turning in circles and I threw up pea soup all over myself.

My body jumped over a massive hole in the floor, landed gracefully on the other side, and followed Smudge Face to one of the few undamaged windows in the building. Coming to a halt, he put both hands on the glass and turned even blurrier, his entire body quaking on the spot. He stood like that for a couple of seconds, then the window turned to dust and fell to the floor like a curtain.

I couldn't even be surprised anymore. I was too terrified.

Wasting no time, Smudge Face climbed out the window and jumped. My body followed, even though I was fighting with all my strength not to, ordering my legs to stop. When that didn't work, I tried going limp, but it was useless. Next thing I knew, I was perched on the windowsill, looking down at a three-story drop.

I'd barely had time to process the fact that Smudge Face wasn't a bloody stain on the concrete below when I was hurled down to my doom.

A scream of terror filled my head.

Heart thundering in my chest, I closed my eyes. My hair flew in all directions, buffeted by the rushing air. I waited for the crack of bones and the pain, but there was only a slight *thud,* and then the pounding of my own two feet.

My eyes sprang open. I was running again, quickly catching up to Smudge Face.

Where were they taking me?

I tried to scream for help again, but my throat didn't obey my command.

Beyond the chain link fence, a black SUV waited, its engine idling. A perfect rectangle was missing from the fence, appearing as if it'd been cut with a laser, Smudge Face's handiwork, I was sure. Christ, what more was this guy capable of? I didn't want to find out.

Crashing sounds came from behind us. Smudge Face threw a quick glance over his shoulder, then sped up toward the SUV.

If they got me inside that car, I was screwed. Trey and I had heard enough stories about homeless kids disappearing after taking a ride with a stranger. No one heard from them again, and they probably ended up preserved and seasoned inside cans of dog food.

Well, I had no time for that. I had to get back and help Trey. I had to get him to a hospital before he... I pushed the thought away. He was going to be fine. He had to be.

Smudge Face ran through the hole in the fence. My body pressed forward, ready to go through it, too, the Shadow Puppet still controlling my every move.

I'd had enough. No creature, no matter how powerful, was going to make me leave Trey. I, Charlotte Rivera, wanted to, had to, *would* stay and help my friend.

Focusing all that I was into a single thought, I formed the word "stop" in my brain. I shaped it as carefully as I could and injected my pure, unadulterated will into it. Then I *thought* it as hard as I could.

STOP!

I came to an abrupt halt a few yards from the fence, my body trembling as if my own personal quake were raging inside of me.

Smudge Face opened the door to the SUV and hopped onto the driver seat. He glanced my way and had to do a double take when he found me frozen on the spot.

"What the hell are you doing?!" he exclaimed. "Hurry up. It's probably the Academy."

I clenched my teeth as my body lurched forward in a jerky step. The Shadow Puppet wedged itself harder into my very being. My other foot began to lift. I tried to keep it firm on the ground, but the force controlling my limbs was too much.

I was losing.

A snarl and a whimper came from behind. I wanted desperately to see what was headed my way, but I couldn't. Then, a massive furry body collapsed against one of the huge abandoned pipes Trey and I often used as a hiding place. The pipe broke—exposing its steel skeleton and falling apart in big chunks of concrete. Sliding down its side like a rag, the werewolf collapsed in a heap, twitched, then went completely still.

What the hell was tougher than a werewolf? I *did not* want to find out.

"Dammit, c'mon!" Smudge Face hissed through his teeth while the SUV's engine revved up.

My tenuous hold on my own body broke, and I staggered forward, arms windmilling. Quickly, the Shadow Puppet drove me toward the hole in the fence, and no matter how hard I tried to stop it, the thread of will I'd had over it was gone.

I was almost through the fence when a flash of blue light hit me, and I went flying sideways, falling and rolling over the ground as if I'd wiped out from my skateboard. As I came to a stop, my shoulders and chest lifted from the ground of their own accord.

Halfway sitting, halfway floating, I watched a dark cloud detach itself from my body and dash like a bullet toward the SUV. Unhinged, I collapsed down with an *umph,* my back hitting the ground.

Tires screeched as the SUV tore down the road.

I blinked at the dark sky, testing my feet and hands to make sure they were mine again. My body ached and my head was fuzzy, but I could move.

"Oh, thank God," I murmured as my toes wiggled.

A dark figure appeared to my side. I flinched, pushed myself into a sitting position, and tried to scurry away.

"Are you okay?" A deep voice asked. It was a neutral question, no real concern or care behind it, like an EMT who was completely over it.

I narrowed my eyes to see better, but all I perceived was a man's outline: tall, broad-shouldered, a cloak billowing behind him.

A warlock?

I knew some of them wore cloaks, even in the middle of the Georgia heat, as ridiculous as that sounded. I'd heard they could be proud individuals, very aware of their heightened status among Supernaturals as well as their ancient lineages.

But to me, he just looked like a guy dressed a bit early for Halloween.

He waited without moving, only his cloak fluttering, stirred by the light breeze that always blew around the building.

"I... I think I'm fine, but... my friend!" I exclaimed, jumping to my feet and nearly collapsing back to the ground.

My head spun. My legs threatened to give out. It took me a moment to find my balance, and when I did, I paused, afraid of falling on my face.

"My friend is injured," I said. "We need to call an ambulance."

The man's head turned to the side and if listening to something, then he said coldly, "Your friend is dead."

My heart clenched in my chest. "No. No. He's not. Trey's fine. He just..."

Tears started falling down my face, and I barely felt them. I wanted to believe this man was lying, but I had seen Trey's blank stare. I had seen a truth I didn't want to admit. My soul broke in two, grief dragging its claws down both halves.

"I need to see him," I stuttered gulping on tears.

"Follow me," the man said, his cloak whirling as he turned.

"No. I need to see, Trey. I need to go to him." I stood rooted to the spot. Only one thought occupied my mind: Trey. I needed to... I had to...

Something moved to my left where the werewolf had fallen. Holding my breath, I slowly turned my head. The beast had gotten up and was about to—

The werewolf leaped toward the retreating warlock.

"Watch out!" I screamed as the creature flew through the air, maw flashing with enormous canine teeth.

The warlock began to turn, hands raised, but whatever he planned to do would be pointless. The werewolf was too fast.

A loud crack sounded. A gunshot. For a split second, the werewolf seemed to hover in mid-air, then dropped to the ground with a muffled *whump*.

The warlock's head swiveled from side to side. I couldn't see his face, but he seemed confused. A second figure, also wearing a cloak, peeled away from the building's shadows. It strolled casually and confidently toward us.

"Rowan," the warlock said in his deep voice. It was a name but uttered as a pissed-off growl.

"Father," an also deep, yet more youthful voice responded.

Father? Who the hell were these people? It didn't matter. Where was Trey?

"What are you doing here?" the warlock demanded.

The newcomer, Rowan, *tsked*. "Is that how you thank me for saving your life?"

"Saving my life?" the older warlock huffed.

"I saved his life, didn't I?" Rowan directed the question at me. "You saw it. The werewolf was about to bite his head off?"

I squinted, trying to see their faces, but managing to see little more than their silhouettes. Was that a spell of some kind?

"Um, yes," I answered stupidly.

"See," Rowan said, holstering a gun into a shoulder strap.

"A gun?" his father asked in a tone that made his disgust and disapproval clear.

Rowan shrugged. "Just giving it a try," he said nonchalantly, though I perceived something like shame in his response.

"You disobeyed me again," the warlock said. "But I will deal with you later. I'm on Academy business, at the moment. Come, girl." He started to walk away once more, acting like someone who was used to having his every little command obeyed.

Well, I wasn't going anywhere with him, warlock or not. I had to go to Trey. I couldn't leave him alone. Turning in the other direction, I marched toward the building's side entrance.

"I think you'd better listen to him," Rowan whispered behind me.

I ignored him.

He sighed. "Don't say I didn't warn you."

I'd only taken a few steps when the warlock noticed I wasn't following him. "I said come with me, *girl*."

He waved a hand, and my body became unresponsive again,

though this time it felt different—more like invisible walls around me rather than cold seeping into my muscles and bones.

"What the hell? Let me go," I said, discovering I had full use of my voice. "I need to go to my friend. I need to—"

"What friend?" Rowan asked. "I can go check." Steps sounded behind me, then Rowan appeared at my side.

"Don't bother," the warlock said, joining us. "Her friend is dead. We need to go. More might be coming."

Again, there was that cold indifference in his voice as if he couldn't care less another human being had died. Maybe he knew Trey was just another homeless kid, nothing but a Regular no one would miss.

Except I would. I would!

"Let me go to him," I sobbed, tears sliding down my cheeks, while I tried to stop them because letting them out felt like accepting that Trey, my big brother, was gone. My heart kept telling me he couldn't be... gone. There had to be a mistake. I would go up and see he was alive, albeit hurt. We'd go to the E.R. They wouldn't turn us away.

"Father," Rowan pleaded.

"I don't have time for this. It's not safe here." The warlock moved closer, and laid a hand on the side of my neck. Everything went dark.

CHAPTER FOUR

FALL SEMESTER
EARLY SEPTEMBER

I awoke to the sounds of AC/DC blaring all around me. Trey was blasting the boom box again. God, he was so inconsiderate sometimes.

I opened my eyes and realized I had no idea where I was.

Nothing about my surroundings made sense. First of all, it seemed like I was suddenly in an episode of *Hoarders*. From the dusty couch I was lying on, I could see nothing but piles of what appeared to be a yard sale gone wild.

At the foot of the couch stood an eight-foot-tall tiki statue with big grinning teeth, a bicycle, and what seemed to be an old phone booth from the 1950s. Next to that was a ceiling-high stack of National Geographic magazines, which soared at least fourteen feet. A stack of afghans lay six or seven deep at my feet.

As I sat up, more piles became evident—mounds of

mismatched shoes, a life-sized stuffed tiger, a naked mannequin wearing only an old fez and a smile.

Where the hell was I?

Behind me, a black and gray ferret stretched and jumped onto my lap. I lurched up with a yelp, unseating him. He scurried under a pile of clothes.

"Oh, crap. Who are you? Where in the hell are we?"

He peeked out from his hiding place. I leaned down and patted his head, and that was all the invitation he needed because he climbed my leg and began sniffing in my pocket for treasures. He looked a bit rat-like, but at least I knew something was alive in this crazy place.

The AC/DC switched tracks to *Back in Black*, one of my dad's favorites. Not that I needed to think about him right, not when....

Trey.

Oh god.

What had happened to him? Was he still in that building alone? That thought slammed into me like a lead weight. I needed to go back. I needed to find him. I didn't care if those awful people were still there. I had to go back to him.

The thought of my friend made my heart crumble much like the window Smudge Face had disintegrated. If I got my hands on that man... Violent images flooded my brain as I pictured all I'd do.

Tears welled in my eyes, threatening to drown me.

I refused to believe he was dead. It wasn't real, not if I didn't see... his body.

I needed to get out of here and catch a ride back to our building.

Fists clenched, I wound my way through the piles, seeking out their owner. I figured all of this had something to do with the man who had paralyzed me and knocked me out. He could use a good swift kick in the balls as far as I was concerned. Then I'd make him give me cab fare back.

I followed the footpath through the mess, dodging a teetering stack of taxidermied crows, of all things.

As the piles dwindled, an office appeared. It wasn't clean by any means, but it was clean*er*. There was more room to walk and the walls and ceiling were visible—all oak paneling and scrollwork that made the room seem more 19th-century British study than storage room. A giant wooden desk dominated a raised platform and behind that, bookshelves crammed top-to-bottom with books.

Then I saw her.

An older woman on a wooden ladder, reaching for a tome on a high shelf and rocking out AC/DC's *Thunderstruck*.

"Hello?" I tried, but the music was too loud.

Her bottom—in a green, flowered skirt— swayed to the music. She had on orange and yellow striped tights and blue orthopedic shoes. My anger turned to confusion.

"Hello!"

She startled, lurched sideways, lost her footing, and began to fall.

Oh, no! I've killed an old lady.

But in my second of panic, the woman waved her hands and stopped herself mid-fall, then hovered there, staring at me.

I stared back because, well, *magic.*

She waved her hands and, simultaneously, lowered herself and turned off the music. Silence fell around us as we eyeballed each other.

Her face was lined, but in a soft, well-loved sort of way, as if she'd spent most of her years smiling. Bright blue eyes regarded me and assessed me in one sweep. Her gray hair was long and curled in messy waves that fell past her shoulders. A green beanie that matched her skirt sat atop her head and pink beads swayed on her neck. The outfit made me think of an old hippie who had never lost her flower power.

"Um, hi?" I said. I was a verbal genius in odd situations.

"You're awake. Welcome. Please, sit down. I'm sure you have questions." She gestured to an old wingback chair near her desk. It was occupied by a stack of manila folders brimming with papers. I eyed it, then straightened my back. I had no intention of sitting, anyway. I just wanted out of here so I could go back home.

"Oh." She flicked her hand and all the folders disappeared off the chair. The distinct crash of items falling and cascading sounded at the back of the room. Well, that explained the mess in the back. She was a disorganized witch.

There had to be a spell for that, but what did I know?

"Please, darling, sit," the woman insisted.

I stood my ground and, next thing I knew, I was staggering toward the chair as the witch wiggled her fingers in my direction.

What was wrong with these people? Did they think nothing of free will?

Satisfied, she sat across the desk and laid her clasped hands on a stack of papers.

"So, how are you feeling?"

"How do you think I'm feeling? Confused as hell. That's how. Where am I?"

"This is my office." She gestured around the room like I was an imbecile.

"I mean, other than this room, where am I? Last I remember, I was on the street while some guy commanded me to follow him and, since I wouldn't, he knocked me out. So kidnapping, which I'm pretty sure is illegal even for warlocks. I need to get back. Right away."

Just remembering what happened brought the rage back, which the flower power lady seemed to sense. She wiggled her fingers and soothing acoustic music began to play. The lights dimmed and she lowered her voice.

"Yes, that warlock was Macgregor Underwood. He's not really

a people person, but he is very good at what he does. Handsome, too." She tilted her head, smiling as if picturing him.

Macgregor Underwood and his son, Rowan, were the men who had both rescued me and kidnapped me. I made a mental note of their names for later use.

"And you are?" I demanded.

"Irmagard McIntosh. Counselor McIntosh to the students here. I'm... well... the school counselor."

"Students? School?"

"Why yes, dear. You're in the Academy, a bit North of Aberdale, Georgia."

The Academy.

I vaguely remembered Macgregor Underwood had mentioned something about that.

But *the* Supernatural Academy? I couldn't be here.

"No, no, no. You don't understand. My friend..." I choked on the last words. Was Trey alone in that abandoned building, the rats circling his lifeless body? My hands trembled as I gripped the chair for support. "I have to go."

From what I knew, this damn Academy was in the boonies. For most of history, it had been hidden from Regulars to help keep its existence a secret. Though, these days, Supernaturals could build anything they wanted, wherever they wanted. God, it would take me forever to get back.

"Oh, dear," she said, as if reading my emotions again, though this time I was sure they were plain on my face.

When she wiggled her fingers, a strange warmth spread through my chest. I started to protest, but then all my bad feelings were whisked away like leaves in a stiff breeze. A feeling similar to opening presents on a Christmas morning, when my mother was alive and my father actually cared about me, flooded my chest.

I was happy. Almost giddy.

A giggle escaped my lips, and I clamped a hand over my mouth. I wasn't just happy. I was high. "What did you do to me?"

Irmagard ignored my question. Standing up and walking to an ancient rotary phone, she murmured something about "... understanding the necessity under the circumstances."

I fought another giggle, the joy nearly bursting in my veins. I felt like singing, skipping. Was I drugged? If I was, I never wanted to come down. I stood up, then twirled around. The fat ferret wandered up, and I scooped him into my arms, twirling him, too.

I felt *so* good.

"Hello, little buddy. What's your name?" I kissed the ferret's nose.

"Yes, send him in," she was saying, though I wasn't paying too much attention. My dance partner wanted out of my arms, but I had decided to keep him.

Irmagard set the phone down and stood beside the desk, watching me dance with a withered expression on her face.

"Your guide is on his way. He'll get you situated. In the meantime, while you're feeling so... jolly, I think it best if I give you some news."

"Hmm?" I dropped my ferret dance partner, but nothing could quash this mood.

Irmagard sighed. "Your friend, Trey Goodwin, is dead. He was killed by one of the subversives who attempt to snatch up young talent and use them in causes to thwart the Academy. Your friend's body has been collected and cremated. Dean Underwood thought this would be the best course of action. The ashes will be delivered to your room."

"Okay." I knew I should feel sad about what she was saying, but all I could feel was extreme happiness. I grabbed one of the feathered hats from a pile next to the chair and tried it on, grinning.

"Also, the building where you lived has been condemned and

destroyed. You cannot return there. It was structurally unsound, and from what I understand, full of rats."

"Rats!" I pressed my hand to my mouth, giggling again. There were questions I should be asking, hundreds of them. I could feel them piling as high as Irmagard's magazines, yet all I could do was giggle.

"Oh, my. I think I've overdone it. You are quite delirious."

"You're telling me," I said, before falling into the chair in a fit of laughter.

The door opened and footsteps headed our way. When I glanced up, one of the most attractive young men I'd ever seen was staring down at me.

His jaw was angular, his eyes intense and brooding. Dark brown locks fell around his perfect face in such a way that made them seem effortless messy. His outfit was similarly styled, sloppy chic, in a plain, white V-neck tee and jeans. A very expensive and ancient looking medallion hung at his throat.

The jewels in that thing alone could pay anyone's rent for a year.

I stared at his physique—he did not skip gym days—and smiled.

Trey, I've met the one, I thought.

"You are a hottie," I confessed, knowing that I should be embarrassed, but unable to feel any of it.

"And you are sauced," he said, unamused. "Counselor McIntosh, I believe you have over-served our guest."

Her hands fluttered about like trapped birds. "Oh, Rowan. Oh, dear. I have, but I can't turn it off now or she'll feel rather bad, I'm afraid. Best to let it wear off. She'll be fine in the morning."

Rowan. One of the men from last night. He glowered as if he didn't agree with Counselor McIntosh's assessment of my condition.

"Can you take her, dear?" Counselor McIntosh asked Rowan.

"I have an eleven o'clock appointment with some very disgruntled parents."

Rowan acquiesced, gesturing that I should follow him, but I was quite enjoying the way the colors were dancing on the upper stained glass windows at the moment. He took my arm and led me out of the office like a mother with a child who would not leave the toy store.

"Of all the people," he muttered, weaving me around Irmagard's piles.

"Where are we going?" I asked giddily.

He glanced at me. "You're going to see my father."

"Your father?" I suppressed another giggle. "Is he mad?" I made a pouty face. "Are *you* mad? You seemed a lot nicer last night."

Rowan frowned. "Last night, my father wasn't forcing me to babysit dubious witches."

Huh? I knew there were also questions I should ask about that, but I couldn't bring myself to care.

As soon as we were out of the room, he shut the office door, whirled me around and snapped his fingers.

All the bad feelings Irmagard's spell had spared me from came rushing back in a wave.

The wall of pain, embarrassment, and sadness hit my heart like a freight train. I gasped, clutching the wall as icy fingers of sorrow dug into my heart. Tears streamed down my face as I struggled to fight the sobs that shook my chest.

The pain. So much pain. Trey. Oh god.

I could barely breathe. The pain pressed on my chest like an anvil, crushing my heart into pieces.

When the intensity subsided a little, I glanced up at Rowan. He had done this to me. Counselor McIntosh had said it should wear off slowly. He gave it all back to me in one blow.

I stared up at him through my tear soaked eyes. "Why?"

His unaffected gaze drifted away as his jaw remained fixed.

"Best to deal with these things head-on. No use putting it off. Rip the Band-Aid off so to speak. Now, let's go. You do not want to keep my father waiting."

One thing I knew for certain, Rowan Underwood may have been hot, but he was mean through and through, and I would never let him see me vulnerable again.

CHAPTER FIVE

FALL SEMESTER
EARLY SEPTEMBER

SORROW WAS a dagger piercing the center of my heart as I followed Rowan down a long corridor, away from Counselor McIntosh's office. I wanted to cry, curl up on the floor and bawl, but I wouldn't let this Rowan guy see me that way. He was cold and uncaring, a rich brat with a heart made of ice.

Besides, he knew the way out of this labyrinthine hell they'd brought me to.

He would take me to Trey... to his ashes, and he and I would get out of this place and go back home. They couldn't have demolished our place overnight. They were lying.

Whatever building we were in, Counselor McIntosh's office must have been at the far end because we'd crossed several corridors already. As we went, I tried to focus on my surroundings, doing my best to push grief aside for now. I was strong, and I wasn't giving this guy the satisfaction of thinking otherwise.

The corridor we walked along was wide and decorated in a very Victorian style. A plush crimson rug ran beneath our feet. Paneling and scrollwork covered the walls just like in Counselor McIntosh's office, except here, they were dust free and reflected the light from the many sconces affixed to the walls. Someone spent a lot of time polishing that wood, for sure.

Oil portraits and black and white photographs sat in gilded frames, displaying stuffy old dudes or groups of people. Students, maybe? This was the "Academy," after all. As I remembered from a news feature I'd watched a while back, the place was *old*—even if, we, regular humans had only learned about it ten years ago—so lots of Supernaturals must have studied here throughout the years.

I still remembered the day I learned about the existence of Supernaturals. I'd been seven years old, eating my breakfast at the kitchen counter, while Mom and Dad got ready for work. A panicked announcer had interrupted the traffic news on the radio to report that a band of Supernaturals had requested an audience with the president.

Of course, at first, everyone had thought it was a hoax. It wasn't until the president himself backed their authenticity that people started to believe. And, even after that, it took lots of *seeing* for most to truly start *believing*.

Supernaturals had been sick of living in the shadows and had decided the world needed to embrace them.

Oddly enough, there'd been no panic. People had actually been excited to find out the creatures from their fiction books were actually real. Of course, their numbers were negligible since only a small amount of the population carried the special Supernatural DNA and they regulated themselves with Magical Law Enforcement to make sure no bad guys hurt humans or stole all our money. I'm sure it would have been a different story if we'd started running into Shadow Puppets and vampires at every corner, or warlocks starting robbing our banks.

And yet, they were dangerous as I clearly saw last night.

Now, I was in the presence of many witches and warlocks. I glanced around, trying to see if some of the other Supernatural creatures roamed the halls, but I didn't see any werewolves or zombies. Maybe they were hiding. Maybe they had their own school. Either way, I was glad none were around. Witches I could handle. A werewolf, not so much.

After crossing several more closed-in corridors, we made it to one with huge windows on one side. I was surprised to see daylight seeping in since all the dim-lit sconces elsewhere had made it feel like night time.

I squinted at the sun breaking through the tall, glass panes. Each window, one after the other, had to be about twenty feet tall. Beyond them, a manicured lawn as large as a football field sprawled in all its green glory. Stone paths cut through the field, lined by perfect bushes and colorful flowers on either side, while a huge fountain sprayed water into the air. Past the fountain was a line of stately buildings, and further still, a forest of thick trees stood grand and luscious as far as the eye could see.

The wealth was extravagant, sickening even. How many meals had Trey and I missed since we'd become homeless? How much did this stupid Academy spend every day in upkeeping and watering their useless lawn?

Finally leading me through a massive open area, Rowan crossed past a grand staircase. His leather shoes squeaked on the white marble floor as he picked up his pace, but I reluctantly slowed down to admire the elaborately carved banisters, the gigantic crystal chandelier that hung between the two sets of stairs, and the grand entrance set right under the second-floor landing.

"If you're casing the joint, don't bother. The anti-theft spells are legendary." Rowan said over his shoulder, an impatient expression on his face. "C'mon, girl. I don't have all day."

I bit my tongue to hold back a well-deserved insult, realizing that arguing with this jerk would be a waste of time. As soon as I had Trey with me, I would be out of here, so why waste my breath? He'd seemed decent enough last night, but first impressions couldn't always be trusted, at least not mine. I'd thought Trey was an airhead the first time I met him, then discovered his goofy behavior was only a coping mechanism to deal with all the shit life had thrown his way.

Beyond the fancy foyer and across another hall, Rowan finally led me to a carved door with a nameplate on it reading, "Dean Underwood." There, he knocked twice, then went in, leaving the door ajar for me to follow.

I hesitated for an instant, then stepped inside, inhaling deeply and telling myself I would soon be out of here.

Once inside, the door closed behind me. I glanced back, thinking I'd find someone standing there, but nope. Magic was more convenient than that.

Slowly turning my gaze forward, I took in the floor-to-ceiling shelves filled to the brim with books, and the large desk that dominated the office. Rowan stood next to the desk, hands at his back.

Behind it, a middle-aged man of about fifty—Macgregor Underwood, I assumed—sat in a high back chair. He had gray hair at his temples, a Roman nose, and thick eyebrows. Piercing blue eyes assessed me with cool detachment.

"What is your name?" he asked.

I pressed my lips together, my gaze sweeping over the desk, searching for anything that may contain ashes: an urn, a box, a bag... There was nothing.

"I asked your name," the man repeated.

Why should I give him my name? I didn't trust these people. For all I knew, they would turn me over to social services. I was still six months shy of eighteen, and these kind of people were always trying to "fix" your life just so they could feel good about themselves. Besides, Counselor McIntosh had known Trey's name, wouldn't they know mine, too? I bet this was just some sort of power play.

"See what I mean?" Macgregor Underwood said to no one in particular. "It's so unfortunate what life on the streets can do to a young person's mind. And they think sorcery is evil. Illicit drugs are the bane of our society. "

I had never done drugs in my life. At least, Trey and I had exercised enough common sense to stay away from them, but this man could believe whatever he wanted. I wasn't here to perform tricks for him. Tricks were *his* job, and he could keep his circus, for all I cared.

"Where's my friend?" I demanded.

Rowan and his father exchanged a glance.

"Counselor McIntosh did hit her with a powerful soothing spell," Rowan said with a shrug.

And you undid it, you jackwad!

If anything had truly addled me, it was the abrupt change. Joy to complete misery in a finger snap. My chest still felt tight as if I was about to have a heart attack or something.

"The hippie lady said you would give me my friend's... ashes," I said.

Rowan's mouth tightened as if he were repressing a smile at the term I'd used for Irmagard. His father lifted an eyebrow and seemed slightly amused as well. I got the feeling they didn't respect her, which probably meant she was twice the human being that they were.

"Well?" I said.

Macgregor Underwood stood from his chair, pulling on his cuffs.

"Ms. whatever-your name," he came around the desk, walking in front of his son without even saying *excuse me*, "as the Dean of Admissions, I am obliged to register you as an Academy student, which I cannot do without a name."

My mouth went dry. Register me? What the hell?

"I suspect that as well as others of your *ilk*," he continued as my brain did somersaults, trying to understand, "you have no interest in joining our fine institution. And though I would very much like to leave you to your own devices, I'm also obliged to try to persuade you."

"Persuade me?" I repeated dumbly. "But I'm not..." I trailed off.

"A Supernatural?" he said, that haughty eyebrow raised again. "Yes, I realize you don't know what you are, but trust me, we do. You *fractured* yesterday, which is the reason that *Quake* and his *friends* came after you. Also, the reason I was there."

Fractured? Quake? Could this guy speak English?

Rowan seemed to see the confusion in my face because he sighed tiredly, then explained.

"What my father means is that your supernatural powers manifested for the first time yesterday. 'You fractured,'" he made air quotes, "because your powers have been repressed for who knows how long, and you finally cracked under their pressure."

He paused, then said, "Oh, and a 'Quake,'" he made air quotes again, "is someone who can vibrate so fast, they can break just about anything with their touch. The one you met yesterday came to snatch you. Subversives like him have locator spells all over the city to help them detect new magic. They actively recruit Supernaturals in this manner to grow their ranks for criminal purposes. They're not good people. You're lucky we were there to save you. Trust me." He finished with an annoyed huff as if he'd only gone through the trouble to explain everything because it gave him the chance to make me feel inferior and inadequate.

After doing my best not to call him something ugly, I said, "Whether or not I'm a... Supernatural, I have no interest in staying in this place. You people killed Trey, the only family I had, and now you expect me to... *go* here." A puff of air blew past my lips. "No, thank you. Just give me my friend's ashes, and I'll be on my way."

I held Macgregor Underwood's gaze, even as part of me begged me to avoid confrontation.

"We didn't kill your friend," Rowan said.

His father ignored him, and so did I.

For a moment, I thought the man would argue, but instead, he shrugged. "Your loss, our gain." He turned to Rowan. "Get the urn and drive her out of campus." He sat back down and proceeded to ignore us.

I waited for Rowan to retrieve the urn from wherever they were keeping it, but he just stood there, staring at his father with a conflicted expression on his face. He probably hated to be stuck with the task of getting rid of me, but he shouldn't have worried. I had no intention of letting him drive me anywhere.

I crossed my arms and stubbornly stared at the front of his desk.

After a tense moment during which his father continued to ignore him, Rowan finally started walking toward the door.

Before he made it there, though, there was a knock, the door opened, and Irmagard McIntosh came in. She had changed and was now wearing slacks and a blouse, rather than a flower-print skirt. She'd combed and pinned up her hair and removed the beanie, too.

"Dean McIntosh," Macgregor Underwood said, standing.

Dean? Wasn't she a counselor?

"Underwood. Rowan," she said with a smile. "Is this our new student?" she asked, turning to me. "Irmagard told me she'd be here."

Wait, she wasn't Irmagard? I was confused, something that happened often in this place.

Still holding a smile, she walked up to me and took my hand in hers. "Hello, dear. My name is Lynssa McIntosh. I am the Head Dean of this Academy."

I pulled my hand away, unaccustomed to having people touch

me. Normally, they gave me a wide berth and leered at me the way Rowan and his father did.

Peering closer at her face, all I could figure was that Dean McIntosh had to be Irmagard's twin sister. Weird.

"My son was about to accompany Miss—she won't tell us her name—on her way out," Underwood said. "She wishes to leave." There seemed to be a hint of satisfaction in his voice. Clearly, he didn't want the likes of me in his precious Academy.

"Do you truly wish to leave?" the Dean asked.

I nodded, finding it hard to tell this nice lady that her Academy could stuff it.

"And did you explain the risks of her decision?" she asked, turning to Macgregor.

"Not entirely," Underwood said casually. "She barely gave me a chance to explain much."

With a shake of her head and a tired smile, Dean McIntosh gently guided me toward the door. "I think I'll take it from here," she said as the door to Underwood's office closed behind us, leaving the two *a-holes* behind. I certainly was glad to be rid of them.

She headed back toward the grand staircase. "Let's go outside, shall we? We can talk there at ease. Besides, it's a beautiful day."

As we walked between the two sets of stairs toward the massive entrance, one of the large doors swung open, letting in a bright stream of sunlight. I frowned at the door, wondering if all of them were "automatic."

Following the Dean outside, I relished the sun on my skin, feeling as if I'd just come out of a freezer. Besides, I was one step closer to escape.

Dean McIntosh lowered herself to one of the steps that led to a stone courtyard with a huge fountain in the middle, sat and stretched her legs. For her age, she sure seemed agile. All the old homeless folks I knew had horrible arthritis and always complained about joint pain.

"Sit, please," she said patting a spot next to her.

I did, unable to turn her down. She just seemed too nice and welcoming. It had been a long time since someone had been this nice to me.

"Forgive Underwood," she said, looking out toward the fountain. "I apologize if he made you feel unwelcome. He means well for the Academy, but his views of the students we should accept is a little warped and antiquated. Besides, in times like this, we can hardly turn down talent. He knows this, but I'm still trying to change his mind about a few things."

"Talent?" I asked.

She paused and smiled, something she seemed to do a lot. I wondered how it would feel to be that happy all the time.

"So here's the thing, Miss, um..." she let the sentence hang.

"Charlie," I finally said, unable to resist her determined blue eyes. Maybe they knew my name, but they sure seemed determined to get it straight from me.

"Here's the thing, Charlie," she said, holding my gaze. "We need you. In fact, we need every Supernatural we can recruit. There aren't many of us to begin with and, to make matters worse, a big number of young people are being snatched by rogue Supernaturals we call subversives. Our numbers at the Academy are dwindling at a time when there is a dire need for good witches and warlocks to fight the unrest these people are causing. If you leave, it makes an already precarious situation worse—not to mention that it puts your life at risk. What happened to you yesterday, whatever made you fracture, will repeat itself, and then bad people will show up again. Bad people like those who killed your friend."

She paused and let that sink in.

"If you stay," she continued, "I cannot only guarantee your safety from those that would harm you, I can also promise that you will learn to control your powers and that, while you're here," she gestured toward the building behind us, "you will not lack for anything. Hot meals everyday, a roof over your head, clothes. Moreover, you will get a... *well-rounded* education."

I'd thought she finished her little speech when her eyes widened.

"Oh," she added, "and if this gives you any satisfaction, the opportunity to show Underwood and his son how wrong they were about you." She smiled and winked.

Despite myself, I smiled back. Showing those two up sounded almost better than the part where she mentioned hot meals. Still...

"How can you be so sure I belong here? I mean... I'm not a Supernatural. I don't have..." I paused. I'd been about to say I didn't have any powers, but then I remembered the disappearing ibuprofen and the hag who called me a witch.

I tried again. "It's supposed to be in the DNA, right? Well, my mom and dad were normal."

"As opposed to... abnormal?" Dean McIntosh chuckled, then asked, "They were Regulars? Are you sure?"

I shrugged, avoiding eye contact. I mean, I'd always thought Supernaturals *were* freaks, and I honestly wanted no part of that.

"When a Supernatural's powers are small and unnurtured," she said, "a person can go their whole life without fracturing. That could have been the case with one of your parents, if you claim you've never seen anything magical. You, however, are different." Her blue eyes traveled across my face as she smiled gently.

A warm feeling spread over my chest, making me wonder if she was using some sort of spell on me, the way Irmagard had. Though, there was a certain honesty in her eyes that made me doubt it. Either way, no one had looked at me like that in a long time. It felt... motherly—no other word came to mind. My heart softened. I knew I shouldn't allow that to happen, but I couldn't help it. Losing my family had left a huge void in me that I always felt desperate to fill.

"Tell you what," she said, jumping to her feet. "Stay with us for some time, see if you like it. A free trial. Isn't that something people in your world love?"

I shook my head, afraid of the small voice in my head that was saying I should agree, the voice that said this lady was someone I could look up to.

"Are you scared you might like it?" Dean McIntosh teased.

Glancing toward the beautiful fountain, I wondered what there was not to like? Of course, I was tempted. For the past year and a half, I'd been living in a rat-infested building. But what exactly would I be giving up if I stayed?

I didn't know.

To be honest, all I could think of were those hot meals she'd promised. I bet there would be hot showers, too. Though, there was more than that. There was also fear. With Trey gone, I didn't have a home anymore, even if our building was still standing. I didn't want to be alone. Not again.

"C'mon," Dean McIntosh said, heading inside. "I'll show you your room."

My room? I'd once had "my own room" but, considering the shock the words gave me, it seemed I'd given up on the possibility of ever having another one.

Hesitantly, I stood and followed the Dean inside. A few days of comfort wouldn't hurt, right? I could pretend I was at a fancy shelter, and when things got old, I could split. I'd done it before. This didn't have to be any different.

As Dean McIntosh led me up the grand staircase, I ask. "Is the counselor your twin sister?"

"You noticed, huh?" she said with a smirk.

I rolled my eyes. Maybe she thought it was a stupid question, but I didn't. If I was going to stay here for a few days, surrounded by Supernaturals, I should be wary. Irmagard could have been a doppelganger for all I knew.

I was in the Supernatural Academy, not Disney World.

CHAPTER SIX

FALL SEMESTER
EARLY SEPTEMBER

WHEN THE DEAN walked me into my assigned room in the Freshman Dorm, she apologized for its size. I glanced around confused. There was a cherry wood bed frame with a matching dresser and nightstand, a desk, and a built-in bookshelf. Across from that, a small closet and a big window overlooked the manicured lawn.

Why was she apologizing? This was luxury.

Almost immediately, I spotted a plain ceramic urn on the desk, and I nearly collapsed to my knees with despair.

Sensing my need to be alone, the Dean left, though not before encouraging me to read the welcome package.

I had two and a half days to get a handle on my grief, enough to figure out if I was going to start classes or not.

Thankfully, I'd been kidnapped on a Friday, which meant

Saturday and Sunday I had no required classes and was given time to "adjust" to my new surroundings.

I adjusted by desperately missing Trey and crying my eyes out, while the rest of the time I slept on a bed that felt like luxury itself, took thirty-minute hot showers, and gorged myself in the school's cafeteria.

In a way, it felt like the spa Trey and I had dreamed about. And the food, itself, might've been enough to keep me around.

"They had chicken carbonara," I told Trey's urn after my first dinner on campus. "I swear I wouldn't mind bathing in it."

"Gah, you should see the desserts," I told him the next night. "There were five types of pie. Pecan, sweet potato, apple, cherry, and chocolate. You would have loved it!"

Talking to Trey helped me feel less lonely, especially when I strained to remember the last time I'd eaten pie and decided it was probably during the last Thanksgiving with my dad, two years ago. He'd purchased it in the frozen foods section and burned it after getting drunk and falling asleep while it was cooking.

As an alcoholic for most of his adult life, these types of episodes got progressively worse, and by the time I was a teen, Dad was spending most of his days drunk. I was sixteen by then and able to cook, clean, and take care of my own basic necessities. The problem was I didn't have any money. If there were Social Security checks from Mom's passing, I never saw them. Dad had been a teacher during my childhood, but had taken a "leave of absence" when I turned fourteen. I think he'd been fired for drinking on the job, but it was a topic neither one of us ever talked about.

Either way, that Thanksgiving, we had little to eat and, when Dad burned the discount freezer-section pie, I'd had to hold back tears. Mom used to make such great pies.

The pies here were definitely not from a grocer's freezer. I ate three different slices.

Everything about the campus was posh and expensive. Everywhere I went I was reminded of the money these people had that I didn't. Instead of dwelling on my awful clothes and lack of any personal belongings, I took advantage of their generosity. Who knew how long I'd have free access to this stuff? I'd probably only last a few weeks amongst these magical snobs, anyway.

While I dined and roamed, I avoided people and garnered strange stares which I ignored. I'd gotten used to darting glances from life on the streets. These were no different. My clothes and hair were clean, but my outfit still screamed poverty. I stood out like a sore thumb, but it didn't matter. I wasn't here to fit in.

Dean McIntosh had given a few T-shirts plastered with the Academy crest on the front—a shield sporting a lion, a key, a book, and a chalice, all circled by the words "Magicae Vincere Tenebras," whatever that meant. It was a nice gesture by the dean, but there was no way in holy hell I was strutting around looking like a walking billboard for a school I was probably not going to attend.

Something else the dean had given me—the huge welcome package that I was supposed to study—still sat on my desk vastly undisturbed. After a quick perusal that revealed a mountain of folders and brochures, I'd lost interest. All the historical facts about the school and the faculty bios made for perfect sleep aid material and nothing else.

The only things I found that were mildly interesting was the mention of a magical portal on the school grounds (a source of power that made the land the Academy sat on very valuable) and the fact that there were many ways to wield magic, either through spoken spells, an item, hand movements, potions and more.

That was cool, although somewhat overwhelming to consider.

But then, *poof*, my little mini vacay disappeared, magician style, Monday morning.

I had a nine AM class.

That had been one of Dean McIntosh's requirements for my free room and board. I had to attend all my classes unless I was deathly ill, and she assured me she would be able to tell if I tried to fake it.

Magic could be so annoying.

The printed schedule pressed between my fingers, I left the Freshman Dorm promptly at 8:30, followed the map to Cabot Hall, and navigated several long corridors to the third floor. Avoiding throngs of students, I tried to find Room 302. My eyes scanned numbers on wood-paneled doors. Somehow I had skipped from 301 to 324.

Was this sorcery? Why did every hallway have to look the same?

"What class are you looking for?" a voice asked.

My eyes darted up and landed on a very stunning female student staring at me amusedly. With mocha skin and sleek black hair, she appeared to be of Indian descent. Her eyes were big and brown, her mouth painted in bright red lipstick that contrasted with her skin tone perfectly. Everything from her expertly styled hair to her impeccable white dress shirt, black skirt, and expensive high heels let me know she came from money and wore it well.

In contrast, in my thrift store clothes, I was the perfect mark for ridicule.

I'd seen it dozens of times before. Even prior to dropping out of high school and living on the streets, I never had nice things. I wore the same clothes, carried broken backpacks mended with duct tape and was on our school's free and reduced lunch program. Popular kids targeted me. One real peach of a human being by the name of Crissa Vega told everyone I had head lice. Another skid mark of society named Joey Turk took pictures of me in the same outfit I rotated every few days and photoshopped them together in a montage of poverty.

Then he sent it around to the entire school.

Assholes.

So I knew, this beautiful creature in front of me, smelling of designer perfume and clutching a handbag worth more than my life's income, *did not* want to be my friend. She was first of many rich kids like Rowan who would line up to torture me.

Well, second in line. Rowan had the distinction of being the first. My blood boiled just thinking about him.

I shook my head and shouldered past her.

"Wait," she called.

When I didn't respond, I heard her grumble something, but it was too late. I'd already sailed past.

Then my schedule darted out of my hands.

One minute, the paper was securely between my fingers. The next, it soared up over my head. Turning around, I saw it sail into this girl's awaiting hand.

Magic. Damn. I kept forgetting.

"Give it back," I demanded, stalking towards her, but she held out a hand to stop me.

Her eyes skimmed my classes. "History at nine AM? Whoever made your schedule is *not* your friend. Alchemy at ten-thirty is better. Oh, and after lunch, we both have Spells 101 with Dr. Henderson. He isn't hard on the eyes, but his quizzes. Woof." Thick eyelashes blinked up to make sure I was listening.

I did wonder about what she'd said. This was a week or two into the semester, and they were already having quizzes? No, thanks. I held out my hand again, adopting a demanding posture, though she was a witch and I was a freeloader with no lightning bolts at my fingertips.

"Can I have my schedule back now?"

She handed it to me, but didn't release it when I clamped on. "Who are you?"

"Charlie," I said, tugging on the paper. It finally slid from her fingers. I quickly put the paper in my pocket.

Her eyes skimmed my attire. Ripped, stained jeans, a T-shirt with a hole under one armpit, and scuffed Vans.

"Charlie," she repeated. "And are you poor?" Her head dropped to the side, her face quizzical.

I was shocked. Who asked questions that bold? I examined her expression for malice, but she just seemed curious.

"That's none of your business." I tried to walk away.

The girl followed me. "It's alright if you're poor. No judgement. I just haven't met many poor people. Was it hard growing up like that?" Her big eyes studied my face for answers.

Was this girl from another planet? Either way, I was not going to be her token poor acquaintance.

"If you'll excuse me..." I started to walk faster, but man, the girl could book it in heels. She kept pace with me.

"My name is Disha. I'm from New York." She held out a manicured hand.

I shook it to get her off my back, then turned a corner only to find myself at a dead-end. Class was going to start any minute, and I was more lost than I had been before.

"Look, Disha, if you will show me to room 302, I will let you ask me three questions about being poor. After that, maybe we don't have to talk anymore. Deal?"

She cocked her head again. "You have a very unique way of speaking. And, yes. Deal. This way." She held out her hand to direct me.

When we turned out of the dead-end hallway, she started with her first question.

"Where did you grow up?"

We zipped around a group of students in a cluster. A blue light pulsed from inside the circle, but Disha didn't even blink. Apparently, that kind of thing happened all the time around here. Another thing to get used to.

I answered Disha's question in as little detail as possible. "I grew up in Conyers, Georgia. Not too far from here."

She frowned as if expecting a different answer before asking her second question. "What was your house like?"

"Small," I responded. "Two bedrooms. It was messy if that's what you're asking."

"Hmm." She knit her brows together and then pointed for us to take a left at the staircase. "Last question. Are you here on a free scholarship?"

The last question hit me like a blow to the chest. Did she think because I was poor I wasn't worthy of being here? A pity case? I didn't know if I had what it took to make it at the Academy, but I certainly didn't need Miss Perfect to wave it in my face. I'd gotten nearly perfect grades before leaving high school. Dean McIntosh had looked over my 1500 SAT score and excellent high school transcripts, the ones that I completed before dropping out, assuring me that though the requirements were a bit different at the Academy, she thought I would do fine. I'd offered to take the GED, but she said my transcripts were good enough to prove I could hack it.

The magic part? That was another story.

Either way, Disha could stuff it. I had taken her rude comments as her being oblivious, but maybe it was meanness after all.

"Yes, I'm here on a scholarship," I answered curtly. "That's your three questions, now if you'll excuse me I see my room."

There was 302 and I had fulfilled my end of the bargain. Now, I didn't have to talk to Disha again.

I strode into the room just as a horrible scream rent the air.

As I came to halt at the doorway, my eyes landed on the life-less, floating body in the center of the room.

Desks were knocked over. Books scattered. A clump of cowering students quivered in the back of the classroom, their eyes on the pair of beings in the center.

I didn't understand what I was seeing. The levitating body was clearly human, but the creature beside it was unlike anything I'd ever seen. Its face was skeletal, covered by what seemed to be moss and decaying leaves. Huge horns of bone curled out of either side of the skull like a goat, a tarnished gold crown resting between them. Old, moth-eaten robes in dirty blue trailed to the floor in tatters. Its eyes were vacant holes, housing green fire. Similarly colored flames curled up its right hand as its left held a golden scepter.

He looked like a king, long buried, then brought back to life. Yet, his eyes burned with a horrible vibrancy, glowing brighter as he circled his boney index finger around and around. As he did so, a noose of green light trailed around the floating body's neck.

The body belonged to a girl, probably a student. Her limbs sagged as she floated above the floor. Her dark locks fluttered in a wind I couldn't feel. She seemed unconscious, but held up by some magical force.

As the green noose tightened, her skin contracted. Her bones began to appear beneath her skin. Her hair withered like old flowers.

He was draining her dry.

"Stop!" I screamed.

The creature's head snapped in my direction. Then, the full power of his vacant stare locked onto me.

The girl fell in a heap to the ground as the dead king held out his boney finger. His vacant eye sockets pulsed swamp-green, holding me captive like tractor beams.

An invisible noose tightened around my throat, choking me. My air dried up. I gagged, trying to suck air, but none would come. My hands scrambled at my throat, trying to loosen the noose, but there was nothing physical there.

My very being began to slip away. I could feel my life draining from me, seeping out like blood from a mortal wound.

My legs sagged. My arms drooped. I could barely keep my eyes open. My panic was slowly being replaced by intense exhaustion. As I drooped like a ragdoll, my body began to contract as if every atom was being yanked from the inside out. My heart had been replaced by a black hole, everything swirling into oblivion.

Still, I fought. I stared into the dead king's eyes, willing my lids open. I would not go quietly.

A rumble began behind me. Then a strong wind. It started as a breeze and then turned into a gust that blew everything against the walls. Papers fluttered. Students ducked as chairs flew. The far window blew out and glass shards rained.

And the best part was my senses returned. I could move. Breathe.

I dropped to my knees as whoever was making the wind stepped forward. I blinked at expensive high heels, then followed up a smooth calf, trendy skirt, a beautiful face set with determination, and an arm extended in a spell, blasting the shit out of the dead king.

Disha was a badass.

The king flew back, his robes plastering to his skeletal body. Hands covered his mossy face as the wind blinded him and objects bombarded him.

Then Disha planted her feet and threw her arms out as if shoving an invisible boulder at him.

The wall blasted open. The dead king's crown shattered to pieces, then he blew through the hole in the wall, plummeting out of sight.

Disha dropped her arms, exhausted. The wind stopped.

I got up on my hands and knees as the people at the end of the room ran out, screaming.

Panting, Disha looked at me, her expression drained, giddy, and a little bit terrified as if even she hadn't known what she was capable of.

"Is it dead?" My voice came out in a choked gasp.

Realizing she didn't know, Disha ran to the open wall, stood at the edge, and stared down. I crawled over to her, careful to avoid the broken glass and bits of drywall.

"Is it dead?" I repeated.

Disha shook her head, smoothing back her hair. "I... I don't know."

I got up, and we stood together, peering down three stories at the zombie king's crumpled body in the bushes below. It certainly appeared dead, but who knew?

A tall African American woman in her mid-forties ran in, scanned the room and spotted us. She sprinted over and peered down at the creature now ringed by a crowd of students, a leather-bound book held tightly in one hand.

"What was it?" I asked the woman. I really hoped she was a teacher and could tell me what the hell just happened.

The woman's voice was level, but carried an undercurrent of fear. "It was a lich," she said, staring at its slowly disintegrating body. "But the real question is, who let it in?"

CHAPTER SEVEN

FALL SEMESTER
EARLY SEPTEMBER

WELL, that didn't take long.

My first day, and I was already in a teacher's office. Not that I was a troublemaker. I tried to avoid being noticed, but tragedy always seemed to follow me around, even before. Like that day Crissa Vega face-planted on her ravioli, and she accused me of tripping her, when all I'd done was wish for tomato sauce on her *Abercrombie and Fitch* T-shirt.

Did the *supernatural-ness* Dean McIntosh insisted I had cause this?

I mean, I had yet to believe her claim that I could wield magic. Disappearing ibuprofen does not a Supernatural make. Besides, wouldn't the moment when one is being strangled by an anorexic king with a fiery hand be the perfect time for someone's powers to manifest?

I would think so.

Disha and I sat next to each other in front of an empty desk, waiting for a teacher by the name of Dr. Henderson, a guy Disha said taught *Spells* at all levels and an introductory class on *Supernaturals and Their Lore*.

While I picked at a rip in my jeans, Disha was primping her hair and checking her makeup in a small mirror. Tons of questions swirled in my mind, but I was still too shocked to string more than a few words together.

"Can't ever be too presentable for Dr. Henderson," she said, winking at herself, then snapping the mirror shut and putting it away.

I wrinkled my nose but said nothing. I never understood girls who went for teachers, but to each their own.

The door behind us opened, and someone walked in. I remained still, staring at the oil painting of the Academy that hung above the desk while Disha crossed her leg and swiveled in her chair, part of her shapely thigh exposed through a slit in her black skirt.

I rolled my eyes. Really?

A guy in a blue suit and silver tie rounded the desk. He appeared to be in his early thirties, tall with brown hair and an angular face. He had perfect skin, warm brown eyes and an open expression that immediately made you feel at ease. He stood straight, exuding class, though not arrogance—the complete opposite of Macgregor Underwood, whose haughtiness was like a slap in the face to impoverished humans like me.

This man gave us a brilliant, welcoming smile that made something tingle in my gut.

Damn. I take it back. I take it all *back.*

If I had to go for a teacher, I would definitely go for this one.

Disha gave a knowing glance, then faced the desk again.

"Hello, Ms. Khatri and Ms. Rivera, I presume." He gave me a slight bow.

"Um, yeah," I said, feeling a swirl of emotions inside.

The guy was at least fifteen years older than me, and here I was, wondering how much he could bench. I mean, it seemed like he must hit the gym every day, but how many hours did it take to look like that? Did he do cardio or pump iron? Hmm, maybe he swam and ate nothing but baked chicken and salad. Would that make a guy boring? And what if a girl wanted to go to McDonald's for some fries? Would he nag about nutrition and counting carbs?

I shook my head, shooing away my irrational thoughts.

"Nice to meet you, Ms. Rivera," he said as he took a seat in front of us, unbuttoning his jacket. "I'm Dr. Thadeus Henderson. I am the Spells teacher. I'm so sorry your first day turned out like this. It's not a common occurrence, not normally."

Not normally? I waited for him to elaborate, but Disha spoke next.

"Is Marybeth going to be okay?" she asked.

Dr. Henderson nodded. "I've been to see her already. Nurse Taishi is taking good care of her. She will need to rest for a few days—the lich sucked a lot of energy from her—but she'll recover." He turned to me. "How about you? How do you feel? I understand the lich attacked you, too."

"I feel fine." I placed a hand on my neck. "Just a bit, I don't know, tired."

"Understandable," Dr. Henderson said. "That was extremely brave of you to call the lich away from Ms. Baggarley."

"More like stupid," I said under my breath.

Disha seemed to hear me, though, because she said, "Yes, extremely brave. I don't think Marybeth would still be alive if it weren't for Charlie. One second longer, and the lich would have sucked Marybeth dry."

I squirmed on my seat, uncomfortable with the attention.

"I didn't do anything. Disha was the one who..." I fluttered my hands in the air in demonstration.

"Indeed," Dr. Henderson said, a huge smile stretching over his face. "I see our extra lessons have been paying off."

Disha sat straighter, looking pleased with herself.

Extra lessons, huh? No wonder she'd been so kick-ass out there. Apparently, she wasn't only a great dresser, she was also an academic overachiever.

Dean McIntosh had explained that students who came from known supernatural families already had a certain level of training. Since their skills were nurtured pretty much since they were born, they never repressed them—hence, they didn't "fracture." Depending on the strength of their powers, some began their first year at the Academy with advanced skills. All the signs pointed to Disha being from one of those families.

"Now," Dr. Henderson leaned back in his chair, steepling his fingers, "Tell me exactly what happened."

We did as he requested, each sharing our own recollection of the events. While we talked, Dr. Henderson just nodded, occasionally stopping us to ask a question.

When we were done, he said, "Everything agrees with what the other students said."

"Does anyone know how that thing got in?" Disha asked.

"Unfortunately, no." Dr. Henderson shook his head. "Most students were in the classroom waiting for Professor Middleton when the lich descended from the ceiling."

I tentatively lifted my hand to ask a question.

Dr. Henderson waved dismissively. "You don't have to do that, just shoot."

"This is probably a stupid question, but what exactly is a lich?" I asked.

"There are no stupid questions, Ms. Rivera," Dr. Henderson said. "At least not under my tutelage." He turned to Disha. "Why don't you explain, Ms. Khatri?"

"Sure," Disha said, turning slightly in my direction. "A lich is an undead witch or warlock—"

"Like a zombie?" I interrupted.

"Not at all," Disha said. "Zombies are stupid, no more than

animated bodies. Liches retain their intelligence after they die and store their soul in some kind of object that had meaning to them when they were alive. This lich's special object was his crown. That's why I went for it. I used a spell I just happened to learn last week. That was great timing, Dr. Henderson. Don't you think?"

"Indeed, Miss Khatri. Indeed. From its description," he continued, "it sounds like he was an ancient lich. Perhaps a king of some sort."

"But what would it be doing here?" Disha asked. "We never had kings in America."

Dr. Henderson shrugged. "He could have also been a madman who thought himself king. Anyone who chooses to become a lich cannot be in their right mind."

"Um," Disha's dark gaze darted between Dr. Henderson and me. "I don't mean to scare Charlie, but... is the school safe? This is the second time an evil Lesser got in. How were they able to get through the Academy's magical defenses?"

Lesser? I frowned at the new term, unaware of its meaning.

"That is the question we are trying to answer," Dr. Henderson said, appearing concerned. "As far as the Academy being safe, well, I can assure you both that, even as we speak, Dean McIntosh is working diligently to reinforce the protective charms around campus."

After a lot more reassuring, Dr. Henderson dismissed us with the advice that we should rest.

So much for my first day of class. All I wanted to do was go to bed and sleep, except maybe that was a bad idea, what with the school being a hotbed for nasty creatures. At least my rats never tried to suck the life out of me. "Free trial" or not, I didn't sign up to become a desiccated corpse.

I was deep in thought, walking away from Dr. Henderson's office and considering if I should pack and split, when someone called behind us.

"Disha, wait up!"

She glanced back, then stopped. "Rowan," she said.

Damn! The day kept getting worse and worse.

Without turning, I pressed forward.

Disha put a hand around my arm. "Wait, don't leave yet. We should talk."

I almost said I had nothing else to talk to her about but, even though I wanted her to leave me alone, I also didn't want to get on her bad side—not after seeing what she was capable of. So I waited, hands in my pockets, face turned away from Rowan as he approached.

"Hey, I heard," Rowan said, his voice gentle and full of concern, nothing like the way it sounded when he talked to me. "Are you okay?"

"Yes, I'm fine," Disha said. "Rowan, have you met Charlie?"

I gave him a sideways glance. His face went from pleasant to constipated-looking in a flash.

"I have," he said as if having met me had caused his constipation.

His presence made me extremely self-conscious. My ripped jeans and T-shirt bothered me more than normal, and his good looks made me wish he had a wart on his nose or something. He was insufferably handsome. How was that fair?

Disha didn't seem to miss anything as her inquisitive eyes went back and forth between us. She huffed. "There can't possibly be bad blood between you two already?"

"Oh no, nothing like that," I said. "Rowan has been *extremely* nice to me since shooting that werewolf."

"You shot a werewolf?!" Disha asked excitedly, giving Rowan her full attention.

Mission accomplished. Surreptitiously, I took two sidelong steps, planning an escape. But, as I was leaving, Disha stopped me.

"I have a feeling we all have a lot of talking to do," she said, hooking an arm through mine and the other through Rowan's and dragging us down the hall and into a large room.

The place seemed to be a lounge. On one end, there were three comfortable sofas arranged around a big coffee table. At the other, several people sat at long tables, looking into their laptops or studying from large textbooks.

Disha led us to the empty sofas and practically pushed us into one of them. We landed next to each other, while she planted her bottom on the coffee table right in front of us.

Rowan gave my thigh a covert glance as it brushed against his. We both jumped as if the sofa were electrified and moved apart, adding a few feet of distance between us. I crossed my arms, looking at anything *but* Rowan. Talk about awkward.

"Ooh," Disha said, "I sense sparks."

"Don't be ridiculous," Rowan said.

If I'd known either of them better, I'd have said something snarky, but I figured the less I opened my mouth, the quicker I'd get out of here.

Disha quickly changed subjects. "Tell me all about this werewolf."

Rowan shook his head. "No, you tell me about the lich first."

Without protest, she proceeded to repeat what had happened. Apparently, she cared more about recounting her own adventures than listening to those of others. She seemed to revel in Rowan's attention, in fact, *any* attention.

After Disha finished explaining what Dr. Henderson had said about the Dean fortifying the protective spells around the Academy, Rowan remained deep in thought for a few minutes.

At times, I caught him glancing in my direction, then turning away when I discovered him. His ill-disguised interest made my skin tingle, and I hated myself for it. No matter how spell-binding his eyes, I had to train my body to grow cold rather than warm when he looked at me. I couldn't deny the guy was hot—hotter than anyone I'd ever met, what with his perfect chin, soulful eyes and amazing body—but more than that, he was a jerk who had decided to hate me because I was poor. No wonder he seemed to be friends with Disha. She certainly had a sizable bank account.

At last, Rowan said, "We should talk later."

He stood, giving me a sideways glance that made it clear he didn't want me as part of *that* conversation.

"I sense some reluctance," Disha said, narrowing her eyes, "so I should tell you, I've decided Charlie is going to be my BFF. Sooo... whatever you need to say to me, you can say it in front of her."

The what?

My mouth opened and closed. People were weird here. Who just up and decides you'll be their BFF without even consulting you?

"You can't be serious, Disha," Rowan said. "You barely know her. You don't know where she comes from."

"Yes, I do," Disha said. "She's from Conyers. Not far from here."

"That not what I mean," Rowan said, giving her a pointed look as if to say "*she comes from a rat-infested building, and you might catch the black plague from her.*"

I blinked a few times and, snapping out of my surprise, I stood, too. "Um, that's nice of you, Disha, but I don't think I'll be staying here much longer."

Fists clenched in a effort not to punch Rowan's nose in, I walked around the coffee table and headed for the door.

"Now look what you've done," I heard Disha say behind me.

"It's for the best," Rowan replied.

I ground my teeth so hard, they creaked. Red flashed in front of my eyes, and I felt ready to explode from fury. Picking up my step to avoid making a scene, I walked out of the lounge area into the corridor and promptly ran smack into somebody.

The pain of something like an ax splitting my chest in two nearly dropped me to my knees.

My vision went black. Images popped inside my head like a slideshow on steroids. They moved so fast I barely could make sense of them. First, there was a dark shape, a man's silhouette against a bright background. That was followed by tattered fabric floating as if in a pool of water, then a skeletal face with a tarnished crown on its head.

The metallic smell of blood flooded my senses, making me want to gag.

My hand flew out. I got hold of something, fighting to recover my control. A hand squeezed mine, grounding me, keeping me from the dark pull of those images in my head.

I came to with a gasp. Had I fractured further? Dean McIntosh had warned me weird things might keep happening to me.

A man's face hovered in front of me. "Blimey, are you all right?"

Eyes as blue as an iceberg stared into mine. I stepped back and took in the person I'd run into. He wore a black suit—a teacher, for sure, since that seemed to be their dress code—and appeared to be in his mid-forties. He had blond hair and dark lashes, and his eyes were serious but his lips seemed ready to break into a mocking smile.

Disha and Rowan came out of the lounge area and stared at my hand locked in the man's. I pulled it away and stuck it in my pocket.

"Professor Answorth," Disha said. "I didn't know you were back from London."

"Ms. Khatri. Mr. Underwood," Professor Answorth said, inclining his head and giving Rowan a forced smile, though his expression softened when he focused on Disha. His British accent was almost entrancing and did nothing but improve his good looks. Was every teacher in this Academy an ex-supermodel or something?

"I see you've met our new classmate," Disha said. "Charlie, are you okay?"

"Oh," he said, turning his attention back to me. "Charlie Rivera, correct?"

"You know her?" Rowan asked with an air of distrust in his voice.

"No, dear chap," he said with annoyance at the stupid question. "Dean McIntosh sent an email to all the staff. A new student starting this late in the term is unusual, but I hear I can expect good things." His smile fell on me, but the icy chill still ran down my spine as memories of those dark images replayed in my mind.

"It's good to meet you, Ms. Rivera," he said. "I look forward to seeing you in my classroom. Maybe I can help you release your... *repressed* powers."

Great! Apparently, Dean McIntosh had told everyone I was repressed or something. Was that as bad as it sounded? From the contempt in Rowan's face, it appeared so.

Professor Answorth straightened his jacket, then, with a wave goodbye, kept on his way.

When Rowan walked off, there was no wave, but his expression suggested he'd have liked to give me a raised middle finger.

Back at you, Douche baguette!

Disha rolled her eyes. "Let's go, *Charbroiled*. I must fill you in on all this male drama."

And again, Disha's arm hooked through mine as she led me God knew where.

CHAPTER EIGHT

FALL SEMESTER
EARLY SEPTEMBER

"DON'T JUST STAND THERE GAWKING in the hallway, *Charmander.*
Come in and shut the door." Disha waved me in as she settled on
her queen-sized four poster bed.

But I couldn't help but gawk. If I thought my room was nice,
it was a roach motel compared to Disha's. Hers was double the
size and decked out with furniture twice as nice. Seriously, her
chest of drawers must've come from Queen Victoria herself,
judging by its elaborate carvings and polished sheen. And were
those twenty-four karat gold drawer pulls?

When I walked forward to get a better look, Disha popped up
to close the door behind me. Perhaps she was worried I might slip
out. And her worries were not unfounded. Her desire to make me
her new BFF made my stomach squirm. She may have saved my
life, but I still wasn't sure about her motives.

"How did you get all this?" My eyes drifted from the expensive white duvet to the crystal chandelier hanging over her bed to the closet stuffed with designer clothes and shoes. On the wall opposite the large windows, a fancy desk held the entire contents of a drugstore makeup counter in scattered piles. Above it, a mirror ringed by exposed lightbulbs looked like something out of a Broadway dressing room. I mean, the room had *mood lighting*.

The space seemed more like a set of MTV's *Cribs* than a college dorm room.

Disha glanced around as if she'd forgotten she went to sleep in the Taj Mahal each night. "Oh, this? Daddy had furniture shipped in. Anyway, tell me, how did you get off on such a bad foot with Rowan? He looked like you boiled his bunny or something."

"You mean he isn't that charming with all the new girls?" I said in mock surprise, picking up a shiny black high-heeled shoe from the floor and examining it. How girls clomped around in virtual stilts all day baffled me.

"Do you like those?" Disha asked, nodding at the shoe. "You can have them. Or better yet..." She ran to her closet and disappeared in the fabric folds. When she reappeared a few moments later, she was clutching several items.

"Makeover!" She waved a handful of dresses and skirts like pompons.

"No. Oh, no." I backed up, but bumped into the wall as she plied me with cashmere tops and flowery scarves.

After I refused most of her clothes, the only way to get her to stop trying to dress me was to agree to take three tops, two pairs of shorts and a pair of really kick-ass black Converse All-Stars that she swore she had in three other colors. I hated taking charity, but she insisted, and if I was going to avoid the mockery I'd suffered in high school, I needed more than one outfit, besides the very nice and dorky school T-shirts from Dean McIntosh.

"I'm going to dig out more," she said, jumping on her bed once again.

I tucked the clothes in a bag she'd given me, a reluctant smile on my face.

"And tomorrow," she added, "we can tackle your hair."

I touched my brown ponytail self-consciously. "What's wrong with my hair?"

"Nothing," Disha said, throwing back her luxurious curls. "You're a total babe. It's no wonder Rowan stares at you."

"Stop it," I said. I'd spent the last hour trying to forget his painfully handsome face. "He stares at me to know how to construct his voodoo doll in proper proportions. What was the dude drama you mentioned earlier, anyway?" I settled on the tufted chair across from her bed.

"Oh, yeah." She leaned forward, laying on her stomach, propping her head up, and kicking her feet back like we were in a made-for-TV movie. "So, get this. Apparently, there's a lot of bad blood between the Underwoods and Professor Answorth, the teacher who helped you in the hallway. Rowan told me his dad thinks that Professor Answorth is behind the breaks in security."

No wonder Rowan seemed to get meaner when he saw my hand in the Professor's.

"If you ask me," Disha said, "I think the Underwoods suspect him because he's a Lesser."

Lesser. That word again. I frowned. "What exactly is a Lesser?"

She stared at me as if I were from Mars.

"In case you haven't realized it," I said defensively, "I didn't grow up in *your* circles."

Her eyebrows went up. "You mean the outside world doesn't know the difference between Lessers and Supers?"

I shrugged and marveled at how disconnected from the *real* world she was.

"Well, let me educate you. It's really easy." She put out her right hand. "Witches and warlocks... Supers." Her left hand went up next. "Everyone else... Lessers."

"That sounds... awful," I said, wondering if my comment would make her decide she didn't want to be my BFF anymore. Though that would be fine, even if I was starting to like her. Anything that smelled of discrimination, for whatever reason, wouldn't fly with me.

"I know," she said. "I know some very nice vamps and succubi."

I sighed in relief, glad she wasn't a bigot, then asked, "So, what is Answorth exactly?

"A fae," Disha said.

"Really?"

"Uh-huh."

I gestured toward my ears. "But don't fae have—"

"Pointed ears?" Disha interrupted. "They do, but he uses a glamour to disguise them and some of his other non-human features. Mind you, Charmander, you shouldn't believe everything you see." She tapped her nose.

Pondering, I took her words to heart.

Following her previous line of thought, she said, "Can you imagine if it's a teacher letting creatures like that lich in? Mary-beth could have died."

I *could have died*, I thought quietly. I was told I'd be safer here than on my own, but maybe not. Another reason my thirty-day trial might be coming to an end sooner rather than later.

"So, what do you think Dean Underwood is going to do about this Answorth guy?" I asked.

Disha sucked in a deep breath before continuing. "Rowan says they have no real evidence, just a hunch, and that Dean McIntosh trusts Answorth for some reason. They need real evidence, which is why Rowan's confided in me. Because of my extra training with Dr. Henderson." She worked her eyebrows up and down in a knowing fashion. "I'm the best trained freshman here. Plus, Rowan trusts me. Our families go way back."

Disha blew on her polished fingernails and buffed them on her shirt. I rolled my eyes. A sliver of her confidence could keep me going for a year, I swear.

"So Rowan wants you to investigate?"

"Yep."

She twisted her hair into a bun at the top of her head and somehow tucked it in on itself to secure it. The fact that the bun was both messy and still extremely attractive was sorcery in itself.

"Rowan tells me things and I keep my eyes and ears open. No one talks about anything around him since he's Macgregor's son, but me..." She held her arms out as if to say *What's not to like?*

"And the great part is now you can help us," Disha said excitedly.

"Me?"

"Just think about it. Who is less assuming, less of a threat, than you?" She gestured to my *all-ness*.

Oh, geez. Here we went again. For a girl as smart as she seemed to be, Disha could be pretty dumb when it came to saying offensive things. So much for wanting me as her BFF. Apparently, she only wanted to exploit me.

"Look, if you're going to use me as some sort of stooge, a get out of jail free card, then I'm out." I stood up.

I'd seen this before. Who would be a better target than the poor girl? Beautiful Disha could break whatever rule she wanted and then pin it on me. Because, of course, I was a criminal, a thief, or whatever they needed me to be.

As I made for the door, she jumped up. "Wait, wait. What did I say now?"

I narrowed my eyes. "You really don't know?"

"No," she said, waving her hands as if in desperation. "I say things and they always come out wrong. I'm sorry. I didn't have many... playmates growing up."

"Playmates?" I raised an eyebrow.

"You know what I mean." She flopped on the bed, appearing defeated for the first time. "We moved a lot. I had a private tutor and didn't even go to school for several years. Then the ones I did go to, the girls were so... "

"Rich? Stuck up? Bitchy?" I offered.

"Yes! You get it." Her shoulders slumped. "I'm bad at this. I really am. My father had to literally pay people to attend my sixteenth birthday party. It didn't hurt that he'd hired The Black Eyed Peas to play."

It was shocking to hear her confession. What I'd taken for popular girl meanness was just lonely girl awkwardness.

And, boy, did I know about that.

I sat back down on the bed beside her. With Trey gone, I literally had no one, and it sounded like Disha didn't either. And how could I fault her for being born into wealth any more than I wanted to be faulted for being born into poverty? Besides, I needed someone else besides Trey's ashes to talk to.

"If I let you do my hair, can you promise not to make me into 2007 Britney Spears?"

Disha sniffed and then giggled. "Your head is too oblong for a shaved style, babe." She lifted my ponytail and let it drop playfully. "Will you help me with the investigation?"

"Do I have to talk to Rowan?"

She shook her head.

"Then I'm in."

"Goodie." She clapped her hands. Honest to God, clapped them.

I laughed despite myself.

Then she grabbed a curling iron. "Now, let's see that hair."

———

AN HOUR LATER, I was spectacularly coiffed and on my way to my room, having survived as much preening as I could stand. It did not escape me that both of my best friends had insisted on trying to makeover my appearance. Maybe life was trying to tell me something.

Or maybe everyone else was way too fixated on physical appearance.

Either way, I'd only let Disha curl my hair and apply a little bit of lipstick. It had cheered her up and given me time to think about all she'd told me.

When I'd experienced that episode in the hallway, it was Answorth I had bumped into. I hadn't told Disha the visions I saw or the feelings. And yet, somehow I thought Answorth had been the one who pull me *out* of the visions. But maybe bumping into him had also been the reason I went into them.

What did that mean? Were Rowan and his father right to suspect he was behind the lich attack? Was Answorth one of the bad guys? A subversive? If so, was it too much of a leap to think he had any connection to the people who had tried to kidnap me? If he was at all responsible for Trey's death and my near-desiccation on my first day of class, I needed to know. Maybe this deal with Disha wasn't such a bad idea, after all.

A large grandfather clock I passed made me aware that I'd missed lunch, which was fine considering my huge breakfast this morning. I'd been excused from my afternoon class because of my brush with the lich, so I had some free time. Apparently near-death experiences had their perks.

Back in my room, I took out the clothes Disha had given me and showed them to Trey.

"What do you think?" I pressed a pair of shorts to my body. "I think you would like Disha. She has a thing for hair and makeup, too. Plus, she's pretty. Maybe you would have been *into* her."

I smiled sadly, then put my new clothes in my new closet.

After that, I dug out all the pamphlets Dean McIntosh had given me. It only took me a few minutes to find Professor Answorth in one of them. There was a super short bio that said he had left his fae home at a young age due to a keen interest in humans and their occult arts. It also mentioned he was a Mentalism professor, which apparently meant studying things like psychic abilities, telepathy, telekinesis, and mind control, all pretty terrifying subjects in the hands of the wrong person. Below that, the pamphlet went on to list his office hours and location. He'd be in for visiting hours at two PM, thirty minutes from now.

Perfect.

I thought about telling Disha my plan, but realized it would be easier if she wasn't with me. I could feign ignorance and ask more questions that way. What new student didn't need guidance, especially one who'd had such a traumatic first day?

As I went to put away the brochures, I spotted a picture of Dr. Henderson's smiling face. He appeared just as charming as when I'd met him in his office. Curious, I read his bio and deduced he was some sort of magical prodigy who had graduated from the Academy at the tender age of eighteen. After that, he'd traveled the world and studied at other Supernatural colleges around the world. He was known for creating his own spells and mastering those of old powerful witches and warlocks. Go figure. The Albert Einstein of the supernatural world. No wonder Disha was learning so much.

With my plan as well thought out as it could get, I grabbed a muffin I'd swiped from the cafeteria and headed out.

Down the stairs and out of the dorms, I walked across the quad to the Humanities Building, a grand structure on the north end of campus, right across from the Enlightenment Fountain, the massive, beautiful water feature that dominated campus.

As I walked my way across several huge lawns, I stewed a bit, having second thoughts about what I was doing. What kind of noob would thrust herself into an investigation with a mentalist? Did I want to almost die twice today?

I pushed my fears away. All I had to do was play it cool and make sure he didn't suspect my ulterior motives.

Right, and cool was my specialty.

The weather was hot, but beautiful, another sunny afternoon in Georgia. The sun burned the top of my head, but I was used to that. Besides, I wouldn't stay hot for long because the great thing about campus was that every building had air conditioning. The grass was watered daily, so it stayed green and luscious. Flowers in beds outside the stately brick buildings filled the air with perfume.

You wouldn't know, in a place this beautiful, that an ancient king might pop up to drain your essence.

A boy whizzed past me on a skateboard, the wheels clacking on the pavement. I felt a terrible ache in my gut. My board had been left back in the abandoned building and I didn't suppose Disha had an old one lying around.

The ache was deeper than that, though. The skateboard reminded me of Trey, and my life as a homeless teen. Was it over? Would this trial period convince me to stay and let my old life go up in smoke? Well, it wasn't like it would be the first time this had happened to me.

Nothing was permanent. Nothing lasted.

Boy, I could use a hit of whatever spell Irmagard had given me in the counseling office right about now.

Emotions swirling in my chest, I rushed toward the Enlightenment Fountain and leaned against its outer wall. The size of a backyard swimming pool, the fountain was round and robust with water spraying out of the center and five animal statues ringing around it. The marble beasts all contorted in different positions.

A lion with its paw outstretched was closest to me. It was regal and aloof and—according to one of the many brochures I'd briefly perused—symbolized ferocity. Next to it was an eagle, its mouth open and talons out in what appeared to be an attack. It represented freedom.

I walked around the basin to get a better look at the other three statues—a woman with one arm, her face blank as if stupefied. I couldn't remember what she represented. A turtle standing on two legs, the front two up as if in defense. It symbolized protection. And the last, a fish with bulging eyes that stood for adaptability.

The fountain sure had character and felt like each of its creatures must have some elaborate story centered around it, some sort of Academy lore I should learn. Maybe I needed to carefully read the entire pile of material Dean McIntosh had given me, but who had time for that?

I went on staring at the creatures, all so strange, so... puzzling. Yet, I was drawn to them.

Obeying a strange impulse to dip my fingers in the water, I reached out.

As soon as my skin brushed the surface, a jolt snapped through me.

Just like before, my vision darkened and the slideshow of horror ran in my mind's eye showing me every terrible magic event I'd experienced since the attack—Smudge Face, the lich, the werewolf, that same dark, faceless figure from when I ran into Answorth. Trey being slashed across the chest, his face going slack.

A scream stuck in my throat, choking me. I couldn't breathe. I couldn't move. Was I fracturing further? Was it the fountain?

Something bashed into me, knocking me off my feet. When I stumbled forward, my hands went out to catch my fall, breaking my contact with the water.

The images stopped. My eyes fluttered open, and I sucked in a huge gulp of air.

When I glanced up, no one was around, but then I spotted the dark shape of a man cutting a swift path across the quad away from me.

And from behind, that person looked distinctly like Rowan Underwood.

CHAPTER NINE

FALL SEMESTER
EARLY SEPTEMBER

I WAS FREAKED out enough to almost talk myself out of going to Professor Answorth's office, but I was no chicken. If living on the streets had taught me anything, it was to be brave. Not as brave as Trey had been, but brave enough to find his killer, plus the lich monger.

What could the *posh* professor do to me for asking a few simple questions?

Nothing.

Even as I hurried to the Humanities Building and tried to focus on its ornate facade, the image of all those Supernaturals—or were they Lessers?—trying to get to me became stuck on repeat inside my head. My spine tingled, and without meaning to, I glanced back toward the fountain. I wasn't sure what was up with that thing. Was it possessed or something? Because it wasn't me. *I* wasn't possessed. Been there done that with the Shadow Puppet, and that felt completely different.

A group of students walked out of the Humanities building as I made my way inside. One of them was laughing after she blinked her eyes at a guy's backpack and it started bouncing up and down.

"Quit it, Olivia," the guy said in a tone that actually sounded as if he was happy the girl was messing with him.

I shook my head, then stopped to get my bearings. Inside, the building seemed more utilitarian than what I'd seen so far. It was still fancy, but the foyer was not some grand affair, just a simple space with some benches and planters. It quickly branched into halls leading to offices and classrooms.

Squinting my eyes and wiggling my nose, I tried to tap into magic to somehow discern the way to Answorth's office. Nothing happened, unless I counted feeling stupid. Apparently, I was starting to buy Dean McIntosh's story about my Supernatural DNA. There was more than disappearing ibuprofen now. There were also visions, so maybe she was onto something.

I resigned myself by reading the directory on the wall rather than the magical GPS I wished I had. Answorth was the first name on the alphabetical list. His office number was 1015.

Making my way down the hall with a sign that read 1000 to 1015, I took several deep breaths and told myself there was nothing to be afraid of. I was just going to have a friendly talk with my professor. I was in his Mentalism class, after all, and visiting him during office hours was natural. No problem.

Even if he could turn me into a mindless zombie with a twiddle of his fingers.

Every office I passed had a number and a plaque with the teacher's name on the door. I expected to see or hear some activity, but the hall was deserted, permeated by an eerie silence that gave me the creeps.

Professor Answorth's office was at the end of the hall, its door closed just like all the others. His sign read "Julian Answorth, PhD."

I knocked, wondering if he was a PhD in the real world or only in the Supernatural one. What could he possibly be a doctor of in the Supernatural world? Magical brain surgery?

I knocked again with a bit more insistence. No response. Rubbing the back of my neck, I surveyed the empty hall, then tried the doorknob. It turned.

Inching the door open, I called, "Hello? Professor Answorth?"

There was a quiet creak as the door swung wide. The office was dark, its only illumination the sunlight seeping through a set of wooden blinds.

With one final scan of the hall, I stepped inside, my eyes drinking in Answorth's domain. There were the usual shelves filled with books, and a desk with one leather chair behind it and two out front for visitors. But that was where "usual" stopped.

I was drawn to the shelves first, which contained books, but also some very interesting "bookends."

There were several decks of tarot cards, a crystal ball with murky depths, a jar full of small bones, a turban with a red jewel affixed to the front, half-burned candles, a 3D model of a brain with parts that could be taken out of its skull cradle, and more.

Were these the tools of a mentalist? They appeared more like a cheap fortuneteller's knick-knacks.

Turning from the shelves, I listened intently for footsteps and, when I heard nothing, I moved toward the desk. A large tome lay open on its surface, a full cup of tea to the side. It seemed Answorth had left in the middle of some light reading. Though, hadn't he just gotten back from London?

Squinting, I leaned over the book. Keeping my hands at my back to avoid touching anything, I took in the illustration that filled the entire left page.

A lich.

My heart quickened as I recognized the skeletal features, its teeth bare as if in mockery. Tattered clothes floated behind it and skeletal hands held a scepter.

The headlines on the other page read "Conjuring and Controlling a Lich" and "Vanquishing a Lich."

When a violent chill cut across my back, I decided I'd seen enough. Rushing out of the office, I eased the door shut behind me.

Heart still sputtering, I walked down the hall, relieved to find it empty.

I was down by office 1011 when there was a laugh, the door opened, and someone came out.

"You are certainly right, my dear fellow," a man said.

I froze as Answorth stepped into the hall.

Catching my presence out of the corner of his eye, he turned and blinked in surprise.

"Ms. Rivera," he said, closing the door to the office he'd just vacated. "What brings you to this side of campus?"

"I... I was looking for you." I hooked a finger over my shoulder to indicate his office. "But you weren't there, so I was leaving."

"Well, I'm here now," he said with a smile. "Come, let's go back. I hardly get any visitors during my office hours. That's why I was chatting with Professor Fedorov. Nice chap. From Saint Petersburg. You'll have him Junior Year if you make it that long." He gave me a cheeky wink as if he meant the comment as a joke, but I shivered all the same.

He herded me back toward his office, and I saw no other alternative but to go with the flow.

As we walked in, he flipped the switch and four lamps came on, one in each corner. He also turned on the desk lamp and promptly sat in his chair, inviting me to take a seat across from him.

I sat and, trying not to over-act, I let my eyes rove around the room, frowning slightly. I paid special attention to the shelves as if I'd never seen them before.

"Fascinating artifacts, wouldn't you say, Ms. Rivera?" he asked, noticing my interest.

I nodded.

"I've collected them over the years," he explained. "They're curiosities that Regulars believe help with divining people's thoughts and future, but you and I know better than that, don't we?" He winked again, drawing an involuntary smile from me. His blue eyes caught the light from the desk lamp, and they practically sparkled.

He was good at setting people at ease, or was it his skill in mentalism working on me? I sucked in a breath, determined to stay cool. My eyes landed on the huge tome that rested in front of him.

His gaze fell to the book as well. "Something else that's fascinating is liches." He pushed the book in my direction, flipping it so I could read. "Not for the faint of heart. It says here," he pointed to a paragraph down the middle of the page, "that it takes very powerful magic and deep knowledge of the creatures to be able to control them."

With a pensive expression on his face, Answorth stood, strode to the window, and opened the blinds. He peered out at the woods behind the building, rubbing his chin, lost in his own thoughts, likely wondering who could have taken control of the old, undead king. Either that, or feigning it so I wouldn't suspect him.

"At any rate," he said, snapping out of it. "What brings you to my office, Ms. Rivera? How can I help you?" He returned to his seat, giving me his full attention.

"Well..." I trailed off, casting out for something to say. He'd distracted me to the point that I couldn't remember my excuse for visiting and, instead, I found myself saying, "Professor, I thought you might know about this...vision I had."

He lifted a blond eyebrow.

"I mean... I don't know if that's your area of expertise," I said.

"But I thought since you teach Mentalism, you might be the right person to ask...um... you know, since the visions are in my... head." I shut my mouth.

God, let the ground split and swallow me whole. Apparently, being homeless had done a number on my social skills.

He nodded sagely, oblivious to my blunders. "I can try to help, Ms. Rivera. Visions are definitely a subject that pertains to my studies. Tell me about them, please." He beckoned with one hand.

"Um," I paused, painfully aware of my screw up.

I had to tread carefully here. I couldn't trust any of these people. For all I knew, he'd played some mind trick on me already, and that was the reason I'd turned into a loose-tongued parrot.

"It's only happened once," I lied, speaking carefully. "And maybe it's not a vision, but more like a magical memory. I keep seeing the lich and this werewolf that attacked me."

I figured Dean McIntosh would have told the entire faculty how I ended up at the Academy, so it was probably safe to mention the werewolf. I did leave out the part about the dark figure that seemed to accompany the images, which was what made me think they were visions and not just memories. That dark figure was nothing like the Shadow Puppet. I was sure of that. It felt infinitely more evil than that, and I had a feeling it was responsible for what was going on here.

Answorth nodded. "Those must have been two very traumatic situations for you, so I'm not surprised the images of what happened keep rearing their ugly heads—not to mention you're still *fracturing*. But you shouldn't worry too much about it. Just give it some time. Now that you're being trained to use your magic and when you're done fracturing, these visions should stop. Also, consider that you're in a new environment. It's a big change for you. Lots of stress, though I have no doubt you'll be just fine in the end."

His words sounded confident as if he had peered into my future and had seen me rocking those Academy T-shirts Dean

McIntosh had given me, while walking around campus with a big smile on my face and a train of adoring friends who wanted me to help them with their homework.

Despite myself, I found my heart feeling lighter and more hopeful about the prospect of staying here.

"Thank you, Professor Answorth," I said. "I'll give it some time."

"Good, good," he said, smiling. "Time heals everything, Ms. Rivera, even the worst wounds." His smile fell a little as if he were remembering something which time hadn't fully healed for him.

So much for suspecting Professor Answorth. He seemed far too kind to be responsible for nearly killing a student.

A few minutes later, I left the Humanities Building. It was a beautiful day out, and I hadn't spent much time amongst the lush flower gardens. Almost absently, I found myself drawn to a hedge garden I'd seen on my way here. Its entrance was a gravel path lined by two rows of miniature bushes in the shape of upside-down cones.

I strolled in, relishing the sunlight on my face and thinking of all that had happened to me in the expanse of four days. Trey's loss felt like a huge welt on my heart that even time's healing qualities wouldn't be able to bandage, much less get rid of. What would I do with his ashes? Keep them? Toss them into the wind? Neither option felt right.

The further I walked, the taller the hedges grew, and I realized the garden was actually a labyrinth. I took a right, making a mental note, determined not to get lost.

After a few more turns, I heard footsteps. Someone was following me.

My heart sped up as I pictured another lich, its bony hands reaching for my neck. What if I couldn't find my way out? And what in the world had made me come in here in the first place? A mind trick from Answorth?

Quickly, I inserted myself between two tight hedges. Their

branches scratched my face and arms, but I clamped my lips shut, held my breath, and stood as still as humanly possible. I waited, peering between the tightly-packed leaves.

Gravel crunched lightly under someone's careful steps. My heartbeat picked up as my overactive brain worried about worse things than a lich or a werewolf, something like a zombie that could suck my brains and infect me so I would crave brains, too.

Then the threat entered my line of vision.

It was Rowan Underwood.

CHAPTER TEN

FALL SEMESTER
EARLY SEPTEMBER

I WATCHED, barely breathing as Rowan Underwood slunk through the labyrinth, his dark eyes searching.

He *was* following me. I knew it was him at the fountain. What was his plan now? Get me alone and jump me? I'd marked him as a jerk, but maybe he was the one attacking students, letting in liches, and wanting to erase evidence. He must think I knew something, and visiting Professor Answorth, a Lesser, couldn't have helped my case.

Trembling with rage and anticipation, I tracked his movements as he stalked down one path, circled around and walked back the other way, his feet crunching quietly on the gravel.

Good, he'd lost me. If I was lucky, he'd go away, and I'd get the hell out of this maze. That was, if I could find my way out. In the commotion, I'd forgotten what turns I'd taken to get myself here.

Rowan came back into view, his eyes still searching, his

expression even and calculating. I tried desperately not to notice his perfectly tousled hair and the vee of skin visible above his white T-shirt. Sun glinted off his medallion as he turned. He was so handsome it made me angry. He probably got everything he wanted with a wink and a smile, not that he needed charm since he had money and a father on the payroll.

He had everything, and he was trying to push *me* out? Me, who had literally nothing but an urn of ashes containing my only friend!

Fists clenched, I fought the urge to rush out and punch him in his Hemsworth-brother face.

Suddenly, the ground shook, trembling like an earthquake was splitting the maze in half. But, instead of cracks forming in the ground, the hedges began to shift. As I watched, the high shrubs lifted up like giant green arms and slammed down in different positions.

"Shit," Rowan said, whirling. He held his hands out as if getting ready to either perform magic or slap box some bushes.

The greenery I'd shoved myself into began to rise, clawing at my skin, dragging me upwards with its *branchie* fingers. I tried to scramble out, untangling from twigs that tugged at my shirt and weaved into my hair. I broke branches with my hands, bending and twisting as my feet lifted off of the ground.

"Hey!" Rowan yelled, surprised or angry, I wasn't sure, but he raised his hands at me ready to throw a spell.

I twisted violently and broke out of the remaining branches. Hitting the ground hard, I gasped for breath as Rowan ran over.

"Stay back!" I grabbed a handful of gravel and threw it at his eyes.

He ducked, throwing his arms over his face for protection.

Scrambling up, I took off down the first path I saw, and ran straight into a dead end. When I whirled around, Rowan blocked my way out.

"Leave me alone," I said, casting about for an escape. I could try to slip through the hedges again, but these looked exceptionally dense. Climbing over wasn't an option as they were nearly ten feet high. Plus, the ground was still trembling, letting me know the hedges were still moving.

"Charlie, stop." He held his hands up, chest heaving. His eyes darted around as if searching for something. "We need to get out of here."

We? I wasn't going anywhere with him, even if he held the only map to the maze.

A buzzing sound filled the air as if hornets had been disturbed in the hedges' shift. I sensed the beat of wings and a poke on my neck. Swatting, my hand brushed something far too large to be a hornet.

Instead of an insect, a large, winged animal *thing* dodged my blow, whirled out and darted toward Rowan.

"Pixie minotaurs! We've gotta go. Come on." He turned on his heel and sprinted into the maze.

Pixie minotaurs?

I knew what pixies were, little fairies I assumed. And minotaurs were those half-bull, half-man animals from Greek mythology, right? But, the creature buzzing toward me was somehow a combination of both.

Fairy wings flapped in a blur behind a brown body with human hands and cloven hoof feet. Small horns curled out above a twisted and ugly face with human eyes but a bovine snout. Its body was about eight inches tall, so I wondered why Rowan had turned tail and run. I could bat that sucker out of the air with one swat.

He was a coward. Fancy that.

As the pixie minotaur flew closer, I realized it was carrying a small spear-like weapon in one hand. That explained the poke. Okay. I could still deal.

"Come at me, you nasty bugger. I'll knock your socks off." I raised my hands, ready to fight.

But instead of ramming at me with its spear, it stopped, hovered in midair, and waved the thing like a wand.

A strange sensation tingled all over my scalp first, then my face and neck, spreading down my body. Horrified, I lifted my hands and watched small hairs sprout from my skin. The same tingling rippled along my collar and under my shirt, giving me a sneaking suspicion that more hair was growing in unwanted places.

"What did you do to me?" I asked, blindly swatting the air as heavy bangs grew down, obscuring my vision. Hair was growing rapidly on every surface of my body.

"Charlie!"

I whirled, pushing strands out of my eyes. Rowan rushed back to me, shooting spells from his fingertips as a swarm of pixie minotaurs flew after him. There were at least a dozen, and they were all firing from their tiny spears. As I watched, Rowan dodged a few, but lurched back as if struck. His eyes went wide as his head began to swell to enormous proportions.

A cry of anger bursting from his throat, he threw both hands up and slashed them sideways, blasting the swarm into a nearby hedge. Then he whirled on me.

"What are you doing? We need to—Oh." His anger turned to shock and then mockery. "Hit you with a capillum spell, did they? Wow." He put a fist to his mouth to cover up his laughter.

"You're one to talk," I said through the hair, gesturing to the top of his head that had swollen up like Violet Beauregarde in *Charlie in the Chocolate Factory*.

He reached up, feeling the extended top half of his head.

"This is your fault. If you had run when I told you to, the swarm wouldn't have gotten me." He waved his hands and his head shrunk down to its normal size.

I held out my hairy arms, waiting for him to do the same for me. He smirked and offered no such spell.

"Come on, Cousin It. We go this way."

Great.

Fuming, I followed him. What else could I do?

Holding my locks to either side so I could see, I trailed behind Rowan as we wove through seemingly unending turns. After fifteen minutes, I was sweating, my new hairdo sticking to most parts of my body.

"Why does this maze even exist? It's a nightmare." I said out loud, more to the universe than to Rowan.

Still, he answered me in a very *tour-guide-esque* manner.

"It was a present from Head Dean Erodot to the new Head Dean Fitzpatrick in 1955. It was supposed to be a gesture of goodwill, but in actuality the maze is hexed. Dean Erodot had been ousted because of his role in the vampire uprising and the subsequent fallout, so this was his revenge. The labyrinth is so carefully cursed, no one has been able to remove it. It has moving walls and mischievous creatures that live inside them. Thus, the pixie minotaurs. Thank god, Dean Erodot had a conscience and didn't want anyone to die."

"And yet, no one thinks to tell the *new student about this?*" I shouted. "How do we get out?"

"It's difficult, but I can do it. Advanced magicians can sense the opening." He straightened his shoulders as he finished his boast. "And, by the way, the welcome package talks about this and other such places on campus. But clearly, you haven't bothered to read the material."

I narrowed my eyes, forgetting he couldn't see my eye-roll beneath all this hair. I'd read *some* of the brochures.

"Whatever, just get us out. This spell is killing me."

Rowan stopped beside me, flexed his fingers and did a complicated gesture. When it was finished, tingling broke out along my body again. Slowly, the hair receded.

I ran my hands down my smooth arms and then my face. The hair on my head was a mess—poor Disha and her curling makeover—but it felt so much better not to be a walking toupee in ninety-degree heat.

"Thanks," I said reluctantly.

Rowan shrugged. "Don't mention it. Seriously. I don't need people knowing I helped you."

Oh god, he was so insufferable.

He started down another path, and I contemplated running off again. I couldn't stand another moment staring at his smug face or hearing his rude comments.

When I opened my mouth intent on telling him so, he turned the corner and disappeared behind a hedge. A loud splashing sound was followed by a garbled cry.

Without thinking, I ran around the corner to find him stuck in a hip-deep pool of impossibly blue water that seemed to have appeared out of nowhere. As I stared, Rowan sank lower, the water acting almost like liquid quicksand, inching him further down by the second.

His hands scrambled through the gravel at the pool's edge, attempting to stop himself from being swallowed up, but there was nothing for him to grab onto. Then he began waving his hands as if attempting to perform magic, but it appeared as if nothing was working.

The water drew him in slowly, climbing up to his stomach.

"Rowan, what do I do?" I asked, running up in front of him. He would drown in seconds if I didn't help, and I couldn't have that on my conscience, no matter how annoying he was.

He scowled as if my offer of help was an insult. "Nothing. Back up."

He took a deep breath, held his hands out like a maestro ready to conduct an orchestra and made two large sweeping gestures. But something went wrong. Rowan cried out as if in terrible pain, grasped his chest where his medallion hung, and collapsed.

The water dragged him down even deeper.

"Oh, crap."

I knelt, grabbed Rowan by the arms, and tried to haul him out. He didn't budge. In fact, he sunk lower, his chest going under. He'd said this place wasn't supposed to kill anyone, but it surely was trying. Was this different? Another attack like the lich's?

I pulled again. Nothing. It was as if there were an equal force working against me.

Glancing around, I didn't see any rope or branches to assist in dragging him out or at least holding him in place until I could get help. In fact, there was nothing around me but tall, green hedges.

When I glanced down at the water for another solution, a face blinked back up at me. She smiled and blew a bubble kiss.

I did a double take, realizing that there was indeed a creature inside the pool—some sort of water nymph with blue-green scales and long flowing aquamarine hair. Her eyes were glassy opals that shone like sea glass and her teeth, when she smiled, curved inward like an angler fish. Her scaly fingers dug into Rowan's clothes as if she were attempting to claim him. I had no doubt she was trying to kill him—to eat him or simply drown him, I didn't know.

What I did know was if I didn't get him out soon, he would die.

Keeping one hand on his arm, I used the other to try to shake Rowan awake.

"Rowan. Rowan, wake up!" I slapped his face, but his head just lolled from side-to-side. He was out.

The nymph laughed at my little attempt, bubbles floating up to the surface, and yanked harder. Rowan slid down until only his head and arms were above the water.

"Stop," I said, glaring at the water nymph. Angry, I reached into the ice cold water and tried to pry her scaly fingers off. Instead of letting go, she reared back and bit me.

"Ow!" I shouted, yanking my hand up. "Knock it off!"

A shockwave rolled with it. Just like when I'd willed the Shadow Puppet to let me go back at the abandoned building, my intense impulse had some effect on the water nymph. She shivered, eyes blinking rapidly as if she'd been shocked. Her fingers let go of Rowan, and she plunged down, disappearing.

Just as I was attempting to pull him out, the pool exploded in an upward rush of water. I was blasted back, pummeled by the icy spray.

When it was over, the pool was gone. Rowan lay face down in the gravel.

I ran over and put my fingers to his neck. Was he dead? Terrible dread settled over my body, but his pulse beat strong. He rolled over, coughing up water. As he did, his hand patted my arm, then rested on it.

A quiet thank you. I almost couldn't believe it. Apparently he was only 99.99% douche.

I was drenched to the bone and so was Rowan, but at least the pool had disappeared along with the murderous water nymph.

His eyes fluttered open. When he saw me and how we were touching, he lurched up, pulling away.

"What? I... You..."

"You passed out. I saved your life," I said matter-of-factly. Then I softened my tone. "What happened? Why wasn't your magic working? And that spell you attempted... it looked like it hurt. Are you alright?"

He glowered at me, before standing up, brushing wet gravel from his clothes. "It's none of your damn business, but it was probably your fault."

Then he whirled on his heel and marched away into the maze.

My fault? His magic had failed him when he needed it must, and it was *my* fault?

Nope. I was wrong to give him credit. He *was* 100% douche.

CHAPTER ELEVEN

FALL SEMESTER
MID SEPTEMBER

"He did *WHAT*?" Disha asked, tossing a bag of clothes on my bed.

"He ran off and *left me in the maze*." I threw up my hands in a can-you-believe-it gesture.

I'd just finished recounting my time in the labyrinth from yesterday afternoon, including the part where, after I'd saved his life, Rowan ran off and left me to find my own way out. After that, it had taken me two hours to find the maze exit and, by then, I was too pooped to do anything but fall into bed. Disha had showed up at my door at eight AM, dying to know what had happened.

"Why is it so hard to believe that Rowan abandoned me in the maze? I know you think he's some hottie prince charming, but he's actually a major douche."

"Well," she said, looking conflicted, "maybe you shouldn't

judge him too harshly before you know more about him. It's not easy being Rowan."

"Whatever." I turned to the bed, not wanting to argue. "What are these?" I pulled a frilly pink top and a pair of very expensive-looking jeans out of the bag she'd brought.

"I cleaned out my closet while you were gone." She waved her hand dismissively at the sack like it was nothing to give someone dozens of designer clothes that had cost her family a small fortune. "Tell me more about the labyrinth. I've never gone in there. I heard a freshman nearly died last year. Sucked into a vortex or something."

"And no one thought to *tell me*? And forget the stupid welcome package, who reads that anyway?" I said, falling back on my bed. "What other mysterious places exist on campus that might cause my demise?"

"Do you want me to list them *all*?" she asked, honestly serious.

"Oh, my God. This place is a death trap." My abandoned warehouse had been safer than here.

"Go back to the part where Rowan was following you. Why would he do that when I'd already told him about having you help us dig up the truth?" Disha tapped her finger on her perfect chin.

"Because he hates me and wants me dead?" I offered.

"If that were true, why would he have run back to save you when the pixie minotaurs attacked?"

I threw up my hands. "Sudden conscience. A wish to rifle through my corpse. I don't know."

"Don't worry. I'll just ask him at lunch."

Man, I envied her ability to make everything seem like it wasn't a big deal, even murderous classmates and near death experiences.

"Whatever, just leave me out of it," I said. "Dean McIntosh wants to meet with me at lunch anyway. Probably to ask how it's going." I gave Disha two thumbs down. "This is what the Dean will get from me. I've had one too many brushes with death to give this place my seal of approval."

Disha gave my shoulder a playful shove. "What are you talking about? I doubt you've ever had this much adventure. Besides, you haven't seen any of the good parts yet, which is why I'm here, to escort you to your nine AM class, Spells 101 with Dr. Henderson. Hubba hubba." Disha waggled her eyebrows.

Disha loved Dr. Henderson, and it wasn't hard to see why—he was the youngest faculty member by at least ten years, coming in at just thirty years old. Yet, he was also regarded as one of the most powerful wizards here. Disha claimed that as a teen, he'd studied abroad with seven of the top ten witches and warlocks in the world, real magical prodigy.

Plus, he was freaking gorgeous.

Warm brown eyes, impeccably styled hair and cheekbones carved out of rock, Dr. Henderson could be a GQ model.

It was hard to fault Disha for her interest.

"Get dressed," she said, nudging the bag of clothes at me. "I want to snag coffee before class. Mama needs her go-go juice."

Disha was already dressed in a flowy sundress that showed off all her curves, gold bangles, and a necklace that dipped into her cleavage. It wasn't lost on me that the full makeup and hair were likely for a certain professor.

I pulled out the least frilly T-shirt and shorts from the bag, opting for my Vans since the Converse were still wet. Bathed in nymph water, yesterday's outfit didn't exactly smell lemony fresh. I needed to find out how to do laundry unless Disha had a spell for that.

I could tell she was impatient and wanted to leave, so I ran a brush through my hair and swished some mouthwash, and mentally said goodbye to Trey's urn, which Disha always tried and failed to ignore, casting furtive glances in its direction. Fortunately, she never said anything about it and respected my privacy in that regard.

As we left and headed to the dining hall, Disha didn't even gripe about my appearance since she was so eager to pull me out of the door. Once there, we queued up behind a gaggle of sleepy students, some still in pjs and barely awake. The girl in front of us kept wiggling her fingers and shooting them at her face, swearing under her breath every time her spell failed.

Disha leaned over to me. "Noob. She's attempting an alertness spell but getting the motions all wrong. Plus, this building has spell blockers in place." My friend rolled her eyes as if to say *Can you believe the ignorance of some people?*

Yeah, I could. I was so ignorant I'd nearly gotten myself lost in a hexed maze yesterday. I didn't know about alertness spells or blockers. Talk about freshman ignorance.

Speaking of freshman, I scanned the crowd for Rowan, but didn't spot him. Maybe he was hiding around a dark corner watching me. Or maybe I was being paranoid. Either way, I was going to keep my eyes open.

We got our coffee and a pastry, swiping our student IDs in the machine near the cash register. It was baffling how some things were magical and some were simply normal, and I had no way of knowing which to expect. It was unnerving to say the least.

Like for instance, when we headed out across the quad and came upon two dudes hovering two feet off the ground. As we watched, they took turns kicking out, trying to crash into each other while a small crowd watched. One rammed his friend, sending him flailing. The winner threw his hands in triumph and a whoop went up from the crowd.

Disha rolled her eyes. "So immature."

I had a feeling maturity was kind of her thing, considering who we were rushing off to see.

I expected to head to one of the many buildings reserved for classes, but Disha led me to a circle of trees on the east side of campus. When we got closer, I noticed students filtering up and down a set of stairs that disappeared underground, almost like a subway entrance but cut directly into a freshly mowed lawn.

"Class is down there?" I asked.

Disha slipped into the line, holding her to-go coffee cup in one hand, while adjusting her leather clutch in the other. "Apparently, the magical current is stronger down there. Also, if we cause a cataclysmic rift, it won't suck up the entire campus."

"Cataclysmic rift. Sounds fun." I shouldered the book bag Disha had given me, swallowing hard. This was technically my first class since the lich had tried to kill me yesterday. It was hard to believe, after all that had happened, that this was indeed only my second day of classes.

Disha led us into the underground hallway, which was lit by scores of dancing lights that ran along the ceiling and twinkled like floating fireflies. By the way they swirled, and made me feel as if we were descending into another world, I could tell they were magical.

Another spectacular feature was the images that appeared on the walls as we moved past. Magical billboards displayed recorded messages that changed as we walked by. The first one was an advertisement for the weekend's school football scrimmage. After that, a male student in a stereotypical jersey held a football and invited us all to the Rumble in the Jungle, a homecoming game that would take place around Halloween. This was followed by an image of Dean McIntosh reminding all not to venture into the lake at night or face drowning and dismemberment... oh, and to have a good day.

I'd never heard a warning about death sound so cheerful. These people were certifiable.

We finally entered an area where the ceiling opened up, soaring all the way up to a glass skylight at least eighty feet in the air. The rest of the cave walls were rock, but here, flowering vines wound up their craggy surfaces, filling the whole space with perfume and color. The dancing lights congregated on the ceiling here as well, weaving in and out of the flowers like glowing honey bees. At the far end, a small waterfall trickled down a rocky ledge and filled a pool at its base. A few students clustered around it, staring into its depths.

I skidded to a stop, staring up in awe at the splendor. "Holy moly."

Disha, noticing I wasn't beside her, circled back and grabbed my hand. "We can gawk later. If we want a front row seat in Henderson's class, we need to get there now."

"Geez, obsess much?" I muttered under my breath.

She didn't notice, yanking me into a cave entrance.

The room, if you could call a hollowed out cave that, was the size of a typical college lecture hall, though instead of wooden desks, there were hunks of stone cut into rows that ringed the main floor area.

"We have to sit on hard stone for an hour?" I griped, feeling cranky and out of my element.

But when Disha pulled us to the front and plonked us down, I realized the stone was as soft as cotton. My rear sunk in a few inches, letting me settle in comfortably. Surprised, I glanced up at Disha, but she had a mirror out, checking her lipstick and hair.

Good god. The girl needed to get a grip.

Just then, I spied Rowan Underwood slinking in the door. His eyes locked on me and then darted away as he stalked toward the back of the lecture hall.

I grabbed Disha's arm, yanking her to me. "You didn't tell me Rowan was in this class," I hissed.

"Every freshman is in this class," she replied, snapping her compact shut. "How do I look?"

Before I could answer, Dr. Henderson strolled in.

Disha straightened. I could nearly feel the heat baking off her body.

"Dr. Henderson." She waved her hand.

He smiled and walked casually over, nodding at us. "Disha. Ms. Rivera."

"I got Charlie here early. Front row. We are ready for whatever wisdom you want to bestow upon us." She grinned with perfect white teeth.

If Dr. Henderson knew she was flirting, he didn't show it. He turned his charming smile and big brown eyes on both of us in a kindly teacher way. "So good to have you, Charlie. Disha is my best student, so there isn't a better study buddy in class."

Disha bristled with joy.

"Thank you, sir," I said. "I look forward to filling in the gaps of what I don't know because, frankly, I don't know a lot."

He nodded kindly. "Why don't you be my assistant today? I'll be demonstrating a simple spell and if you're up here with me, I bet you'll get it a bit quicker."

Disha blinked rapidly. Would she be mad at me if I said yes? But then, how could I say no? I really needed to learn as much as I could just to defend myself against liches and water nymphs... and Rowan.

"Sure."

As more students filtered into the room, I followed Dr. Henderson up on the platform. But up here, where everyone could see me, my stomach suddenly filled with thousands of butterflies. I could feel everyone's eyes on me, the new girl. When I glanced up, Rowan was indeed staring. He dropped his head to his open book as if it was suddenly fascinating.

Panicked, I decided I wanted out. I tapped Dr. Henderson on the shoulder.

"Excuse me, sir, but maybe you should ask Disha or someone else. I really don't know what I'm doing, and it's probably better if I just watch."

Glancing up from a stack of notes he was reviewing, he smiled and put a hand on my shoulder. "Charlie, you're going to do fine. It's easy. I promise. I won't blow up your eyebrows like I did my last assistant."

"*That happened?*" I said, shocked.

He laughed. "No, I'm kidding. Relax. I swear it'll all be painless. Cross my heart." He drew the X over his muscular chest.

I felt myself blushing all the way to my toes. Dumbly, I followed him to the center of the stage. Maybe I would have even turned over my first born if Mister Handsome asked.

With a hand movement similar to tai chi, Dr. Henderson pressed his fist to his throat, sending his voice booming throughout the room. "Ladies and gentlemen, please find your seats. The lesson will soon begin."

The students filtered in until the room was nearly full. Many females sat in the front rows, eyes wide as they watched Dr. Henderson's every move. I purposefully did not peer up to the top corner of the room where I knew Rowan would be throwing eye daggers at me.

"Now, class, my assistant for today is our new student, Charlie Rivera. Please give her a hand."

I smiled awkwardly at the smattering of applause, now wishing I'd spent a little more time on my appearance since this was the first time the whole Freshman class would be introduced to me.

"Today, we are going to work on levitation, a simple enough spell, though, concentration and a balanced chi are needed to do it properly. Charlie and I will demonstrate."

Dr. Henderson strode away ten paces, whirled around, and faced me. "Charlie, please repeat my motions as closely as you can. Understand?"

I nodded, feeling sweat trickle down my back even though the cave was cool.

As I watched, Dr. Henderson performed several tai chi motions—arms pushing invisible air, one foot stepping out, his body pivoting. When he blew out, pushing both arms down, his body began to rise above the platform.

"Simple," he said.

After he brought himself down, he gestured to me. "I'll do it again. This time, Charlie, you copy me."

I shook out my hands nervously.

Together, Dr. Henderson and I did the motions. "Breathe, Charlie," he said. "Center yourself."

Center myself. I searched inwardly, trying to do as the professor instructed, but all I sensed inside of me was a turmoil, like a big ball of yarn that was all tangled up and had no beginning or end.

I inhaled a deep breath and blew out, but, as I did, my eyes landed on the exact spot where Rowan had been sitting. Only, he wasn't there.

Taken aback, I pushed my hands down, and... *shot myself into the ceiling!*

I soared up like a runaway rocket, banging into the overhead light fixture and tangling in the wiring. Lights popped. I flailed, tangling myself up even more and causing the chandelier to vibrated. Then my pants caught on something and tore to expose my backside.

Oh, my god.

I dangled there, stuck and exposed for all to see. Heat burned across my face as I tried to pull my arms from the chandelier branches to no avail.

"Oh no! Charlie, I'm so sorry. Stay put. We'll get you down." Dr. Henderson began an elaborate set of hand gestures that would hopefully levitate me down.

Well, it seemed I had finally fractured all the way and the full strength of my powers was now out—just like Dean McIntosh had said it would. But why, oh why, did it have to happen here?

All I could think about was how much of a fool I'd made myself out to be in front of the entire class, hung here with my pants ripped like an idiot while everyone stared and laughed.

Well, not *everyone*. As I looked out at my classmates' upturned faces, I realized that, at this height, the auditorium's top doors were visible.

It was there I spotted Rowan Underwood, clutching his chest and limping away like an injured animal.

CHAPTER TWELVE

FALL SEMESTER
MID OCTOBER

SHAME. Complete and utter shame.

That was what life at the Academy became for me after the levitation debacle in Dr. Henderson's class. Over a month had passed from the time I got myself tangled in the Spells' cave and exposed myself to the entire Freshman class, and not a day had gone by that I wasn't reminded, painfully, that no one had forgotten. I was a subject for ridicule here just as much as I had been in high school, just for an entirely different reason.

I had missed my mother dearly during those awful days in high school, just like I now missed Trey. They'd both known how to make things like this seems insignificant. Back then, I had talked to a portrait of mom, asking for advice. These days I talked to Trey's urn more than I'd like to admit.

Had I inherited this crazy gene from Mom? From Dad? I wanted to believe I'd gotten it from Mom. She'd always been my favorite parent, and I'd never been embarrassed to admit it. Mom had been our rock and our compass, without her, our foundation crumbled and our path went blurry. After her death, family had become but a concept, and I still missed the real thing.

She would have told me to forget the whole thing and taken me for ice cream. I think even now it would have helped. Instead, I was obsessing over my quick descent into ridicule.

I had wanted to blame Rowan for what had happened. I mean, I'd shot to the top of the cave like a crazy rocket after a harmless push with my hands, and I'd hung like an unsightly Christmas ornament while everybody laughed. There was no way *I* had done that. That would have required controlled magical power, which I wanted to believe I didn't have and Rowan did—not to mention he'd run out of the classroom, looking as if he'd exerted himself after attempting to drive my head straight into the rock ceiling.

But, as much as I wanted to believe Rowan *Hates-My-Guts* Underwood was to blame for the big "L" figuratively painted on my forehead, Dean McIntosh had eventually relieved me of the misconception when she showed me what I'd done wrong and then had her assistant, Priscilla Fordyce, teach me the proper way to levitate.

It had taken six weeks of remedial classes every Tuesday and Thursday for me to get the hang of it and learn the trick of lifting off the floor a few inches rather than blasting off into the stratosphere.

"I swear it'll all be painless," Dr. Henderson had said. *"Cross my heart."* He'd even drawn the sign over his chest, a smile on his GQ face.

Such a liar!

Well, it wasn't painless. It hurt a lot. Maybe not physically, but psychologically I was scarred for life.

They'd even given me a nickname.

"Hey, it's Yogi Bare," someone said as I crossed the quad back toward my dorm. Bare, not Bear, mind you, since everyone had seen my backside. I didn't even know people my age remembered that prehistoric cartoon, but apparently so, because they all thought it was hilarious.

Ha, ha.

It wasn't funny the first time, and much less the thousandth time. Damn it!

The mystery of why Rowan had run out of the class was still unsolved, though. I'd mentioned it to Disha, and the expression that crossed her face made it clear she knew something about it. However, she didn't share her thoughts with me, whatever they might have been.

Now, walking across the quad, I lowered my head and pressed forward, clutching my books tighter to my chest. How was I still here? The free trial had expired, and I hadn't left. Had the comfy bed and regular meals made me soft?

No.

If I had to put the blame on something, it would have to be the fact that I had actually learned to freaking levitate. For real. Not some yogi with a propping stick or some optical illusion crap, but the real deal.

Dean McIntosh had been right. I carried the Supernatural gene. I belonged in the Academy, and every new day felt more right than the last. So—even though I was known as Yogi Bare, the clueless, homeless kid who hadn't even known she had powers —I'd decided to stay and prove to anyone who thought their fancy-schmancy Supernatural family made them better than me, that they were wrong.

I did need remedial classes in every subject except the non-magical ones, but I was working my butt off, doing extra home-work and practicing at any chance I got. It was exhausting, but also satisfying, and I had never felt more alive in my entire life.

But, alive or not, when I made it to my room, I shut the door behind me, discarded my books on my messy desk, and collapsed face first on the bed.

Dead.

And I would have remained a corpse until the next day if not for the insistent knocking, followed by shouting, at the door.

"Open the door, *Chardonnay*. I know you're in there."

I groaned and rolled onto my back.

"Go away, Disha," I said. "My bones are crying in agony. That's how tired I am."

"There's no way you're missing tonight, girl," she said, while still pounding on the door. "Everyone, and I mean *everyone* is going to be there."

"Precisely," I said under my breath.

We'd already been over this several times. I didn't want to go to the Rumble in the Jungle homecoming game, no matter how amazing it was supposed to be. I just wanted to stay in my room and sleep for twelve hours straight. I didn't even like football.

"Charrrrrrlieeeee," Disha growled.

Oh, crap! She was using my real name, and she only did that when she meant business.

I groaned again and got to my feet. If I didn't let her in, I would pay for it later. I'd learned the hard way that the girl didn't take *no* for an answer. A week ago, when I hadn't felt like studying for a quiz, she'd hexed my ears so that every word anyone spoke sounded like Ewoks talking at a million miles per hour. Disha got creative with her hexes. I had to grant her that.

Heaving a sigh, I opened the door.

Disha charged in, dressed in a sexy Halloween costume that made *me* blush. She wore tight short shorts, mesh pantyhose with knee-high socks over them, a striped black and white, low-cut shirt, and eye black to complement her glittery makeup. She was stunning, her every curve a work of art. I could already imagine all the guys at the game ogling the hot football referee.

Twirling back to face me, she threw a yellow flag at my feet and blew a whistle.

"Unsupportive BFF. Five-yard penalty. Third down," she said, jutting her hip out and scanning me up and down with more attitude than a recently-crowned Miss America.

I closed the door and dragged my body back to bed—except Disha didn't let me collapse onto it as I'd intended and blocked my way with an extended arm.

"Where's your costume?" she demanded.

"You know I've barely slept for the last few weeks, Disha. Tonight is my chance to get some rest. I have no homework, for once."

She rolled her eyes. "That's because the teachers want everyone to attend the game. It's a tradition. The only game of the season worth attending, really. Faculty against students. Don't you want to see Dr. Henderson in tight pants and shoulder pads?"

I considered for a moment, and I must admit my eyelids fluttered a bit as I imagined him leaning forward, waiting for the snap at the line of scrimmage.

Disha nodded knowingly. "Besides, the Rumble in the Jungle theme has me intrigued." She rubbed her chin. "I vote for trees all over the field with vines for Dr. Henderson to swing from while wearing nothing but a loin cloth."

"A loin cloth? Dr. Henderson? Don't you think that's a bit much?"

She waved a dismissive hand at me as if saying, "*Nothing could ever be too much.*" We were talking about Dr. Henderson, after all. He was practically a god to my friend. She probably thought he would look hot in diapers.

From what I'd learned, the homecoming game always had a surprise theme to make it more interesting. Last fall, according to the sophomores, the theme had been "Bunny Slopes." Football on skis. Imagine that. Of course, to make the events all the more interesting, magic was allowed.

"Disha, please, I'm tired," I said. "See this," I pointed at the purple circles around my eyes, "Not part of a zombie costume or anything. These are real."

"I'll teach you the Ewok hex," she said in a singsong voice.

I blinked and gave her an skeptical stare. "You will?"

"And how to block it," she added to sweeten the deal.

She'd almost driven me crazy with that spell. It would be nice to know how to block her. Plus, I was terrible at hexes. Apparently, I lacked the *finesse for small things*—Priscilla's words not mine. It seemed I had enough power to shoot myself into outer space but lacked the subtlety to do the little things.

"And you will work with me until I learn it?" I asked, narrowing my eyes at her.

"Pinky swear," she said, hooking her little finger and offering it to me.

I hooked my own finger with hers. "May all your hair fall off if you break your promise," I added.

Disha hesitated for a short instance, then shrugged and sealed the deal.

"Now," she said, glancing around the room. "What shall you wear for a costume?"

CHAPTER THIRTEEN

FALL SEMESTER
MID OCTOBER

I was practically naked, wearing a sheet and a pair of white panties.

That was it.

Maybe in a previous life, I would have been embarrassed, but tonight, I found that I didn't give a flip. It was possible the lack of sleep was impairing my judgment, but I wasn't even cold. The cool fall breeze felt good as it slid up my legs and into my airy toga.

Where Disha had learned to turn a simple sheet into an actual garment was beyond me, but I had to admit I didn't look half bad. The toga wrapped over my right shoulder, leaving the other one bare, then flowed down in graceful folds and stopped mid-thigh.

Paired with a golden belt she'd fetched from her closet, and a laurel crown she'd fashioned from a few branches, my costume made me feel like a Greek goddess.

Not bad for Yogi Bare, I thought with a lifted eyebrow.

"Wait up," Disha said, touching my arm to make me stop.

Other students filtered around us, headed for the football stadium, their costumes each more amazing than the last.

Disha took my crown off and waved her fingers over it, turning it a brilliant gold.

"There. That's better," she said. "It matches your belt now."

"Thanks," I said, examining the crown. It was heavier and appeared as if Disha had turned it into real gold. Now, that was a spell that would have come in handy a year or so ago. Trey and I might have had good food to put in our bellies if I'd known how to turn rusty nails into gold.

God, Trey would've loved tonight. What he would've given to be here. I smiled, then realized that the days of being gutted every time I thought about him were behind me. I guess talking to his urn and pretending he was still around had helped curve the crippling pain.

I turned the crown from one side to the other. "Is it—"

"Real gold?" Disha finished for me. "Nah," she waved her hand at the air. "It will wilt in a few hours. Tops."

"Oh." So much for that idea.

I slipped the crown back on as we started walking behind a girl with bark-like skin and little birds circling around her head, and guy wearing a black cape that fluttered with a life of its own.

When we entered the stadium a few minutes later, a trumpet blared a fanfare as if announcing the arrival of medieval knights, but all I could see were football players. We climbed up the stands as they ran onto the field, wearing yellow pants and navy blue jerseys, the Academy's colors.

The bright lights above were blinding, impeding the view of the night sky. The place was small in comparison to other college stadiums, but it was grand like the Roman Colosseum, with arches, carved stone, and majestic columns.

We found two empty spots among a group of people dressed

like the Scooby-Doo gang—one of them so similar to a Great Dane that it was obvious they'd used magic to accomplish the look.

"Just in time!" Disha said excitedly. "The faculty is coming out." She jumped up and down and started cheering. "Go, Thad!"

From the other end of the field, the Academy's faculty strolled out, wearing regular clothes. They waved, while half of the students cheered and the other half booed.

"Is that what they're wearing?" I asked, frowning.

They made a sorry lot for a football team, half of them gray-headed and with pot bellies, and the rest wearing dresses and ballet flats.

I rolled my eyes. "This is ridiculous."

Disha gave me a sideways glance and patted my shoulder as if to say "*You don't know anything, little girl.*"

"Are you ready to *rrrumbllle*?" A loud voice asked over the speakers just as the song *Welcome To The Jungle* began to play.

The crowd went crazy, screaming and cheering, and I found myself catching their excitement, too.

I was waving my arms up in the air when a sense of being watched made me glance a few rows down. There, staring up at me, was Rowan, wearing what looked like a gangster costume, fedora and all. His intense brown eyes met mine, then traveled to my naked shoulder. My cheeks heated up, and as much as I hated it, my silly self-consciousness made me glance away.

Shifting my attention to the field, I told myself to ignore Rowan's presence, which wasn't all that hard to do considering that only one football team was lining up to play. Huh? The students prepared to receive the kick off, while the faculty still sat on the bench, presided by Dean McIntosh, who seemed to be giving them instructions of some kind.

Professor Answorth sat at one end of the bench, his blond hair resplendent under the stadium lights. Dr. Henderson occupied the opposite end. He was the only one wearing semi-sporty clothes rather than a suit like the other male teachers. He looked youthful, almost like a real player. Professor Middleton, my History teacher, sat next to Nurse Taishi. And my very personal torturer and Dean's Assistant, Priscilla Fordyce, was in the middle, flanked by teachers who taught upper level classes.

It looked like everyone was there, the only one conspicuous by his absence was Macgregor Underwood, who probably thought he was too good for a homecoming game.

A whistle blew, marking the beginning of the game. Dean McIntosh sat and, suddenly, a second team appeared on the field. My jaw hung open. A virtual zoo had materialized in front of the student team. There were gorillas, cheetahs, rhinos, bears, and even a giraffe.

A huge, silverback gorilla kicked the ball toward the opposite end of the field, then the animals charged.

I watched, hypnotized as the faculty sat on the bench, some twirling their hands, others murmuring with their eyes closed, yet others clinging to objects that channeled their energy. I'd learned in the last weeks that everyone was different, and each witch and warlock found their own way of wielding their magic. I'd tried all kinds of things myself, but nothing had seemed to make a difference. Maybe, I was supposed to find a special object like Professor Middleton who held on to a leather-bound book, while hovering a hand over it and focusing on the gangly giraffe.

How the student team didn't turn tail and run the other way at the sight of gigantic rhinos stampeding in their direction, I didn't know. All I knew was that I would have ran faster than the cheetah now chasing the guy attempting the punt return.

But all was fair on the field, the students were using magic, too, and seemed to have wings on their feet as they ran and jumped.

For the next hour, we cheered and screamed bloody murder until our throats grew hoarse. The game turned out to be one of the most exciting things I'd ever witnessed, and I openly admitted to Disha that I was glad she'd dragged me here.

At some point, my friend left and came back with two hotdogs and two drinks. I gobbled both barely aware of how fast I ate, but fully conscious of how delicious it all tasted. The best hotdog and the best... I stared into the cup.

"What was this, Disha?" I asked.

"Witch's Brew," she said as she pumped a fist in the air. "Go, Thad!" she screamed at Dr. Henderson's bear. We'd pretty much figured out which animals went with each faculty members.

Witch's Brew? A drop of something black and viscous was left in the cup. I blinked as the speck seemed to inch up the side of the cup like a worm.

A burp escaped through my lips. My vision blurred. Heat climbed up from my chest to my neck, then my cheeks. Of their own accord, my eyes wandered over the crowd, searching for Rowan, but he wasn't there.

I licked my lips, scanning the stadium. Everything appeared fuzzy, and the crowd's chants faraway.

"I need... I need to use the restroom," I said, feeling woozy.

"Sure. Go ahead," Disha said, her attention locked on the game and *Thad*, of course.

I vaguely wondered why she was calling Dr. Henderson by his first name, then staggered down the steps and into the corridor that ran around the stadium.

My toga dress slipped off my shoulder. I giggled and pushed it back into place. Seeing double, I blinked at the signs overhead.

"Where's the restroom?" I mumbled to myself.

A strange heat whirled in my chest, radiating into my limbs. I bit my lower lip and ran a hand down my warm neck. I felt on fire and longed for cold water to splash over my face.

The corridor was completely empty, which struck me as odd, even though it was obvious no one wanted to miss one minute of that insane game. I hunched my back, my arms hanging limp, and made a gorilla sound. I laughed, then walked aimlessly, glancing all around and tripping on my own two feet.

Am I drunk?

I hiccupped.

Must be.

A dark shape crossed the corridor ahead of me and, as it went out one of the exits, I caught sight of a head of blond hair.

Professor Answorth?

I shook my head. I'd just seen him sitting on the bench, staring at the field while his lips moved at a prodigious speed.

Shrugging it off, I kept searching for the restroom, then caught sight of someone else.

A gangster.

He seemed to be slinking behind the other figure but stopped when he spotted me.

"Charlie, what are you doing?" Rowan demanded.

"Rowan," I said, my voice a low purr.

Guided by some foreign force, I sashayed in his direction. His eyebrows twitched as he watched me sway toward him. He took a few steps back as I got closer, and promptly ran into a wall.

"What a great costume," I said, adjusting his tie. "It suits you."

"Uh, thanks."

Smiling, I ran a hand down the side of his face. He hadn't shaved, probably to match the costume, and the roughness of his stubble felt wonderful to the touch. Rowan swallowed, his brown gaze falling to my lips.

"Your costume is great, too," he said, his fingers landing softly on my shoulders.

A shiver ran down my spine. His touch felt electric. I drew closer, my body pressing against his. His other hand snaked around my waist and held me in place.

"What are you doing?" he asked again, though this time the question had an entirely different meaning and seemed to come from deep in his chest.

What was I doing? That was a good question. I'd barely talked to the guy lately, even if I always caught myself searching for him around campus and stealing glances his way whenever he was around.

"I'm just..." Trailing off, I let my fingers weave into his hair. It was as soft as feathers just like I'd known it would be. The woody smell of his cologne whirled around me like an invisible rope and pulled me closer into his solidity. He sucked in air through his teeth.

Breathing me in, his quivering lips lowered to mine.

"Charlie," he said, my naming sounding like a plea.

My lips were millimeters from his. Our hot breaths mingled.

Then he wrinkled his nose. "Are you... are you intoxicated?" he asked.

"Oh, yes," I said, placing a hand to the back of his head, attempting to pull him closer.

To my immense disappointment, he disentangled himself from my embrace. "What did you drink?" The tone in his voice brooked no argument.

"Witch's Brew," I said, trying to grab his shirt.

He dodged away from my grabby hands. "How many?"

"One," I said.

He frowned. "But it was your first, right?"

I nodded. "It was so delicious."

Rowan sighed and ran a hand through his hair, looking oddly disappointed.

"C'mon," he said. "I'll take you back to Disha."

"But I—"

"You're drunk and shouldn't be wandering around alone."

"I'm drunk?" I giggled. "I really am drunk!"

He rolled his eyes, pulled me up the stairs and delivered me to Disha. "Watch your BFF, all right? She'd never had Witch's Brew before."

"Oh, shit!" Disha said. "I didn't know." She laughed and helped me sit as Rowan left me there, feeling abandoned.

"Sorry, *Charcoal*." Disha patted my head. "It'll pass."

I stared at the field and noticed Professor Answorth still sitting at the faculty's bench.

"Disha," I pointed toward the blond teacher, "did Professor Answorth go anywhere while I was gone?"

She frowned. "No, but I wish he had. His rhino has dropped two passes from Thad."

I scratched my head, then slouched on my seat, exhaustion hitting me like a wrecking ball all of a sudden.

The stadium swayed. My stomach tumbled. Then, for the rest of the game, I did my best to keep the Witch's Brew on the right side of the world.

CHAPTER FOURTEEN

FALL SEMESTER
MID DECEMBER

"Dee, just eat. Come on." I shoved a plate of muffins across the table towards her.

Disha stared at the plate, no light in her eyes. Sugary breakfast treats were normally her morning routine. How she stuffed down three muffins and still rocked her size four figure I had no idea.

Things had been going along pretty well for the last month and a half. No supernatural creature had tried to suck my essence, and I hadn't tangled myself into any chandeliers in front of my entire class. Then, all of a sudden, Disha lost her sparkle. Her normally buoyant self became a deflated shell who couldn't be coaxed out by makeovers or bad puns.

The worst part was I had no idea what was wrong, but whatever it was, she didn't even think up inventive nicknames for me anymore. I'd never wanted anyone to call me Charmander so much in my life.

Now it was nearly winter break and soon she'd be headed off to New York and I'd be stuck here alone for two weeks. If I was going to figure out what was wrong and try to fix it, I needed to know now.

"What is going on? Will you please tell me?"

Disha shook her head, dark bangs falling into her eyes. Over the last three days, puffy circles had gathered there that no concealer seemed able to hide.

The muffins were doing me no good.

Desperate, I glanced around the cafeteria for ideas. Spotting the pizza line, my mind drifted back to Trey's pizza parties. He'd been a champ at getting me out of my funks. Hmm, would a picnic with handmade crafts cheer Disha up? Maybe, except I sucked at paper crafting.

Besides, dancing garlands and twirling snowmen had already been *magicked* by the staff around the ceiling of the bustling eatery —one more reminder that Christmas holidays were upon us and I would be left alone while my classmates went home to their parents' houses.

I didn't exactly have one of those and there was no freaking way I was going to let Disha's parents pay for a flight to New York.

Scanning past the clumps of co-eds chatting over coffee, I caught Rowan staring at us across the cafeteria. A red blush burned up my neck as I averted my gaze. We hadn't spoken since I attempted to kiss him during the Rumble in the Jungle. Nearly two months had passed with us awkwardly avoiding each other. Not an easy feat, but I was dedicated to dodging any painful conversations about my drunken come-on.

How had I been so stupid? Witch's Brew or not, what deranged part of me had thought that making out with my arch nemesis was a good idea? He'd been playing the same game, too, skirting around me in the hallways, leaving rooms when I entered and generally treating me like I had Ebola.

It didn't matter. Disha mattered and something was wrong with her.

I pushed coffee in her direction, but got no response. I could only think of one other option: enlisting Rowan's help.

Ugh.

Once again, I turned my attention to his table. His gaze was locked on Disha.

Rowan was concerned. I could tell by his expression. He was a good friend to her even if he was a jerk to me.

"Disha," I said, shaking her limp shoulder. "Would you tell Rowan?"

She shook her head. "I can't tell anyone."

"Arg!" I smashed my fist on the table. "This is stupid. Just tell me. How bad can it be? Did you get kicked out of the Gorgeous Indian Girls' Society?"

Disha moaned.

Reluctantly, I waved Rowan over, feeling my stomach clench around my meal.

He sprung up and walked deliberately to our table. He was wearing a heather gray Henley that somehow brought out the deep chestnut brown of his eyes and hugged his muscular body at the same time. Was the shirt magical, designed to trick women into desiring him against their better judgement?

To prove my suspicions, many heads turned as he cut around the busy cafeteria tables. Two girls leaned in and whispered to one another as he strode past, their eyebrows disappearing into their bangs as they regarded his jean-clad backside. The medallion hung at his chest and reflected the sunlight streaming in the windows. Disha had told me that he was an item warlock and that necklace was what he used to channel his power. She, on the other hand, commanded the magical forces with hand motions and concentration alone, a much harder skill.

And me? Well... I had no magical item and continued to suck

at hand magic despite Assistant Fordyce's remedial efforts. Lucky me.

Rowan loomed behind me, his cologne invading my nose. My heart began to beat against my ribcage as he sat down and turned his full attention to Disha. His dark gaze darted to mine for an instant, and I could swear his breath caught—probably as he suppressed the desire to murder me.

"Disha, hey. How's it going? I've noticed you've been a bit upset lately," he said, kindly placing a hand on her arm.

My friend raised her head, made a distraught face and dropped it back on the table.

"Go away, Rowan," she said into her arm.

"Listen," he continued softly, "if this is about that..." his eyes darted to me before continuing, "that *thing* we discussed. Don't worry. It'll be alright."

What was this? They were keeping secrets from me? Anger and embarrassment mingled together in my gut.

Disha lifted her head, blowing hair out of her face. "It's not about Answorth and the item you think he stole."

Rowan shook his head. "No, not that—"

"God," Disha went on. "Answorth is not behind the attacks. Your dad is just being prejudiced. Just because he's a Lesser, that doesn't mean he's a thief."

Rowan shushed her, his head lifting to scan the nearby area as if spies might be listening. "We don't need to discuss that here."

"In front of me, right? Is that what you're implying? Can't trust Charlie. *Nooo*, she's not trustworthy. Still a useless street rat." Anger bubbled up, reminding me once again that he was a grade-A asshole.

Disha whipped her head up. "Get over it, Rowan. Charlie isn't some secret agent." Then she turned to me. "A magical item was stolen during homecoming. Something very powerful. If used by the wrong person, it could literally destroy the entire school. Rowan and his dad think Answorth stole it and have been tracking him ever since. But Answorth has the perfect alibi. He was at the game. Everyone could see him there."

"Disha," Rowan hissed. "Enough."

"Wait, Answorth?" Memories flashed through my brain—the hallway as I searched for the bathroom, a blond head darting away looking very much like Professor Answorth.

Then again, I was drunk.

Rowan's dark eyes zeroed in on me. "Do you know something about Professor Answorth?"

"No... not really." I paused, trying to figure out if it really was the professor I saw or someone who looked like him, or if I'd just had an intoxicated hallucination.

Rowan screwed up his face in disgust. "Just what I thought. Covering up for your mentor?"

"My mentor?" I replied, incredulous. "What gives you *that* idea?"

"I saw you go in his office early in the year and a few other times," he said.

Rage flared like a white-hot sun in my chest. "Are you still following me?"

His answer was a sneer.

He was exaggerating. I'd been in Professor Answorth office only one other time. Assistant Fordyce had sent me there to talk to him about improving my concentration.

My fists clenched and I wished there wasn't a spell blocker in place so I could zap Rowan with the thunder spell Assistant Fordyce had taught me last week.

"I should give you a taste of your own medicine," I said through clenched teeth.

Rowan narrowed his eyes, his medallion glowing. "Try me, Rivera." He lifted his hand and, as he did so, the skin of his forearms came into view. Blue veins snaked up his skin, disappearing under his shirt.

I grimaced involuntarily. What in the holy hell was wrong with his arms? Those dark blue veins looked sickly.

"Stop! I can't take it anymore." Disha leaped up and darted out of the cafeteria.

"Disha, wait!" I went after her and so did Rowan, but I didn't have time to argue that he should butt out. Disha needed her friends. With him at my elbow, we raced after her as she left the building.

She was running, which was so unlike her. She often told me sweating would make her hair go limp.

Down the path and across the quad, she cut through clusters of students, even ignoring the group that seemed to be growing a *Jack and the Beanstalk* type vine in the middle of their circle.

"Disha!" Rowan called.

She turned but didn't stop running. "Leave me be. I want to be alone right now."

"Disha, can we just stop and talk?" I was getting winded. The girl could run. Damn those long legs.

Seeing we were still behind her, she ducked around a hedge. Shoot. This was a full on chase, and I was wearing slip-on shoes.

Panting, I skidded to a stop, gripped my knees and sucked wind. Rowan took off past me. Angry, I shot up. There was no way I was going to let him be the knight in shining armor while I was the chick who failed gym class.

I ran around the hedge only to find a shed with the door thrown open. Disha and Rowan had to be inside. But what was that strange smell?

Praying I wouldn't find pixie minotaurs, I dashed inside.

The interior was dark, lit only from the door behind me. Ahead, I could just make out a large store of gardening equipment —hoses, rakes, fertilizer, and a riding lawn mower. I had the brief thought that someone should invent a spell for grass clipping when I heard a moan and a yell coming from behind a row of shelving.

"Disha, no!" Rowan's voice called.

A pulse of energy rocked the shed. Shovels clattered to the floor. A shelf tipped over and spilled. I froze, feeling the energy growing stronger, ebbing and flowing like a giant heartbeat.

Some serious magic was going down.

While everything in me told me to flee, I walked deeper into the shed, I wound around the tilted shelf to find Rowan staring at Disha who stood in the middle of what appeared to be a Satanic animal sacrifice.

My eyes darted from the giant pool of blood on the floor to the ancient runes sketched in salt around it. The carcass in the center appeared to be a dog, but it was too mangled to tell. Judging from the horror on Rowan's face, this was not typical magic.

Unfortunately, Disha seemed to have stumbled into the middle of the circle of runes and was stuck, her arms out at her sides like a marionette, her hair floating as if she were underwater, and her feet dangling slightly off the floor.

I did the only thing I could think of. I yelled at Rowan. "Get her down!"

His head whirled in my direction, and his expression told me what a mess we were in.

"Get out!" He shouted, waving me away. "Go get help."

"No!" Disha cried. "Get me off. Now. Now. Now." There wasn't time to get help. The spell was intensifying. It reminded me of the lich, making me think that if we took too long Disha could be sucked dry.

Without hesitation, Rowan acted. Extending his hands, he shot magic at Disha's body. She sagged, her body dipping down and her arms going limp. For a split second, I believed he'd done it. Then her body spun, slowly bobbing up like a balloon as the room throb faster.

When she revolved back toward us, I gasped. Her eyes were gone. Well, not gone, but vacant. Milky white. Her hair flowed behind her like sentient snakes, accentuating how elongated and horrible her face now seemed.

Then she opened her mouth far too wide and let out a tortured scream.

Staggering back, I threw a hand over my face. "What's happening?!"

"She's possessed!" Rowan threw out another spell, his medallion pulsing on his chest, but I could tell it wasn't working. Those blue veins I had seen earlier grew darker and more pronounced. Now they were creeping up his neck, too. He was going to kill himself and Disha if I didn't do something fast.

My magic was useless here. I knew that. So, instead, I raced toward Disha, grabbed her waist, and tried to yank her out of the circle.

The magical heartbeat locked into me, pulsing through my body like a live wire. Images ran through my mind on a erratic slideshow—the lich, the werewolf, a dark figure. My muscles stiffened. My teeth snapped together. Disha, in my arms, vibrated as if she were having a massive seizure. We were stuck. We were dying.

A body hit mine, knocking us to the ground.

I lay there for what seemed like hours willing my body and brain to wake up, but it felt as though it had been replaced with cotton. As my head cleared, I realized that Disha, Rowan and I were lying in a clump on the shed floor. He had knocked us out of the circle.

I became aware of his chest under my head. The rise and fall of his labored breathing. The feel of his skin on mine.

I was laying on top of Rowan, our bodies intimately entwined.

Springing up, I untangled myself from the pile of arms and legs. Disha was limp, appearing unconscious. Rowan sat up, shaking his head. The blue veins were dark lines tracing up his neck. I didn't know what that was about, but it couldn't be good. One problem at a time, however.

"Help me," I said, grabbing Disha under the arms.

He stood and lifted her feet. Together, we carried her out of the shed and set her on the grass. In the daylight, she looked even worse—pale, sunken and definitely unconscious.

"We need to go to the dean," I said. "Or Nurse Taishi."

Rowan shook his head. "My father can't know about this. We should go to Henderson."

"Henderson?" Disha would kill us if we took her to her crush as disheveled as she was, though that was a minor concern compared to her well-being.

"He'll help and be discreet about it. Besides, he'd do anything for Disha. Hurry." He waved his hands and this time the spell worked. Disha hovered off the ground and disappeared, allowing us to push her invisible body along the grassy area towards Henderson's office, I assumed.

I wanted to ask why we needed to be discreet. Disha hadn't done anything wrong but time was of the essence and we had to hurry. Still, I glanced over at Rowan. He seemed exhausted and more shaken up than I was. The blue veins stood out like a map of angry rivers climbing out of his shirt. There was something very wrong with him, and it seemed to intervene with his magic.

"What was that *thing* in the shed?" I finally asked.

Rowan's expression darkened as he quickly navigated Disha's body around a tree. "Dark magic. Looked like someone was attempting a summoning spell, probably something similar to what brought that lich onto the school grounds. All of this... it's not good."

"But why would Disha run in there?" I asked. There was no way my friend was associated with something like that.

"I don't know. She seemed drawn to it. A spell like that is sometimes set up to trap a victim, someone to help power the spell. If we hadn't intervened, it would have drained her entire life force."

"She would've died?" I thought about the lich and what it felt like as it sucked the very essence from my body. No wonder Disha was unconscious. "Will Henderson be able to help her?"

Rowan nodded, seeming distracted.

I looked up at the set of buildings I hadn't noticed before. "Wait, what is this place?"

"Staff housing," he said, pushing Disha's hovering body against the brick of one of the three-story dorm-like buildings.

"How have I never seen this place before?" I had been on campus for months now and had never seen this particular structure.

"It's restricted, magically hidden so students don't track down teachers that give them bad grades and hex them in the middle of the night. I can get in because my father lives here and sometimes sends me up on errands. Now, stay with her. I'll go up and find Henderson. If anyone asks, tell them you got lost or something."

Of course he wanted me to tell a lie that made me seem like an idiot, but I didn't object. We needed help for Disha.

"Hurry," I said.

Rowan ran up the porch and disappeared. I put my hand on my invisible friend's body.

"It's going to be okay, babe. Just get better and I'll let you give me as many makeovers as you want."

Voices from around the other side of the building caught my attention. Stiffening, I worked on my lie, trying to make myself appear as confused as possible. But then I recognized one of the voices, and it happened to belong to Dr. Henderson.

I jogged along the building and turned the corner only to see him and Professor Answorth clustered together in a dark corner, locked in a heated conversation.

"I don't think you understand the severity of what we're dealing with here." Professor Answorth leaned towards Dr. Henderson with a stern look on his blue eyes.

Dr. Henderson, expression angry, shot back with a finger in his colleague's face. "You don't know what you think you know, Answorth. And I don't appreciate the threat."

Professor Answorth softened. "Look. I want to help you. We're in this together." Then he leaned in and whispered something in Dr. Henderson's ear.

I needed to hear what they were talking about. Maybe Answorth was the thief and he was trying to get Henderson on his team. Creeping forward, I didn't see the trashcan until my hip banged into it. A loud clang echoed through the courtyard.

Both men whipped their heads in my direction, fear and guilt written all over their faces.

CHAPTER FIFTEEN

FALL SEMESTER
MID DECEMBER

STINKY GARBAGE LAY between the angry-looking professors and me. I thought about throwing myself into it. Anything was better than this.

Professor Answorth stared down at the waste I'd spilled, then up at me. I stood frozen, my heart thudding.

"Um, hi." I lifted a hand and gave them a lame little wave.

"What are you doing here?" Answorth asked, his tone unfriendly, nothing like normal.

"I... was... looking for Dr. Henderson." God, sometimes I sucked at coming up with lies.

Dr. Henderson glanced up from a rotting banana peel, which he'd been staring at with an expression of shame etched in his features. He frowned at me, clearly surprised by my need to see him.

"Is that right?" Professor Answorth said. "It couldn't have

waited until his office hours? Staff housing is off limits to students. For good reason." He gave Dr. Henderson a disgusted glance.

Oh god! Was he insinuating that I... ? That Dr. Henderson and I... ?

The heat of shame and distaste rose to my cheeks.

"I didn't know that," I said, my words coming fast. "I just have a question about... uh... about Satanic sacrifices." I cursed inwardly. "Um, something weird I read in a book."

Shit! I'm such an idiot. With a capital "I".

The blond professor shook his head and started walking in my direction. As he passed, he waved a hand, and the garbage can righted itself, while all the spilled junk floated back into it. He stopped in front of me, his face stern. I wrung my shirt and stared at the ground, hoping Disha was still invisible behind me.

"I think..." Answorth said, measuring his words, "you have a good head on your shoulders, Ms. Rivera. I dearly hope you do not prove me wrong. Good day." The heels of his fancy leather shoes tapped against the stone courtyard as he walked away.

I groaned and rubbed a hand down the side of my face.

"What is this about Satanic sacrifices?" Dr. Henderson asked in an irritated tone that made it clear he didn't believe my excuse.

I shook my head. "Nothing. It's really about Disha." I turned and pointed toward the wall where Rowan had left her.

"What kind of joke is this?" He frowned toward the empty-looking spot.

"It's not a joke. She's invisible," I said, just as the building's front door opened and Rowan walked out.

"Oh, thank God!" Rowan exclaimed, joining us. "Dr. Henderson, Disha was sucked into some Satanic sacrifice, and she won't wake up. You have to help her."

He took a step back, his eyes searching for the proof.

Rowan waved a hand, causing Disha's invisible shape to flicker for a second.

"Oh, Disha!" Henderson exclaimed, panic thick in his voice. He glanced all around nervously. "Let's go through the back." He led the way, hurrying us through a service entrance and quickly guiding us into a small studio apartment.

He slammed the door behind us and instructed Rowan to lower Disha onto the queen-size bed that dominated the space. I glanced around the tiny kitchen, the sitting area beside it, and an open door that led to a bathroom.

"What kind of Satanic sacrifice are you talking about? Where would she run into something like that?" Dr. Henderson asked as he leaned over Disha, checking her pupils and pressing a hand to her forehead.

I walked closer to the bed, my steps small and hesitant. Disha's hair was plastered to one side of her face, which was paralyzed into a grimace of fear. Her hands were twisted into claws, and she seemed as stiff as a wooden plank.

"I don't know what kind," Rowan said. "She was trying to hide from us and ran into one of the gardening sheds. That's where it was."

Dr. Henderson seemed to grow as stiff as Disha for a second, then sprang to his feet and ran to the little kitchen. From the cabinets, he retrieved several items and hurried back. He thrust a blue box of Morton salt into Rowan's hand, and a matchbook and four candles into mine.

"Underwood, draw a circle of salt around her. Rivera, light candles north, south, east, and west of her," he instructed as he picked Disha off the bed and deposited her on the hardwood floor.

Rowan opened the box's spout and quickly poured a circle of salt around Disha's body. When he was done, I lit the first candle and placed it above Disha's head.

"No. Outside the circle," Dr. Henderson ordered.

I moved it right away and hurried to set the other three candles in place. As soon as I lit the last candle, I stepped aside and stood next to Rowan. We exchanged a worried glance and watched Dr. Henderson remove his shoes and socks, then take a clock from the wall and lay it in the circle next to Disha. Stepping in himself, he planted his bare feet on either side of her's.

Without pause, he started reciting something in what sounded like Latin. "Vade retro satanica potestas. In nomini lux. Exorcizamus te, immunde spiritus."

He put his hands out, palms facing Disha and repeated. "Vade retro satanica potestas. In nomini lux. Exorcizamus te, immunde spiritus."

At first, nothing happened. Just as I was beginning to worry, white light shot out Dr. Henderson's hands and hit Disha right in the chest. She began convulsing, her legs and arms lashing out, but staying within the salt circle as it seemed to burn her when she got too close.

Disha groaned. Her body came off the floor—her legs, arms, and head dangling. The light *whooshed* around her like a comet. Her hair swung as it passed through it. The light rose to the ceiling, hovered there for a moment, then plunged back into Disha. She glowed for an instant, then jerked and collapsed back on the floor.

Everything went still.

Rowan seized my hand, squeezing it tight. My eyes opened wide in shock. I stood frozen, wondering if he even knew what he was doing.

Dr. Henderson was a statue, except for his lips which still moved silently.

Was it done? Had it work?

My answer came in the form of a black shadow that shot out of Disha's mouth. The apparition swirled like smoke above her for what felt like an eternity, then dove into the clock beside her.

Rowan exhaled and let go of my hand, clearing his throat. My gaze remained locked on Disha. I wanted to ask if she was okay, but I didn't know if I should talk.

"What the hell was that?" Rowan asked, breaking the thick silence.

Trembling, Dr. Henderson stepped out of the circle and sat— or more precisely, collapsed—on the bed. He took a few minutes, panting and rubbing the back of his neck, before answering.

"A time demon," he finally said. "When they possess some-body, they steal their time, taking over and leaving no memory of what they made their victims do. Undetected, they can live inside someone as long as they please. It's fortunate you were with her when it happened. She might have..." He trailed off, peering down at Disha with tenderness and relief.

Rowan gave me a sideways glance, then asked, "How did you know what type of demon it was?" His voice was full of accusa-tion and suspicion.

Dr. Henderson blinked up and focused on Rowan. "Something else that was fortunate," he said. "In a staff meeting yesterday, Dean McIntosh warned us a time demon was on the loose. Someone released the creature from an old clock at an antique shop in Atlanta. Apparently, it'd been wreaking havoc in the city. I made an educated guess."

"How did it make it here?" Rowan asked.

"That is anyone's guess," Dr. Henderson said, leaning forward and putting his head in his hands.

"Is Disha okay?" I asked.

"She'll be fine," Dr. Henderson said, without lifting his head. "She just needs rest, and I do, too. I'll make sure she gets back safely when she wakes up. Now, if you please, would you leave and let us rest?"

"But—" I began.

Rowan put a hand on my shoulder. "It's all right," he assured me. "We should go."

We walked to the door, but not without a few backward glances at our friend.

"Use the back door," Dr. Henderson ordered before we left.

―――――

Rowan and I were sitting on a bench by the Enlightenment Fountain, staring at our feet.

No words had passed between us since we'd left Dr. Henderson's apartment. We'd walked here in a sort of stupor, lost in our own thoughts. The events since we'd chased Disha out of the cafeteria kept playing in my head over and over, a hundred scenarios of how she could have died adding themselves to the horror. Damn my overactive imagination!

"I don't believe him," Rowan finally spoke in a low growl. "Do you?"

"Dr. Henderson?" I asked, still feeling awkward. We hadn't spoken about him grasping my hand after Disha's exorcism, yet I felt it hanging between us.

"Yeah," he nodded, angling his body in my direction. "He knew right away what to do, what kind of demon had possessed Disha. How?"

"You heard him. Dean McIntosh warned the staff about it."

Rowan stood and started pacing in front of me. "That's if it's even true. I don't trust him."

The late morning sun shone on his brown locks, making them appear golden. My own brown hair was darker, so it would never look like that in the sun. His tight shirt allowed a precise view of his chest as he breathed in and out in agitation. I blushed as my mind tried to imagine his pecs and abs under the Henley. I glanced away and figured I probably needed a plunge in the cold fountain. That should drown my traitorous hormones.

"W-well..." I stammered, "you must trust him enough since you decided to take Disha there," I said. "Plus, he helped her. She's gonna be okay."

"I only took her there because they..." He pressed his lips into a thin line.

"Because... they... what?" I enunciated each word as his meaning revealed itself to me. "Oh, shit!"

"Yeah, shit is right," Rowan said.

"I'm so stupid." I ran a hand through my hair. "Why didn't I see it?"

All she'd said from the beginning of the school year was "Henderson this and Henderson that." It was so obvious now. Why didn't I put it together before? They were having an affair.

Rowan sat back down, sighing in frustration. "I didn't see it either. Not 'til a few days ago. He broke it off, and she lost it."

"So that's why she's been so upset. God, poor Disha."

"It's for the best," Rowan said. "Henderson should never... It's against the rules. They would both get kicked out if anyone finds out."

"Disha would be devastated," I said. "She loves it here."

"Now you see why I don't trust him?"

I nodded. "Still, do you think he would be capable of releasing those creatures inside the school? I mean, that would make him a subversive, and he's a teacher here. Why would he want to hurt the school or the students?"

"Power, Charlie. It's always power, and the Academy has a lot of it," he added, lowering his voice, eyes darting toward the fountain to make sure no one was near. "You know there is a portal on campus, right?"

I nodded. I'd read about it in the welcoming package, which I'd made sure to practically memorize after that incident with the pixie minotaurs. From what I read, there were several portals all over the world, and one of the most powerful was here at the Academy. Portals were interconnected conduits of magic that allowed travel between them but were also incredible sources of magical power. I briefly wondered where the Academy's was located. The package had said few people knew the locations of the portals, and they safeguarded the knowledge in order to keep the world safe from power-hungry crazies.

Just then, it occurred to me that Rowan Underwood was talking to me about the attacks and who he suspected. Did that mean he didn't believe I was one of the bad guys anymore?

"We need to find out if it's true that Dean McIntosh warned the staff about the time demon," Rowan said, his brown eyes dancing around as if searching for ideas.

We?

Well, I wasn't about to contradict him. Rowan knew a lot about what was going on, and the more I learned, the closer I would be to finding out who was responsible for Trey's death. I'd promised his urn more than once that I would avenge him.

"Would your father know?" I asked. "Does he go to staff meetings?"

"Not always, but it's a good place to start. I'll ask him tonight. In the meantime," he stood, "we should go back and get rid of that stuff in the garden shed."

A chill ran across my back. I didn't want to go back in there, which must have shown in my face because he added, "My father said they've received several letters from parents already. They've been questioning the safety of the school. If something bad happens again, the dean will have to close the Academy and send everybody home. That *can't* happen."

He seemed very adamant about this, desperate even. Why? His intensity seemed odd, as if his life depended on it. It was not like he was homeless and would have nowhere to go if they closed the school. Me, on the other hand...

I jumped to my feet. "Let's go then."

Terrifying or not, I helped him clean up the carcass.

———

AN HOUR LATER, we headed to Dean Underwood's office. When we got there, Rowan instructed me to wait in the girls' bathroom down the hall, assuring me that dear old dad wouldn't take kindly to me tagging along. Still, Rowan promised to brief me directly afterward so we could decide what to do.

Mutilated animals. Satanic demons. This was not what I signed up for.

While waiting in the bathroom, I let water rush over my hands as I scrubbed and scrubbed, but I couldn't wash enough times to get that poor, dead dog's blood off. Rowan had tried to convince me it was a badger as we carried its husk out of the shed, deep into the wood and set it ablaze with an incinerating spell, but I knew better. Someone was going without their beloved Fido tonight, all because of some maniac.

A maniac we had to track down before they closed the school.

Images of me sleeping in a burnt-out husk of a building flashed in my brain. No. That simply could not happen. Not when I finally felt like my life was going somewhere. Rowan and I would figure out what was going on.

Rowan and I. That was an interesting phrase. Did he still loathe me, still suspect I was a subversive hell-bent on taking over the school's magic? He must not if he was telling me his trusted secrets.

Like the fact that, right now, he was in his father's office, about to learn whether or not what Henderson had told us was true. Did the faculty know about the time demon being loosed on the world or was that a lie Henderson used to cover his tracks?

But what was taking so long?

I glanced at the wall clock anxiously. It had already been twenty minutes. What were they doing, rehashing old fishing trips?

The clock also let me know I had missed all three of my classes today. Not great, considering I was one of the worst witches here. Disha was going to have to help catch me up when she was well again.

Speaking of Disha, I didn't feel right leaving her behind with Dr. Henderson. If they'd been truly having an affair, was it a good idea for them to be alone? But then, what did I know about healing someone possessed?

Nada.

I walked to the door and opened it, scanning the hall for Rowan. The administration building was pretty quiet, a few people walking in and out, but Rowan was not one of them.

It shouldn't take this long. Something was wrong.

Taking a deep breath, I pushed open the bathroom door and stepped out. Dean Underwood's office was the third on the left. I stared at the polished wood door and the opaque glass inset with his name stenciled on it. Rowan would be mad if his father found me lurking outside, but then, if none of them heard my approach, who would be the wiser?

"Time to put your money where your mouth is," I whispered to myself, readying my hands.

We had learned a simple cloaking spell a week ago in Dr. Henderson's class, and I had nailed it with Disha's help. I hadn't attempted it since, but it seemed only fitting that I do it now, using Henderson's spell to try to ascertain if he, himself, was the thief.

Stretching my fingers, I ran over the motions in my mind, hoping I remembered them correctly. Otherwise, I might come out of this with two heads.

"Here goes nothing."

Taking a deep breath, I performed the spell.

I tilted my hands, blowing out my breath as I channeled the image in my mind—me invisible in this hallway. My concentration was focused on my body and the flow of magic.

A door slammed, jarring me out of my thoughts.

When I came out of the spell and opened my eyes, I found that my body was invisible, but only from the waist down.

"Shit snacks," I murmured, extending my hands to try again.

Footsteps headed in my direction cut me short. No one should see me like this outside of the administrative offices.

Panicked, I jogged away from the footsteps, tucking myself into the little nook that led to Dean Underwood's door.

The door was cracked open, and, without even trying to, I could hear Rowan and his father speaking.

"—disappoint me at every turn. I told your mother you weren't cut out for it, but no, she begged me to take you on, let you get more involved, show you the wizarding ways. She said you could handle it. That you would be an asset to me."

It was Dean Underwood speaking, but he sounded like he was admonishing a soon-to-be-fired employee, not speaking to his son. My stomach twisted at his tone. I'd heard a similar one from my own father when he'd been one or two bottles into one of his drinking binges. At least it sounded like Rowan's mother supported him and believed in him. My mother had been the same, always telling me I could take on any challenge that came my way. It seemed Rowan and I had that in common, *one* parent who truly looked out for us. At least he still had a family while all I had were bittersweet memories.

"I'm doing my best," Rowan said. I could barely see his outline through the frosted glass.

Dean Underwood sighed. "That's the worst part. If this is your best, then what are you even doing to help with this investigation? You showed promise early on, but lately... even your grades are an embarrassment. I should send you back to your mother."

"No," Rowan answered forcefully. Then he backed off a bit. "I'll try harder. I'll get the answers you are seeking, bring up my grades."

"You'd better."

A chair creaked. I could just picture Dean Underwood tilted back in his chair, so nonchalant after browbeating his son.

"I want dirt on *Answorth* ASAP. I want him out. We can't take any more chances. And I want to rub it in McIntosh's face when we do it. Protecting him. Claiming he's only got the school's best intentions at heart. Ridiculous. He's a Lesser for God's sake."

"Yes, father," Rowan answered.

I heard another chair creak as if Rowan were standing up. Footsteps headed my way. I had to get out of there. But Dean Underwood's last words stopped me in my tracks.

"One more thing, son. That foolish Rivera girl. You'll stay away from her if you know what's good for you."

CHAPTER SIXTEEN

FALL SEMESTER
MID DECEMBER

"Field trip day," I sing-songed to Disha as I plopped down next to her at our regular cafeteria table. I placed her favorite coffee and muffin in front of her, before chowing down on mine.

Disha glanced up with tired eyes, picking at her breakfast.

"Whoopie." She twirled an unenthusiastic finger in the air, before using that hand to support her drooping chin.

My friend was finally well, taking two days to recover in her room before venturing out to classes again. When I'd gone to visit her and bring her snacks, she'd spilled everything—how the love affair between her and Dr. Henderson had started while doing private tutoring, how absolutely infatuated she had been with him, and how he'd broken it off a few days before.

But, when she started describing their toe-curling sex, I waved the white flag. I didn't need to hear about my professor's favorite positions. Gag me with a pitchfork.

This was a case of helping a friend get over an ex, which happened to be something I was good at. I'd helped Trey when the girl from the coffee shop broke up with him via a message written on a napkin. I could help Disha out of this.

"On today's docket... At ten AM, we have a field trip, AKA our final exam. At noon, lunch on the lawn, picnic-style. And at three, I got that cute boy from class to agree to drive us to the salon for manicures." I waggled my eyebrows enthusiastically. I didn't mention I had to sell some of my hand-me-down clothes at the consignment shop in Aberdale to pay for them.

Disha barely moved. This girl had it bad.

"Okay. That's fine. Today is going to be fine," I said to her and myself. "Come on. Let's have a nice walk in the sunshine to cheer us up before the field trip."

"It's an exam," Disha moaned.

"To-mato, to-mah-to." I took her hand and dragged her to the main doors.

Last week, Professor Answorth had explained that our semester Mentalism exam would take place outside the class-room. For that, the class had been instructed to meet him at the school's historical museum on the far side of campus, one of the few buildings I'd never visited because it was such a hike.

The good news was Disha wasn't wearing heels because she didn't have anyone to impress. Her expensive sneakers would speed our walk along nicely.

The twenty-minute trek with her grunting and moaning answers to my questions wasn't exactly pleasant, but we got to the museum without surprises. After the events at the shed, the foun-tain and the labyrinth, I was always nervous on the grounds. Who knew when something would pop up and try to kill you?

This line of thought brought me back to Rowan, who I'd been trying to erase from my mind. To my utter disappointment, he'd failed to show up to fill me in on what his father had said, which gave me the hint that he and I were no longer working together.

Daddy had made that very clear, and apparently Rowan was following his orders to perfection since he'd completely avoided me in the last few days.

I was still steamed about how his father had spoken about me like I was common trash. And Rowan hadn't uttered one word in my defense.

Rude.

As Disha and I walked up to the museum, we clustered with our classmates at the base of the steps, waiting for Professor Answorth. I could quickly see why this structure was separated from the others. Unlike the stately brick buildings and manicured gardens that made most of campus look like a magical Cambridge, this building was... bizarre.

Appearing as if it had been pieced together by four different architects, each section had its own style. The left wing was austere, postmodern, and composed of sleek lines and right angles. The surface shimmered as if made of a million diamonds, forcing me to shield my eyes from the glare.

In extreme opposition, the right wing was constructed of natural materials like wood and stone, with ivy vines climbing up the rounded Hobbiton-style windows. Moss crowded in the nooks and crannies and I half expected to find a gnome or fairy peeking out of one of the many oval windows.

In the center, the main entrance seemed like something straight out of a Salvador Dali painting. The arches sagged and the pillars leaned as if the foundation had shifted in an earthquake and no one had bothered to fix it. Even the steps leading to the entrance tilted, giving me a sick, vertigo feeling.

"Was the architect on drugs?" I asked Disha.

She either didn't hear me or was deep into something on her phone.

Another girl, who I'd seen in class but never talked to, leaned in to answer. She had short, black hair and a nose ring, going for that cute punk vibe.

"That's what I thought at first, too," she laughed. "They'd have to be on drugs to come up with this mess, but I read somewhere that the five heads of the magical schools that founded the Academy created the museum together. Each wing is decorated in that person's style to show that—even though there are different types of magic—they can all work in harmony to create something beautiful." She gestured to the building.

"Oh. That's cool. Thanks." I smiled at her.

"You're welcome." She held out a hand heavy with rings. On her exposed wrist, a *magicked* dragon tattoo slithered under her skin.

I took her hand and shook it. "You're Georgia, right? I've seen you around. I'm Charlie."

She tilted her head at Disha. "And she is?"

Disha tapped on her phone.

"She's... in a funk," I added, patting Disha on the back. "Boyfriend trouble," I whispered.

"Ah," Georgia nodded knowingly. "That's why I avoid them all together."

I snorted, thinking instantly of Rowan who didn't appear to be in attendance yet. Not that I was noticing.

"So... Georgia, did your parents name you for our beloved state?"

She rolled her eyes. "They think they are *so* clever. They won't be laughing when I put them in the world's worst retirement home."

I couldn't tell if she was joking or not, but I liked her style—sarcastic, take-no-prisoners, and funny. I'd seen her in classes before, but we'd never spoken. In fact, I hadn't spoken to most of my classmates, spending all my time with Disha, but with her semi out-of-commission, it was nice to have someone answer my questions with something other than a grunt.

And, yet, there was something off about Georgia. As I studied her further, I realized her hands were trembling as she fidgeted with her book bag and her words were coming out a little too fast. Dark circles hung under her eyes like she hadn't slept in a while. I wondered if she'd been pulling all-nighters to study for the exam or if she was on some drugs to enhance her performance.

"I bet he's testing us on telekinesis," Georgia whispered.

"Hmm?"

"Well, I've been inside the museum and there are lots of artifacts. Lots of things to levitate. I've been practicing." She leaned toward me. "Professor Answorth kind of tipped me off."

I raised my eyebrows.

"Well, he didn't say it in so many words, but he told me after class one day, when I asked him what to study, that I should go back and look at chapter seven in the textbook," she said, eyes big. They were slightly bloodshot, adding to my suspicions.

Chapter seven of the textbook? I'd done the assigned readings, but that chapter was assigned over a month ago. I couldn't remember what it had covered any more than I could remember what I'd had for breakfast the first Monday of November.

"Oh," was all I could muster as my stomach churned. Telekinesis was not my strong suit by a country mile. It required too much finesse. I was going to straight up fail this exam.

My thoughts were whisked away as the class began to shuffle forward. Answorth had appeared and lead us in. Georgia, Disha and I fell into step behind the crowd.

A quick scan for Rowan let me know he hadn't snuck in the back. He was indeed not here and missing the final exam. That would not bode well for his grades. Maybe something was wrong. I thought about the blue veins under his skin and how... unwell they made him seem sometimes.

My eyes were drawn forward as we entered the building. The ivy on the outside wall rippled like verdant scales as if waving us in. Then, inside, an apparition became visible on the entrance's domed ceiling. A floating head that spoke to us *Wizard of Oz* style.

"*Greeeetings*, witches and warlocks. Young and old. Supernatural and human. We welcome you to the American Magical Historical Society and Gift Shop," the chipper floating head boomed. "Please enjoy our magical oddities, artifacts, and historical wonders, but be warned. There are items here that can stop your heart, split your spleen, and turn you into a newt. So please, keep your hands and other appendages to yourself at all times."

Magical artifacts. I wondered, in passing, if this was where the last stolen item came from.

The head talked a bit more about the rules, wished us well and then *poofed* into a cloud of sparkly purple smoke.

"Well, that was something," I whispered.

Beside me, Georgia giggled a little hysterically. Yeah, she was definitely on something. Poor girl. This exam must've meant a lot to her. I wondered vaguely if it should've meant more to me, but there had been so much else going on.

Professor Answorth clapped his hands and waved us forward, deeper into the museum.

"Onward to your examination," he instructed in his British accent.

The halls we passed had so many wonders my eyes and brain could not process them all. I spied large golden goblets, mummified animals, and something that appeared to be a giant purple squid sculpture. There were hallways glittering with jewelry and galleries of artwork. I wanted to wander through everything, but the class kept flowing forward. I definitely had to come back.

Answorth led us into the area that was part of the "drunk architect" section. Oil paintings hung crookedly, matching the slanted angles of doorways and lamps, and giving me that off-kilter feeling again.

Beside me, Georgia put a hand to her head, appearing anxious or ill. I wondered if she suffered from performance anxiety. The pterodactyls in my stomach were proof that I had my fair share of anxieties myself.

We passed a door labeled "Restricted Access." A guy dressed

in a dark suit stood next to the door, looking sullen. He stared straight ahead as if we weren't there. He looked like someone who would be packing heat, or maybe he didn't need to because he could shoot death rays from his pinky toes.

What kind of dark magic lurked behind those doors? Probably the items that could split your spleen. Or worse.

We slipped into a smaller room at the end of the hall. At least here, the decor was hung properly so I didn't feel as though the floor was tilting. It was a smaller gallery room, with many framed portraits labeled with gold plates. There were sculpted busts on pedestals and one life-sized statue of a man riding a snarling manticore in the room's center.

Professor Answorth climbed up on a stone bench and waited as we clustered around.

"Ladies and gentleman, today is your final exam. I will give you ten minutes to look over your notes before beginning. Study wisely, as this task will make up twenty percent of your final grade."

Digging in my bookbag, I glanced back to where Georgia had been standing, intent on asking her for some telekinesis advice, but she wasn't where I'd last seen her. Scanning the room, I realized she wasn't there. Did she realize that if she wasn't back in ten minutes, she would fail the exam she'd studied so hard for?

I went back to examining my notes, trying to cram the entirety of chapter seven inside my stressed out mind. It wasn't working. I was too damn nervous.

I scanned the room again. Georgia wasn't back. Had she gotten ill? She had looked terrible. What if she'd gone to the bathroom and passed out or worse. If she was sick, someone should check on her and let Professor Answorth know she wasn't just skipping.

"Disha, I'll be back in a second," I said, setting my bag down.

Her eyes darted up to me. "You can't leave now. It's the final exam."

"I just have to check on something. We still have five minutes."

Her round stare let me know I was being crazy, but I didn't have time to explain.

Darting out of the room, I scanned the hall for the bathrooms we'd passed on the way in. They were near the front entrance. I could make it if I ran.

Taking off at a jog down the hallway, I prayed Georgia was just washing her hands or something. I really didn't have much ti—

I skidded to a stop, my heart pounding. I couldn't be seeing what I thought I was seeing.

On a second glance, indeed I was.

The doors to the "Restricted Access" section were wide open, and standing in the middle of the room amidst cases of rare and powerful-looking artifacts, was Georgia in the act of stealing one.

CHAPTER SEVENTEEN

FALL SEMESTER
MID DECEMBER

How the hell did she get into the restricted section? Where's the guard? My eyes darted around and quickly spotted him. He was knocked out on the floor, half of his body hidden behind a large planter.

A scream caught in my throat. I should have been calling for help, but I found myself walking closer to take a better look at the guard.

"S-sir," I stammered in a broken tone.

Was he dead? Had Georgia killed him? No, it couldn't be. She seemed so nice.

When I made it far enough to see his face, my veins ran cold. He was unrecognizable, his skin dried and cracked as if a giant tick had suck the life out of him and no amount of water could ever rehydrate him back to life.

The scream that had been lodged in my throat finally escaped. It echoed through the large space, magnified. Footsteps hurried in my direction from the testing area. Help was coming, but, suddenly, I couldn't tear my eyes from the room before me. The place was filled with dozens of pedestals housing cased-in objects. Many magical artifacts hung from the walls while the largest ones sat on the floor—suits of armor, shrunken heads, swords, ancient pistols, sculptures. There was even a large wardrobe in one corner that made me think of Narnia.

Georgia stood inside the room, her hands resting on the glass case that protected one of the artifacts. Her eyes were glazed, her stance robotic. She looked like a zombie.

Professor Answorth kind of tipped me off, she had said.

It was an odd thing for me to remember at the moment, but for some reason, the words echoed a few more times inside my head, making me wonder why he would have shown such preferential treatment. Why give her a hint?

A... *suggestion?*

But wasn't that a mentalist's specialty? Suggestions. Which begged the question: what other ideas could he have planted in her mind?

I lowered my gaze, trying to see inside the case. Something golden rested at its bottom, but I couldn't tell what.

I took a step into the room. Georgia didn't even glance up, too entranced by whatever spell she was casting.

"Ms. Rivera!" A voice called from behind me. "What are you doing?"

My head swiveling slowly, I glanced over my shoulder. Answorth and my classmates were standing on the other side of the doorway, regarding me with shocked expressions. Vincent, the top student in the class, pointed at the dead guard.

"She... she killed him," he said.

What?! Did he mean *me?* From their angle, they couldn't see Georgia, so I must have appeared as guilty as if I held a bloody knife.

Oddly, that didn't seem to matter. Instead of feeling fear or worry, all I felt was deep curiosity about Georgia and the item. Something didn't feel right inside my head, but it didn't seem to matter—not when the tug of the case demanded my every thought.

What was inside? I had to know.

I stepped closer to Georgia. Her hands were planted flat on the sides of the case as her lips moved silently. She didn't matter either, though. My gaze fell on the artifact.

"Ms. Rivera!" Answorth exclaimed, his voice edging closer. He paused. "Everyone stay back." After a beat, he addressed me again, "Mr. Rivera, please, come out of there. It's not safe."

"Charlie, do as he says." This from Disha who sounded scared enough to use my real name.

They had no reason to be scared. The item in the case would fix everything. A warm feeling spread in my chest.

"Georgia?!" Answorth gasped behind me. "No, get your hands off that case."

But it was too late.

The case cracked, the glass making a sound like someone crunching ice between their teeth. Fissures crawled up the case's sides like upside-down lightning bolts.

"We can even break items with telekinesis," Professor Answorth had said one day in class. *"All you have to do is make them vibrate fast enough."*

The case imploded. Glass rained down on the floor with the sound of a thousand diamonds scattering across the tile. Georgia merely blinked at the object she'd released.

An alarm blared, and a metal door fell from the ceiling, slamming Georgia and me in with a score of weird, magical relics.

The *thud* of the metal door should have sent us squealing in fear, but we both just stood there, staring at the golden glow of the item Georgia had liberated. It rested on a black, velvety surface, growing more radiant by the second.

It was the most beautiful thing I'd ever seen.

As if tugged by a leash tied to my heart, I lurched forward to get a better look. At first, I couldn't decide what the item was. It appeared to be two large wedding bands stuck together.

"What is it?" I murmured to no one in particular.

I frowned and cocked my head to one side for a better angle, then realized the rings weren't stuck together. They were separate, and they weren't rings. They were more like... wide bracelets.

Georgia lifted a hand to pick one up.

"I wouldn't touch that," I said—not because I was worried for her safety, but because I didn't want her nasty fingers on them.

They were mine.

She ignored me. I tried to slap her hand away, but she moved fast for a zombie and got a hold of it. Clenching her fist around it, she lifted it up in triumph. Her eyes glinted under its light as she brought it down and started slipping it on her other hand.

"No!" I exclaimed, something inside me cringing at the idea of Georgia wearing the bracelet. *My* bracelet.

I lunged forward, throwing my arms around Georgia's waist and knocking her off balance. We toppled to the floor, me landing on top of her. She recovered immediately and, after pushing me off, she elbowed me in the jaw.

I tumbled to the side, hands flying to my face as I cried out. Still reeling from the pain, I watched her stand and—in one swift motion—slip the bracelet onto her wrist.

She smiled, her face twisting maniacally. But the elation didn't last. It fell from her expression almost as soon as it materialized and morphed into a grimace of agony.

Right where she stood, Georgia's body began to shake. Her arms flailed. Her head whipped back and forth. Her teeth rattled.

I stood, my hands extended in her direction. "Georgia," I whispered.

She seemed to quake as if an electric current were travelling through her. Light burst from her mouth in a silent scream. Then she went still and, for an instant, teetered on her own two legs before collapsing.

As she hit the floor, the bracelet slipped off her wrist—widening to pass over her hand—then rolled away, coming to a stop right in front of me.

I stared at it, Georgia completely forgotten.

The bracelet beckoned me, shapes dancing in its golden, polished surface. My trembling fingers reached for it, while a desperate voice in the back of my mind told me not to do it. I ignored it and picked it up.

It was cool and smooth to the touch. I turned it this way and that, admiringly. There were no designs on it, no encrusted jewels, not a mark of any kind. But it was beautiful, and it was mine.

I put it on, easily slipping my hand through it as it widened for me. Once in place, it tightened securely and comfortably around my wrist. Warmth spread through my body as something inside me seemed to swell.

My gaze fell on Georgia, then on the bracelet at my wrist.

Oh, no. What the hell have I done?

Panic exploded in my chest just as I convulsed once and promptly fell to my knees. I expected light to burst through my mouth like celestial puke, but instead, it came from the pedestal where the other bracelet waited.

Trembling, I stood up and walked to it with slow steps. The second bracelet beckoned me just as the first one had. I obeyed, some powerful force overpowering my will, and slipped it onto my other wrist.

It occurred to me that I could die like Georgia, but for all the world, I felt amazing because my magic—which had always felt like a giant jumble of nonsense inside of me—quickly was falling into place.

CHAPTER EIGHTEEN

FALL SEMESTER
MID DECEMBER

THEY WOULDN'T COME OFF.

Dean McIntosh, Dr. Henderson, Professor Answorth, and even Nurse Taishi had tried, and they had all failed.

The cuffs had made themselves comfortable on my wrists. Permanent, like a bad case of herpes.

Aradia's Cuffs, that's what they were called. They had killed Georgia, and everyone was worried they would kill me next, but I felt fine. Great, really.

Better yet, I was sure they were *my* item, the thing I needed to center and focus my magic. Several times already, I'd used Disha's spell to make everyone sound like an Ewok to my ears, then turned them back to normal without a glitch. I'd practiced it a lot before, and I'd never been that consistent. Now, it felt like that tangled ball of yarn that had been my magic had come unraveled, and its beginning and end were clearly at my reach.

From what I could gather, the cuffs had belonged to an Italian witch, who was supposedly the daughter of the goddess Diana and Lucifer. That should have been enough to scare the crap out of me, but, if the name Diana was supposed to mean divine, then the cuffs were as good as they were bad, just like everything and everyone—Dean McIntosh's words, which I agreed with but for one point. Only Rowan was pure darkness, no good in that one.

I was in Dean McIntosh's office, a large space with tall mahogany bookshelves on three of its walls, wood floors sectioned off by three Persian rugs, a fireplace, marble busts of old dudes on pedestals, and a desk almost as big as a queen-size bed—a far cry from her sister's office and way less fun. Maybe the dean needed a ferret to liven things up.

I was sitting on a chair while Dean McIntosh, Dr. Henderson, Professor Answorth, and Nurse Taishi fussed over me as if I were ill.

In the back of my mind, I was dimly aware that, despite the fact one of my classmates had died, I was more worried about keeping the murderous cuffs than actually mourning her loss. Something was messed up with that, but I couldn't bring myself to feel the deep sense of loss that should accompany a senseless death. All I wanted was to try all the spells I'd been practicing, and I couldn't do it while sequestered in this office. Clearly, the cuffs and their magic was messing with my head.

"You are wasting your time," Macgregor Underwood said from the window where he'd been standing, surreptitiously watching everyone's attempt to take the cuffs off my wrists while he pretended to stare at the lawn.

They all peered in his direction.

He turned and faced us, his hands clasped behind his back, perfectly coiffed hair shining in the overhead lights. "The cuffs *chose* her. They won't come off until she's dead. Or we find a clever spell."

I held my breath. Was he trying to scare me? Was it a threat or something? Maybe he was planning my murder in order to place the cuffs back under a glass case.

"The last witch who wore them did so for over thirty-five years," he said. "Since the Academy acquired them, anyone who has touched them has died. That is why they were in the restricted area. That is why they killed Georgia. The only reason this girl is not dead as well is because, for some ungodly reason, Aradia chose her."

Dean McIntosh dismissed him with a wave of her hand. "That is just legend, Macgregor. It's not been officially documented."

"I guess this is our chance," he said, gesturing toward me. "Exhibit A, no known spell has been able to remove the cuffs. Exhibit B," his dark eyes, so much like Rowan's, bore into mine, "do you happen to feel mighty and capable of everything, by chance?"

Four additional pairs of eyes angled in my direction. I blushed and stared at my shoes.

"Um, not particularly," I lied.

I didn't want them to decide I was dangerous and murder was the only option to get the cuffs off me before I went on a world-domination campaign.

"She's lying," Underwood said.

"I'm not," I protested, but I sounded as convincing as a defendant on Judge Judy.

"Who put you up to this?" he asked as if I were really on trial.

I finally met his gaze. "Who put me up to what? What are you trying to say?"

"If we search her room, I wonder what we'll find. Our missing staff, perhaps?"

Missing staff?

Was he talking about the item that was taken during the Rumble in the Jungle?

"You're crazy," I spat. "I don't know anything about a staff. Search my room if you want!"

Everyone stared at me with raised eyebrows. I squirmed in my chair. I'd yelled at a faculty member, but what the hell? He'd just accused me of stealing.

So much had changed, yet so little.

"Macgregor," Dean McIntosh said, "we don't accuse anyone of theft without proof."

Damn right! I sat straighter.

"Ms. Rivera," she turned to me, "students don't raise their voices to teachers, nor any faculty members for that matter."

Shit. I deflated again.

Silence hung over the room. I armed myself with courage despite the scolding from the dean herself.

"You are all asking the wrong questions," I mumbled.

The sneer I sent in Answorth's direction must've been pretty good because even Underwood shifted his gaze toward the mentalist. Though, too late, I remembered I didn't have any proof to accuse him, which would probably only get me another reprimand.

"Um, like I told you before..." I said, backpedaling a bit, "I went after Georgia because she left the test and was acting weird. I'm pretty sure she was being controlled by... someone."

There. If I kept things vague and let everyone draw their own conclusions, they might just start looking at Answorth more carefully. To my satisfaction, Underwood did exactly that.

"Wasn't Georgia Copeland one of your *most improved* students, Julian?" Underwood asked the blond professor.

Instead of going on the defense as I expected him, Answorth's face fell with sadness.

"She was," he said. "She really cared about her studies. This is bloody awful."

All the others nodded, and, at last, I found my heart growing heavy with sorrow and guilt. Answorth's words were like a slap in the face. The girl had died because of some bastard who was using her for an evil purpose, and it had taken me this long to stop thinking about myself and the damn cuffs.

What was wrong with me?!

Answorth focused his full attention my way, then knelt, placing a hand on the arm of my chair, and peering up with clear blue eyes.

"What makes you think someone was controlling Georgia?" he asked.

I blinked at his spellbinding gaze and shook my head.

"Um... well, she was moving like a robot and her eyes were glazed over. Also, when I talked to her, she didn't seem to hear me."

Answorth nodded sagely. "Yes, very common characteristics of someone under a controlling spell." He stood, pulling on his cuff-links. "Not an easy spell to cast, especially on a strong mind like Georgia's, but not impossible for a powerful witch or warlock. Any of us could have done it." He cast a dark glance in Henderson's direction, which was not wasted on anyone.

With a sharp exhale, Dean McIntosh took a seat behind her desk. "This conversation is hardly productive. We need to decide what to do about the rest of the semester. A student is dead, and there will be hell to pay for our failure to protect her."

"There is no question about what should be done," Underwood added. "The semester should be canceled and the Academy closed."

What?! They couldn't do that, could they? Where would I go? Homelessness was simply not an option. Not again. Not without Trey.

"There will be an uproar amongst the students," Henderson said. "They won't want to repeat their subjects."

Damn right.

"The academic impact is hardly an issue when lives are at stake, Thadeus," Underwood said, walking back to the window. "But they shouldn't have to repeat their subjects. Those who have already passed will keep their grades. Those who were hoping their final exams would help them achieve a passing grade can use the holidays to study further. Then they can do their examination when the school reopens next semester. Meanwhile, we will use the time to reinforce security, do damage control, and, of course, investigate Ms. Copeland's death as well as the other *incidents*."

Dean McIntosh was nodding her head thoughtfully like she believed this was the best plan ever, but it wasn't. It didn't take *me* into account. It left me hanging over the jaws of a canned turkey Christmas dinner at a shelter.

"As far as Ms. Rivera is concerned," Underwood said, not glancing my way as if I wasn't in the room, "she cannot be left unattended until we know what effect those cuffs will have on her."

"Indeed," Answorth said, his cerulean gaze drifting to my wrists.

Underwood quickly added, "Aware of her *situation* as I am, I will willingly offer my home to her during this difficult time. My wife, sons, and I can keep an eye on her to make sure she's safe."

The what...?!

My brain did cartwheels. He'd told Rowan to stay away from me, why do this now? Did he want the cuffs back on that pedestal? I bet that was it. He didn't want a lowly witch like me—someone with blood from an unknown family—to possess one of the Academy's precious relics. He would prefer to put them back in that museum to gather dust.

I shook my head. "I... I don't think that will be necessary. I don't want to impose."

"You have no choice in the matter," Underwood said. "Not while you are wearing school property."

My jaw dropped. I peered toward Dean McIntosh for some sympathy. The guy was saying I was worth less than the stupid cuffs. *Excuse me?* We were talking about a human life over two circles of metal.

But all of this seemed to go over the dean's head because she looked relieved. "What an excellent idea, Macgregor. Will Bonnie mind?"

Underwood waved his hand. "Of course not. You know her. She'll be glad to have another female in the house. She always complains about *all that testosterone,* what with three sons." He said this as if he thought his wife was stupid for feeling that way. Typical male.

Three sons? I had no idea Rowan had brothers. Why didn't anyone tell me anything?

"It's decided," Dean McIntosh said. "Nurse Taishi, could you make sure Ms. Rivera is in good health? Well... besides the... you know..." She gestured toward the cuffs.

"Of course," he said, inclining his head respectfully. He was dressed in blue scrubs, his black hair slicked back to perfection, looking out of place among all the suits.

"And please, can you stay with her until we figure out the best way to keep an eye on her while we establish if Aradia's cuffs will have a negative effect on her?"

"Certainly," Nurse Taishi added.

No no no.

This plan sucked. I didn't need a babysitter.

"Dean McIntosh," I said. "I don't think that will be necessary. I feel fine, and I—"

"Ms. Rivera," the dean interrupted, "I know how you must feel, but please understand we only have your wellbeing in mind. As you've heard, those artifacts are kept in a restricted area for a reason. Many deaths can be attributed to them, including your poor classmate's, Ms. Copeland's. We don't want yours to be added to that unfortunate list."

I swallowed the knot that formed in my throat as I remembered Georgia's expression of terror as she fell dead. That could have been me. It could still be me if the cuffs suddenly decided I was chopped liver.

I nodded. I could take this. Besides, going to the Underwood's lair might yield important information toward Trey's killers. They'd been the ones there to save me when it all happened, after all. I had a sneaking suspicion all of this was connected somehow.

Nurse Taishi and I exited the dean's office, leaving the rest behind to discuss the gory details of what to do next.

Outside, we found a large group of waiting students, Disha and Rowan among them. Everyone straightened to attention, their curious eyes examining every inch of me. I wished for a sweater to pull over the cuffs, but everyone could see them. Some regarded me with fear, but most just wore hard expressions of distrust.

Disha pulled away from the bunch, Rowan trailing behind her. "Are you okay, Charlie?"

"She's fine," Nurse Taishi answered before I could, then guided me toward the infirmary. "Dean McIntosh will soon have news for everyone, so stay calm."

"Can we come with her?" Disha asked, walking behind us.

"It would be better if—"

"Please," I begged. "She's my best friend."

Nurse Taishi sighed and reluctantly agreed.

I threw a narrowed glance in Rowan's direction. What would he think when he heard the news?

CHAPTER NINETEEN

WINTER BREAK
LATE DECEMBER

NEVER IN MY life had I witnessed a more silent car ride.

Macgregor Underwood sat up front, navigating his Mercedes down the highway, while Rowan and I rode side by side in the backseat. It was more awkward than that time I shot myself into the ceiling in Dr. Henderson's class. And that event was in the history books of most awkward moments ever.

Rowan cleared his throat and shifted, making the hand-stitched leather seat creak underneath him. It had been a while since we'd been in close proximity to each other. Sure, the backseat was roomy, but, like any sedan, we only had about a foot of tense air between us. I could smell his cologne, hear the scratch of his jeans as he leaned back.

Jesus, would someone please turn on the radio?

But, then we turned onto a driveway blocked by a wrought

iron gate. Dean Underwood rolled down his window and punched a code into a keypad, causing the gates to swing wide.

This was all too much. I was on an episode of *Cribs*, only I was the observer. These two were the rich snobs who lived it.

Or maybe, I was Little Orphan Annie and he was my Daddy Warbucks.

The thought made my breakfast threaten to lurch back up. Macgregor was the least fatherly figure I'd ever seen and that was saying something, considering my own alcoholic father.

The house came into view, confirming my suspicions. To call it stately would have been an understatement. The mansion that spread out across the manicured lawn was as perfect as a dream. A fountain bubbled on the brick paver driveway, ringed by square hedges and rounded shrubs. I counted twelve windows out front before Dean Underwood pulled us into a giant garage.

I guess knowing magic really paid.

The car turned off. Rowan and Macgregor got out, but I sat there, clutching my bag. How had I gotten myself into this?

Macgregor rapped his knuckles on the window, causing me to jump. The expression on his face was anything but welcoming. "Are you going to sit inside the car the whole time?"

Then he and Rowan strode away, leaving me in the car. I contemplated staying there for the entire two-week holiday. The stink I'd leave in the Mercedes would serve him right.

But then my cuffs throbbed as if telling me more awaited inside that mansion. Maybe answers. Maybe more than long, tortuous days and nights. The cuffs had started doing that shortly after we left the Academy, and it was interesting, to say the least.

I sighed, exited the car, and followed the path to the garage door which had been left open for me. Through it, a hallway led to a giant entryway complete with marble floors, soaring ceilings and a grand staircase that blew my mind. Hallways led in all directions and I had no idea where I was supposed to go.

"Oh, there you are, darlin'!" a chipper female voice called from down the hall.

A petite blond woman came toward me, her high heels clacking on the polished marble. Her hair was perfect, her dress expensive, but her smile was warm and genuine. She pressed me into a hug, flowery perfume invading my senses before she pulled back and gave me a once-over.

"Charlie, I'm so happy you're here! When Mac told me we were having a girl as a guest, I about jumped for joy. You have no idea what it's like to share a holiday with mostly men." She winked at me as if she and I were in on some secret joke. Then she pulled me through a gilded archway into the massive kitchen.

Mrs. Underwood, or Bonnie as she asked me to call her, set me down at a bar stool behind a massive granite counter before plying me with a spread of food that could choke a horse.

"If you don't see something you like, you just holler for Mariana. She'll get you set up. You have a room upstairs, third door on the left and I put some toiletries in your bathroom for you. I have got to go. Running a Christmas charity auction, but I'll be back at nine, okay, darlin'?"

Her lilting southern accent swirled around me like her perfume had. In a flash, she had kissed my cheek, hugged me again and disappeared.

Alone in the echoey kitchen, I stared around, wondering if I should retreat to my room or eat. The smell of smoked meats and buttery pastries won me over. If I wasn't going to enjoy myself, I could at least get some good grub out of the deal.

After I'd eaten, I wandered toward the staircase, intent on heading up, but the pull of seeing the rest of the house was gnawing at me. Each room was more glorious than the last, and, with no one around to stop me, I couldn't help myself from exploring. Plus, there was the constant pulse of the cuffs and that feeling at the back of my skull that there was something here I was supposed to see.

I stepped cautiously into a library lined with more books than Dean McIntosh's office. The polished wood and furniture large enough to sail out to sea on reminded me of the staff offices in the Academy. The desk at the far end of the room had to be Dean Underwood's. If he found me in here, snooping, he'd likely do more than glower.

And yet, a book laid open on his desk and, more importantly, a computer awaited, its screen on.

Glancing behind me, I tiptoed over.

But, the book was titled *Ancient Breads of Eastern Europe*, and worse, the computer screen held an unfinished game of solitaire on it. Useless.

What I did find were several family photos in cherry wood frames. I picked one up, staring at the Underwood family. There was Macgregor looking like the rich villain in a movie, his wife, who seemed blissfully unaware of what a bastard her husband could be sometimes. Beside them stood their three boys. The older two were golden-haired and beaming like their mother—the type of boys who would row crew and wear sweaters around their necks as they cavorted on ivy league campuses. Had they attended the Academy?

Then there was Rowan. Dark, brooding, and off to the side as if he didn't quite belong. Even in this 2D image, one could tell he was the black sheep of the family.

More evidence supported this analysis when I scanned the rest of the contents of Macgregor's desk. Pictures of both older boys abounded. They held up awards, or smiled at ceremonies honoring them in each of the photos.

There were no other pictures of Rowan.

I thought about how his father had spoken to him that day in his office like he was an employee he was close to firing. What must it have been like growing up under his brothers' shadows, feeling like he was never good enough, but intent on trying to prove himself nonetheless.

I had lots of daddy issues, myself, but this took the cake.

Feeling a strange pang of sympathy for Rowan, I turned and strode out of the office. I should find him and mend fences. If we were going to spend two weeks together, we should at least be civil about it.

But first, I needed to use the little girl's room.

I went up the hall and headed to the bathroom Mrs. Underwood had mentioned before she left.

I opened the door and stopped short as my jaw nearly hit the floor. Rowan stood by the shower, soaking wet and bare-chested with a towel covering his lower half. Beads of water dampened his hair and slid down his sculpted body.

Sucking in a breath, a surge of heat pulsed through my body as my heartbeat sped up.

He stared at me, clutching his towel, a shocked expression on his face.

"Oh! I'm sorry," I muttered.

But as I turned to go, my gaze locked on the dark blue veins spider-webbing his torso and arms. I'd seen a few of these before when his shirt had shifted, but this... This was nothing like I'd ever seen. It appeared as if his whole body were infected with some sort of disease that was eating its way out. Forget gangrene. He had gang*blue*.

"Oh, Rowan," I said, realizing, somehow, that this was what the cuffs had wanted me to see.

Before I could think about what I was doing, I reached out and touched his chest.

My cuffs glowed, shooting pain down my arms as visions swirled in my brain—Rowan lurking around a dark forest, a flash of light, a figure wreathed in blue flame with blinding red eyes, that figure blasting him in the chest. Pain. Constant, agonizing pain.

He stepped back, breaking our connection. His eyes were hooded, and I couldn't read his expression.

"Wh... what happened to you?" I asked, unable to draw my eyes away from the roadmap of pain on his chest.

He reached to the floor, grabbed his shirt and tugged it on. It was as if he felt, even now, that he should hide from me.

His answer came out slowly as his eyes sought the floor. "I was cursed. I went on a mission to help my family last year, one that proved... more difficult than I'd planned."

"That *thing* did this to you?"

He searched my face, probably wondering what I knew, how I knew.

"What's the treatment? Your father surely must know how to..." But as I said it, Rowan's tightening expression told me everything.

"Your father doesn't know," I whispered.

Rowan shook his head. "No one knows. Well, except Disha, Nurse Taishi, and now you." He said the last part as if my finding out was an unfortunate development.

"Rowan, you have to tell him."

"Do I?" His voice was hard and his smile didn't reach his eyes. "And have him kick me out of the Academy? What would I do then, Charlie? Flip burgers? Work for my brother's company packing boxes? I'd rather die."

"Well, your wish might be granted," I said, exasperated. My eyes lingered on the veins of blue barely visible below his collar. "They look worse."

"They *are* worse," he shot back, but then he hung his head. "I don't know what to do. The curse is draining my power more each day. Soon... I won't be able to do magic at all, lately it's been spotty at best."

The expression on his face nearly broke my heart. "The first thing you should do is put on some pants," I said, swallowing thickly. "Then meet me in my room. We'll figure it out."

When his grateful gaze met mine, my heart nearly leapt out of my chest. He should have dismissed me off hand—I knew next to nothing about magic compared to him—but he just seemed glad to have someone else on his side, even if it was me. Plus, I had the cuffs now and maybe that counted for something.

I stepped out, closing the door behind me, reminding myself that, under no circumstances should I let myself fall for Rowan Underwood.

CHAPTER TWENTY

WINTER BREAK
LATE DECEMBER

THAT EVENING, we ate dinner together, if you could call it that. Mariana served us a meal fit for a king on the gigantic twelve-seat dining table. Apparently, tomorrow, his brothers would arrive and the house would be busy, but tonight it was Rowan and me.

We ate in silence. Rowan's eyes stayed on his phone, letting me know we should not talk about his curse, even with Mariana out of the room. I guess he also thought we shouldn't talk at all, which was annoying. With no phone to distract me, I spent the time going over the magic spells I knew that could help with Rowan's curse, but soon started to feel pretty useless. If Nurse Taishi couldn't help him, what made me think I could?

Delusions of grandeur much?

Ever since the cuffs had claimed me as their own, I'd been struggling with those impulses. It was as if I'd gotten a serious injection of ego the minute they'd latched on. There was nothing I could not do. No challenge I couldn't defeat.

Until my brain jumped in, reminding me what a terrible student I'd been up until now.

But the cuffs, my ego countered. *They are my item.*

And it was true. All my spells and incantations worked so much better than before.

Yet, would that be enough to reverse a terrible curse?

After dinner, Rowan and I went to our respective rooms. The plan was to meet up in the backyard after his parents had returned and gone to bed.

In the meantime, I called Disha on their landline. She picked up on the first ring.

"Oh, Charlize Theron, I've been waiting all day. Tell. Me. *Everything!*"

"Hello to you, too," I mocked. "How was the flight?"

"Boring. Stop stalling. Are you and Rowan in love yet?"

"Gah, no. Stop it." I wouldn't tell her I walked in on him in the shower. She'd twist it into something it decidedly was not. "No, he's taking huge pleasure in ignoring me. Macgregor, too. But Mrs. Underwood is nice."

"She is. How she can stand her husband I will never understand." Disha blew a breath into the phone. "What's the house like? I've never visited."

"Huge. Probably what you're used to."

Disha sniffed. She was always uncomfortable when I brought up the disparity between me and her. It was like wealth embarrassed her, probably why she always gave me her things.

"Hey, listen, I need to ask you something," I said. "It's about Rowan."

"Mmm hmm," she answered, expectantly.

"He told me... you know, about the curse. Like, the blue veins one," I whispered into the phone.

"Oh." She went quiet for a bit before continuing. "He's really sensitive about it. I've tried to help him multiple times, but it's a really nasty curse. We went to Nurse Taishi after I insisted, but there was nothing he could do either. I told Rowan to tell his father, but he flat out refused."

"That's what I told him." But after what I'd seen in the office, I understood why he wouldn't tell dear old dad.

Disha proceeded to list every spell, potion, and therapy they'd tried together. As she ticked each off, I realized she'd mentioned every single treatment I'd been wanting to try. We'd learned a few things on reverting curses in Henderson's class but, of course, my delusions of grandeur didn't live up to Disha's efficiency.

I had nothing.

I hung up, promising her an update, and feeling more defeated than I had in awhile. What had I been thinking, offering him help? Disha was an advanced witch and Rowan came from one of the oldest and most powerful supernatural families in America.

Stupid cuffs. Stupid Charlie.

My door creaked open and Rowan's head slipped through the crack. He tossed his head back as if to say it was time and then retreated. I heard his quiet footsteps tread away as he headed outside.

I contemplated crawling under my large, four-poster bed and pretending I was asleep, but then my cuffs flashed with heat and light. It was as if they wanted me to follow Rowan. Maybe if I couldn't help him, they could.

Creeping through the house, I descended the back stairs and slipped out of the laundry room and onto the back patio.

Moonbeams and strategic uplighting made the Underwoods' backyard into a dream. The brick patio had two seating areas with large outdoor couches and another huge metal and stone table set. There was a built-in pizza oven, a grill, and a wet bar near the illuminated and sparkling in-ground pool. More paved walkways wove around shrubs and flower gardens off into the distance.

A chill cut across the yard. Yesterday, it had been mild and sunny. But it was December in Georgia so, of course, today the temperature was near freezing. I clutched my sweater to my body and scanned the grounds for Rowan. He'd told me to meet him near the tree line, which I could barely spot beyond the lit grounds.

I walked the path, eyes and ears open. There was a distinct lack of magic in this household, so I didn't fear that, but there was something else lingering around like a bad smell. The house and grounds felt... empty, but I couldn't put my finger on why or what it meant. Maybe it was made to match Macgregor's heart.

Movement near the tree line drew my eyes. There was Rowan in a windbreaker, his shoulders hunched, breath pulsing in the cold. I tried desperately not to enjoy the ruddy glow his cheeks had adopted or the way the wind tugged at his dark hair.

"Hey," he said.

"Hey." I was ever the cunning linguist, I know.

"So, you said we could figure this out, any ideas yet?" Chestnut brown eyes watched me, hope hidden in their depths.

"Well, I did think about it," I murmured, stalling, "but then I talked to Disha and she said you'd already tried the few things I came up with."

"Oh." His shoulders slumped. "Okay, then."

He started to walk back to the house.

I held out a hand. "Rowan, wait."

But when he whirled back, I realized I wasn't sure what I was going to say.

"My cuffs pulse," I blurted.

One of his eyebrows arched.

I sucked in a cold breath and tried again. "My cuffs have been pulsing since we left school and more since I came to this house. Since I've been around your family. It feels like something."

"Something?" he repeated, forehead wrinkling.

I shrugged. "Look, they're new to me, okay? I don't really know what it means, but it feels like it means something."

"Not nothing," he said quietly, pursing lips that were full and red.

I took a step toward him. "Like when I, er, touched you. In the bathroom." Heat ran up my cheeks. I knew they had to be bright red.

He seemed to ponder this. "What did you see?"

You, nearly naked, your chest glistening.

No, Charlie. Bad. That wasn't what he meant.

"A creature ringed in blue flame. You. A forest."

"This forest," he murmured.

"This forest?"

He nodded solemnly. "Why do you think my father built his home here? The trees hide strong magic and supernatural creatures. He wants to be near them, but he fears them, too. That's why he set up the magical perimeter to keep them out."

That was the emptiness I felt.

"So, he sent you in there to investigate?" How awful.

Rowan's lips tightened. "Something like that. I wasn't afraid until I got cursed."

"And you won't tell him because you think he'll make you leave the Academy."

"I don't *think* he'll make me leave. I *know* it. Everyone knows his opinions on weak warlocks. It's not much better than what he thinks of Lessers. And don't get him started on weak witches and warlocks who choose to become Lessers to boost their power. Anyway, he looks down on all of them and thinks they don't deserve basic human rights, much less be allowed to get the best magical education around."

"I don't understand. I thought Lessers were born that way." I remembered the Quake and Shadow Puppet that had attacked Trey and me. Could a witch or warlock turn into one of them?

Rowan shook his head. "Some are born that way, yes. But anyone can become a werewolf or a vampire, if they survive the transformation. They are never respected, though. They're considered trash."

"That clarifies your father's hatred for Answorth," I said.

"That's not the only reason. Answorth *is* up to something, and we'll prove it."

"Oh." My shoulders slumped. This whole conversation had me baffled and feeling bad for everyone. "So what now?"

"I guess we go in, and I try to hide my marks for the rest of the break. It was easy at school since my father barely acknowledges me, but here..." He sighed.

As he started to walk away, my cuffs throbbed again. This time, without thinking about it, I reached out and grabbed his arm.

The cuffs burned like liquid lightning. My body jolted. Rowan stiffened, his eyes popping wide.

Then I was there again, in the woods with him as he came upon the blue creature. It's eyes were tiny drops of hell and devil horns sprouted from its oddly-shaped head. I felt the zap of pain when it cursed him, but this time my attention was drawn to my cuffs as they seared my skin.

I fell to my knees in agony.

Back in the dark December night, my cuffs were indeed glowing white hot. The skin underneath them blistered and smoked.

Aghast, I looked to Rowan for help, but he was too busy staring at his skin. It seemed he had pushed his jacket sleeves up to reveal his arms.

Arms that no longer had blue veins running up them.

CHAPTER TWENTY-ONE

WINTER BREAK
LATE DECEMBER

ROWAN'S MOUTH opened and closed as he stared from my arms to his. He seemed frozen for a moment while I shook in pain, slowly sliding to my knees, tears spilling down my cheeks of their own accord.

My wrists were on fire. The pain was unbearable.

"Charlie!"

He snapped out of his shock and caught me before I fell, scooping me into his arms as if I weighed nothing.

He ran toward the pool and set me on one of the lounge chairs. He tried to examine the burns, but I squirmed in pain, biting my lower lip to stifle a cry.

"Be still," he ordered. "Let me look."

Clenching my fists, I forced my arms to stay steady as the pain throbbed like an extra heartbeat.

He stared at the still-blazing cuffs. Behind his dark gaze, a million questions seemed to pass as he considered what to do.

Then, as if making a quick decision that might not be the best, he clasped both hands over the cuffs. His head jerked back, the tendons on his neck popping out like live wires. My pain redoubled. I squeezed my eyes shut and swallowed the raw scream that rose to my throat.

For a desperate instant, I thought we were doomed. Dead.

His father would find us in the morning, Rowan collapsed on top of me, our bodies as crisp as morning bacon.

But then, the pain subsided. My lungs unclenched, and I could breathe again. My shoulders relaxed as I sucked in two calming breaths. Never had feeling nothing felt so good.

I opened my eyes. Rowan's face was set in concentration, a muscle jumping on his jaw and the medallion on his chest pulsing. His gaze tangled with mine, intertwining so tightly it felt we'd go on staring at each other forever. He was in the thrall of a spell of some kind.

A growl sounded deep in his throat, then he jumped up, letting go of my wrists. He stood, chest heaving, strands of dark brown hair tickling his forehead.

"Shit, that felt good," he said.

Excuse me?

It'd felt like dying.

He must have seen the confusion on my face because he knelt by my side and put on a concerned expression. "Are you okay?"

"No, I'm not okay," I blurted out, pushing up from the lounge chair and walking to the edge of the pool on rubbery legs. The surface of the water sparkled with the well-placed lighting that shone from its depths, but even the beautiful water feature couldn't soothe me. What in the world had just happened?

Rowan came closer, put a hand on my shoulder, and made me face him.

"Does it still hurt?" he asked with a gentleness I'd only seen him express toward Disha.

I nodded. "Not as badly, but yeah."

He took my hands in his, and we both examined my wrists. At the edges of the cuffs, my skin was Christmas red, blisters visible on the tender side, right at the edge of my palms.

"I did a cooling spell on the cuffs," Rowan said with an ill-contained smile. "Let me try a healing spell now."

I pulled my hands away again. "You looked too damn happy to see me in pain," I blurted out.

"What? No." He shook his head. "That's not it at all. I'm sorry. It's just my magic hadn't worked that well since..." he gestured toward the forest, the source of his curse.

"You cured me, Charlie," he said, his voice nearly breaking. He cleared his throat and snatched my hands again. "Now, let me try this and, for once, be quiet."

I opened my mouth to argue, then realized I'd only be proving his point, so I bit my tongue and let him do the healing spell.

Warmth traveled from his fingers into mine, tingling its way up my wrists, arms, shoulders, neck. I inhaled sharply, enjoying the sensation even as an internal voice told me not to get things confused. This was just a healing spell, and the fact that my lips were tingling and the memory of our almost-kiss during the football game was replaying in my mind had nothing to do with any of this.

Slowly, the warmth receded, leaving me cold.

My hands still in his, Rowan admired his handy work, running a finger over the healed blisters. He smiled.

"You might have some scars left," he said apologetically, a chagrined smile gracing his lips.

God, who knew he had such a sexy smile.

Had I done that? Given it back to him?

"I... I guess we're even now," I said, attempting to pull my hands back.

He tightened his grip, my fingers prisoners to his.

He shook his head. "What you've done for me is not so easily repaid, Charlie," he said in a husky voice that should be bottled under a label reading *Entrancing*. Seriously, they could sell the stuff.

"You've saved me from disgrace," he said. "You've redeemed me."

I wanted to blow it off, tell him it was nothing, but I was ensnared in his dark eyes, while his touch schooled my nervous system on the proper way of feeling. I hadn't known I could feel *so* much, that every nerve ending could light up this way.

Rowan took a step closer.

"What are you doing?" I asked.

He inhaled as if taking in my scent, then caressed my cheek with the back of his fingers.

"That day," he said in a whisper, "during the football game, do you remember it?"

I almost said I didn't. He would probably believe me since that was the first day Witch's Brew had entered my system, except I didn't want to lie.

"I remember," I said.

Rowan wet his lips. Heat flared in my chest.

"I've wanted to kiss you ever since," he said, a small blush appearing on his cheeks.

"Oh?"

"Were... you just drunk? Or did you mean it?" he asked, his gaze falling to my mouth.

Oh god.

He'd just admitted he wanted to kiss me. I could do the same. Right?

Except it didn't feel right. I'd just cured him from a terrible curse. Of course, he liked me right now. A lot, probably. Heck, I'd been pretty awesome, cuffs aside. His blue veins were gone. His magic was working again. That made me pretty damn kissable. From all angles.

I took a step back, ending all physical contact between us and breaking the spell of the moment. Rowan looked the way I felt. Bereft. Disappointed. Eager to shorten the distance I'd put between us.

"I did mean it," I said, giving him that much.

"But... not anymore?" he asked as if afraid of the answer.

"I wouldn't say that."

He gave me a crooked, satisfied smile that made me want to slap him and pull him to me at the same time.

"I'm just not sure it's such a good idea." I rushed out the words, sounding snappy and maybe a bit hurtful. I didn't want him to think he had any sort of hold on me. He was probably used to girls falling at his feet, and I didn't intend to be one of them.

"Why not?" he asked, seeming genuinely curious.

"Well, I just... cured your curse, so you're probably impressionable at the moment," I said, trying to sound like Answorth when he taught his lessons. "Also, you and I are from two different worlds. Your father already hates me."

Rowan rubbed his chin, considering. "All those things aren't necessarily bad, Charlie," he said in a serious tone. "But time will tell. Now, we should probably get some rest. Tomorrow might prove to be a taxing day."

———

OVERNIGHT, Rowan's house turned into a Christmas wonderland.

A massive twenty-foot tree bedecked in white silk ribbons appeared overnight in the foyer. It was so large and perfect that I suspected magical elves were involved in its procurement. Its fresh scent permeated through the house, unleashing memories of holidays with my parents when mom was still alive and we were happy. Holidays were when I most missed having a family. And

Trey. God, he loved Christmas and I'd left his ashes back at the Academy.

"Good morning."

I turned from staring up at the tree and found Rowan standing behind me, wearing dark jeans and a gray, short-sleeve T-shirt that hugged his torso and biceps like a second skin. He glanced down at his bare forearms and smiled.

Since I'd met him, I'd only seen him wearing long-sleeves. The change was good. Too good. He looked sporty and relaxed, but it was more than just the T-shirt. His entire demeanor was lighter. Happy, even. Was this the real Rowan? The one before the curse? The pain? The worry?

He came to stand next to me and stared up at the tree.

"Ostentatious, isn't it?" he asked, wrinkling his nose.

I shrugged. "Goes with everything else."

He laughed, a rumble from deep in his chest that sounded foreign. Did I know him at all?

Leaning in closer, he whispered, "I've been thinking about last night."

A thrill traveled the length of my traitorous body.

"I think I'm still... *impressionable*." He gave me a sideways glance that paused on my mouth then rose to my eyes and lingered there for a long time.

"Oh, there you are." Rowan's mom came at us from one of the side hallways, breaking the intense moment. "C'mon, let's eat breakfast before the troops arrive. Things go crazy when everyone gets home. Did you sleep good, darlin'?" she asked, hooking an arm around mine and guiding me away from the tree. "Is Rowan being a good host?"

"Yes, ma'am," I said.

Bonnie was wearing a dress that screamed Christmas. It was red, with lace flowing from the bow tied at the A-line waist, and a calf-length skirt that fanned out like a bell. To complete the dress, she wore pearls at her neck and matching, strappy shoes.

I pulled on my hand-me-down sweater. It was "Disha Nice," but I still felt underdressed.

She led us toward a dining area adjoining the kitchen, where Macgregor sat behind a newspaper and barely acknowledged us.

The spread was magnificent, and I found myself filling my plate with eggs, pastries, sausages, and fruit. Rowan gave me a knowing smile. I guess midnight escapades made you hungry.

Later that day, when Rowan's brothers arrived—the oldest one with a wife and two blond demons erroneously called *grandchildren,* the other one with a haughty supermodel he called his date —things went crazy, indeed.

You would have thought a mansion would be enough for the two granddaughters—I still had trouble thinking of Macgregor as a grandfather—but I suspected the Taj Mahal would not have sufficed.

"Nathaniel and his wife think those imps are angels," Rowan whispered in my ear as the oldest kid, a girl of four with a bow the size of Russia on her head, tried to literally climb the Christmas tree.

With a tweak at a ring on her finger, Bonnie floated the little girl away from the tree.

"No, bonbon. Not yet. It should at least last the day," she said with a giggle, while Macgregor rolled his eyes and promptly sequestered himself with his two oldest sons in his study, without bothering to introduce me or include Rowan.

I didn't know why, but it hurt when Nathaniel's wife gave me a sideways glance and turned to the middle brother's date.

"Lawrence has the worst taste," Rowan whispered in my other ear, throwing a tired sneer toward the supermodel.

Seriously, the woman could be Miss America with twig-like limbs a mile long.

"She has legs up to her neck," he said as if reading my thoughts. "Who likes that?"

Who doesn't? Was he serious?

We followed the women into the parlor. The kids ran ahead squealing and asking when they could open presents.

Rowan shook his head fondly, and I found myself feeling jealous. I was nothing like these people, but, in their own way, they were happy. They had each other and could spend times like this together. I had nothing, expect this feeling that I was an intruder, someone who shouldn't be here.

While Rowan's mom talked about what a success her Christmas charity event had been, I sat on a wingback chair, staring at the crackling logs in the fireplace. A couple of times, I caught Rowan's eyes on me as he played with his nieces, trying to keep them from climbing up the furniture and breaking the expensive vases.

The oddness of the situation struck me suddenly. For the past three months, my life had been filled with supernatural creatures, demonic possessions, and unexplained events.

This, here, was too normal.

Even if it wasn't *my* normal. Even if it felt wrong.

I hadn't managed to find my place at the Academy, to fit in. Of all the students, only Disha made me feel welcome, so when I wasn't with her, I hid behind the anonymity of campus life. As awkward as that was, this was much worse.

Without anyone noticing, I left the parlor. I went in the bathroom where I'd seen Rowan last night and splashed my face, wondering if going to my room and disappearing for the rest of the day would be too rude.

As I blotted my cheeks with a fresh cloth from a shelf, I remembered Rowan's muscled torso, and the white towel wrapped around his narrow waist, water dripping down his smooth pecs. My mouth went dry.

The door opened slowly, breaking me from my thoughts. Rowan, himself, slid in. He closed the door behind him and leaned casually on it.

"You're the girl with the plan," he said. "You've escaped."

I was about to deny it, but he went on.

"Next time, take me with you. Don't leave me at the mercy of those witches and the little devils." He smiled in such a disarming way that I couldn't help but smile back.

"All three of them are witches?" I asked, the idea of "Miss America" being a witch almost sending me into a fit of giggles.

"The worst kind." He paused and scanned my face. "Must be weird for you to be forced to spend the holidays with us. It's weird enough for me and I live here."

"Just a bit," I said, throwing the cloth in a hamper in the corner.

Without warning, he took my hand, pulled me out of the bathroom, and dragged me through the house. We clomped up the stairs, past my bedroom, and into what looked like *his* bedroom.

I planted my feet as soon as we crossed the threshold and glanced around. Undeterred, he pressed on to a double window, which he unlatched and threw open. The wind teased back his hair as he glanced over his shoulder.

"C'mon." He climbed out and disappeared from sight.

I took a few tentative steps forward, my eyes darting from one thing to the next. A perfectly made king-size bed with a gray duvet. A desk with pencil sketches pinned to a corkboard above it. A gaming chair in front of a large TV and three different types of controllers strewn around it. A couple of model planes hanging from one corner and below them a bookcase filled with the kind of tomes I'd grown used to seeing at the Academy.

"Are you coming or not?" Rowan poked his head in and gave me an annoyed look.

Walking to the window, I peered out at the late afternoon sky. Rowan was nowhere in sight. Carefully, I stepped out onto the gabled roof, doing my best not to look down.

"Climb up," he called from his spot at the peak, where he sat staring out toward the adjacent forest and the horizon beyond.

I climbed up, my hands down on the gritty roof tiles.

Don't look down. Don't look down, I repeated to myself.

When I got close enough, Rowan lent me a hand, pulling me up until I perched next to him. I let out a sigh of relief.

"I'm sure you'll agree it's much better out here than inside," he said, his brown eyes fixed on the horizon, his features so relaxed he almost seemed like a different person, like a Rowan from a Bizarro dimension, where all was good and no harm or curses ever came to anyone.

I glanced down at my cuffs and, for the first time, wondered if I'd be better off without them, if I was better off away from all of this supernatural crap. But who was I kidding? I was not a Regular, and if I couldn't find myself in this new world, I was shit out of luck.

We didn't exchange any words. It should have been awkward, but the silence between us was perfect. The changing colors of the sky said it all. There was so much more out there than what we currently had. All we had to do was wait and do our best until we were prepared to go get it. We stayed up on the roof until the sky turned purple, and the rustle of the wind over the trees threatened to lull me to sleep.

After we carefully descended from the peak, Rowan went through the window, then gripped my hand as I climbed in and made sure I didn't bang my head against the frame.

Once inside, he held onto my hands and searched my face until I was forced to meet his dark eyes.

"I think you're right," he said. "I'm very impressionable at the moment." He frowned, appearing concerned. "I'm actually starting to think you're... kind of amazing."

Pterodactyls spread their wings inside my stomach.

I nodded, knowingly, and did my best to sound unaffected. "Maybe you knocked your head."

"I must have," he said, touching two fingers to his temple. "Because you're not really amazing, are you?"

"Nope, not one bit." I shook my head.

"Hmm," he took a step closer, his hand climbing up my forearm, sending chills into every corner of my body.

I laid my hand on his chest and traced a circle, repaying him the favor, and wondering if some Shadow Puppet had taken possession of my limbs again. It certainly felt like it. What ever happened to *"Don't get involved with Rowan?"* I couldn't seem to remember why that was important as my eyes searched his warm brown irises.

He lowered his mouth to mine. My breath caught at the whisper-soft touch of our lips. Fire ignited in my brain at the mere graze of skin against skin. He pulled away, his gaze reaching deep into mine.

"You are nothing like what I imagined," he said, his breath warm on my mouth.

"You aren't either," I said, my voice low and heady. My heart fluttered in my chest and my head was light. I gripped his shirt, unable to let go.

At the tone of my words, he seemed to lose it and kissed me again, this time deeply, his hand on the back of my neck, possessive and strong.

Before I realized it, my fingers were in his hair, relishing its silky feel. Our kiss deepened, growing desperate and more hungry. Grasping my waist, Rowan guided me to the bed, where he eased himself on top of me, and I had to stifle a groan as our bodies molded to each other.

A part of me screamed I should push him away and get off his bed, but his kisses were too good, and his hands chaste, despite the way my traitorous body seemed to want more.

We kissed with abandon, as if the rest of the world didn't exist, as if nothing else mattered. Oddly, it felt right. As right as everything else felt wrong.

CHAPTER TWENTY-TWO

SPRING SEMESTER
MID JANUARY

"*CHARDONNAY*, you really need to be paying attention here. Answorth is about to show us how to possess the frog." Disha jostled my shoulder.

I shook away the thoughts plaguing me and tried to concentrate. Possessing a frog did sound interesting, but my mind was elsewhere and had been since that night last month in Rowan's bed.

Just remembering the delicious press of his body on mine sent shivers to my curled-up toes. His urgent lips. The taste of his mouth as his tongue slid over mine.

Damn. I was definitely distracted.

Our incredible make-out session had been rudely interrupted by Macgregor Underwood. He'd thundered up the stairs, bellowing Rowan's name.

Scrambling, we'd jumped apart and straightened our clothing

as he strode in the door. Macgregor's narrowed eyes and disapproving frown seemed etched in stone as he surveyed the scene—rumpled bed, rumpled us. In an instant, he had demanded to see Rowan in his office, leaving me both unsatisfied and panicked that I would soon be kicked out of the house.

However, that was not to be my fate. I'd stayed at the Underwoods' for the rest of the break. It was Rowan and his father who had not.

I had not seen Rowan since the last backward glance he gave me. He and Macgregor had pulled out of the garage that night and had not returned. Nor had they come back to school at the start of the term.

I had stayed under Rowan's mom's care, which involved lots of tea parties with her friends, preparations for a New Year's event at one of her charities, and even a shopping trip to the fanciest stores in Atlanta. I'd been glad to be back in school, even if Dean McIntosh had grilled me about the effects of the cuffs while I lied through my teeth and promised all they'd done was help me focus my magic, never mentioning the fact that they'd also made me more powerful. The last thing I needed was more babysitting, so really... they'd forced me to lie with their overprotectiveness.

When a full week of classes had gone by with no word from Rowan, I'd grown desperate enough to ask Dean McIntosh if she'd heard from them. She informed me that they were on private Academy business, but they were fine. Rowan would receive credit for the work he was doing with his father. I was not to worry about them.

And yet, there was a tightness in her smile that made me suspect things were not going as well as she claimed. How could they be if Rowan and Dean Underwood had been gone over a month? Everyone knew they weren't relishing in fun daddy/son adventures because they enjoyed each other's company.

The worry gnawed at me during the day and kept me up at

night. It was worse than Disha's moping over Professor Henderson. At least she knew he was still alive.

Had I found Rowan only to lose him? Was I destined to lose every person in my life who I chose to care for?

The ache widened into a cavern that threatened to split me in two. I felt lonely. Not even talking to Trey was helping.

"Char-*lie*," Disha whispered, her bony elbow digging into my side.

"Ow," I mouthed, but I obliged her and attempted to watch as Professor Answorth murmured the incantation again, twisting his fingers and touching the speckled frog's head.

The entire class stared, enrapt as the frog stiffened. Professor Answorth lifted his hands, causing the frog to rise and stand on its two long legs.

"I didn't know frogs could do that," Disha whispered.

I nodded, watching it all with growing unease. Answorth had been cleared of having any involvement in Georgia's death, but that frog's gaze looked eerily similar to hers before her death.

"Now, pay attention," Professor Answorth said with a comical twist of his mouth. Using one hand like a marionette with an invisible string, he kept the frog on its legs. Then he reached for his phone with the other hand. Swiping it open, he started a familiar tune. "Hello, my baby," blared from his iPhone while Answorth directed the frog to strut and kick just like the famous Michigan J. Frog.

The class giggled, but all I could think about was the frog, imprisoned in his own body. A puppet. I knew exactly how that felt. Answorth could command him to jump in front of a car. He could command him to do any vile thing he could think of and no one would be the wiser.

This was wrong.

My hand shot up as if on its own.

Answorth saw me, lowered the frog, and turned off the music, his face sliding from joy to something more serious and professorial.

"Yes, Ms. Rivera."

"Should we be learning this?" I blurted.

All students turned to look at me, disapproval written all over their faces, but I kept going.

"I mean, isn't this dangerous? After all, could witches and warlocks use this to basically commit crimes and get away with them?"

Answorth employed magic to swipe the frog off the table and into his cage as if moving it out of sight might erase what he'd just done. He straightened his shoulders and lifted his chin, although, come to think of it, he looked pretty disheveled for a man who always wore a jacket and vest to class. His clothes were unusually rumpled, his hair uncombed and there was a sallow pallor to his cheeks that suggested illness. I wondered if Georgia's death and the investigation had taken its toll on him.

"Class, all eyes up here. Ms. Rivera proposes an interesting, nay, a very *important* question. Is it ever okay to possess another human? What say you, class?"

There was a general grumbling. I knew I'd just made enemies with nearly every freshman in my graduating class. So much for fitting in.

Disha shot me a worried look and then raised her hand. She was going to fall on the grenade for me.

"Magical Law of 1845 states that it is unlawful to possess any human or supernatural creature. Only the council or Magical Law Enforcement may do it, and they must obtain permission from the high court."

"Excellent, Ms. Khatri. We are not allowed to use this skill on Regulars. I dare not think any of you would *possess* enough power to do so, anyway." He waggled his eyebrows at the pun. "It is very rare for a student to have what is needed. This takes much prac-tice and years of well-seasoned powers."

"But someone did it to Georgia," I said without raising my hand.

Professor Answorth stiffened, and I swear when his gaze met mine, all friendliness had fled. "That is correct. We must never forget what happened to her. It was an unforgivable crime."

"Then why show us? Even on a frog?"

Answorth twisted his neck from side to side as if my question made him uncomfortable. "There are things worth knowing, Ms. Rivera, even if one never uses them. Now, class." He strode around the desk and waved his hand, causing all of our textbooks to flip to the same page. "We will pick up our reading on using mentalism to protect ourselves against a possession."

He was changing the subject and trying to make it seem like his little demonstration had led up to learning to protect ourselves, but I wasn't buying it. There had been a glee in his eyes, when he made that frog dance, that hadn't been normal.

Not natural.

Or maybe I was crabby and taking it out on him.

My cuffs flared as if in response. Crabby, for sure. But that didn't mean Answorth was innocent. And if Rowan wasn't here to keep an eye on him, I would. When he returned, he'd be pleased to know I had kept it up in his stead.

Was I just doing this to please him? Try to remind him what he saw in me that day?

Well, maybe I was, but it didn't make it a bad idea.

Fifteen minutes later, when class ended, Disha and I folded up our books.

"Let's go," she said, heading out of the classroom. "If we hurry, we might catch Mr. Sexy still at his shift in the cafeteria."

Mr. Sexy was Disha's new crush, a senior with blond, surfer boy hair and aqua blue eyes. Apparently, she was picking a new boy toy that was as far from Dr. Henderson as possible.

I casually eyed Professor Answorth who was busily packing up his materials.

"You go ahead. I've got some surveillance to do."

Disha made a face, crossed her arms together Wonder Woman style and cast a bubble of silence around us.

"Are you crazy? He was cleared over Christmas break. They brought in the best investigators the high council has. He was exonerated, Charlie. No involvement. Just like everyone else. Capice?"

I shook my head, both in disagreement and in wonder that she could know so much. Either her parents were well connected and had spilled all the secrets, or she was talking to Dr. Henderson again.

"Are you saying that a powerful warlock like Professor Answorth couldn't fool members of the high council?"

"I don't know, Charlie, but what makes you think that you, a freshman with literally no experience before September, would be able to do better than the best minds in wizardry?"

Her words stopped me cold. I reared back with their bluntness.

She slapped her hand over her mouth. "Charlie, I'm sorry I snapped."

I waved it off, even though it still stung. "It's nothing."

"It's just that... ever since you got those cuffs," she gestured at my wrists, "you've been different."

It was true. My cuffs, and their new found power, had made me daring—reckless even. But, they also made me powerful. More powerful than Disha even knew. I'd told her about their curing Rowan of his curse, but I'd left out how they hinted at things. How they drew me toward people as if they had a *mind of their own*.

Yeah, I'd left out that little tidbit.

When I glanced over my shoulder, Answorth was sneaking out the back door, very Scooby Doo villain-esque. My cuffs flashed hot as if letting me know I was on the right track.

"Come on," I said, grabbing Disha's arm. "Just trust

me, okay?"

She gave me an are-you-kidding-look, but finally nodded.

I smiled with the glee of having her by my side and the opportunity to use my new-found power again.

Grabbing both her wrists, I tapped into my magical wellspring. It was as if I had batteries cuffed to my arms. The minute I focused my mental energy in their direction, the cuffs produced a stream of energetic bubbles tripping through my veins. I mumbled the spell we had learned in Henderson's class, with a few added tweaks of my own. Then I pushed the charm out over Disha and myself.

The minute she blinked out of existence I knew it had worked.

"What did you do?" she whispered at me.

"You can talk normally. No one can see us and only you and I can hear each other. It's a cloaking spell."

"What kind of cloaking spell is this?" I couldn't see her face, but alarm and amazement tinted her voice.

"Don't worry about it, okay? We need to move. He's slipping out the back."

Pulling her along, we darted around groups of students and exited the building through the front door. Then I headed around the side to the back exit. Answorth was already outside, cutting a swift path north.

"He's not going to the staff housing. What could he possibly want at the north end of campus?"

Disha's disembodied voice appeared at my left shoulder. "Wide open spaces? All that's up there is a field and then the woods."

So he wanted to be alone? Interesting.

We jogged after him. Disha panted at my side, but she didn't protest, a sign that she was now as intrigued about his field trip as I was. And when we saw him slip into the tall trees at the edge of the property, my suspicions felt all but confirmed.

"He's being sneaky for sure," I said, casting my eyes about for Disha even though there was nothing to be seen.

"I have to admit, you may be right. Do we follow him? That forest is chocked full of dangerous creatures and spells gone wrong. Plus, there are blocking spells around to keep students out. If we step into one of those, we'll be sucked in and transported to Dean McIntosh's office."

I rolled my eyes. As if she'd cared about following the rules when she'd been having an affair with one of the teachers.

"Yes, we follow him. We need to know if he's the one letting demons in and stealing items. Dean McIntosh certainly thinks he's innocent. Maybe they're in it together."

"Charlie," Disha's voice admonished, but I could tell she was keeping pace with me as we headed to the tree line.

We slipped through the first tall trees with Answorth in sight. I was glad it was still broad daylight because the moment we walked under the tree canopy the sun disappeared, casting everything in long, creepy shadows.

Hands wrapped around my arm and I yelped.

"Told you it was scary," Disha said as she pulled close.

"We'll just see what he's doing and then get out," I said, my chest tight. She was right. The magic around us felt old and unstable, like ancient dynamite. One wrong move and we'd be in deep trouble.

As we walked, it felt as though eyes were watching us from the trees. We were cloaked, but I'd learned in class that some magical creatures could see past any type of cloaking spell. Memories of the lich and the werewolf crept up like icy fingers.

"There," Disha said, squeezing me tight.

Answorth had stopped in a clearing up ahead. The area he picked was small and dim, far enough from the main campus that anyone passing wouldn't see him. Definitely perfect for some nefarious bullshit.

We scooted up closer, keeping track of all his movements. His briefcase, that should have held his books and papers, sat on the forest floor, pulsing with a sickly yellow light.

Disha's nails dug into my arm and my cuffs warmed as if to say *See, I told you so.*

Answorth reached down and opened up the case.

A long wooden object shot up four feet into the air and hovered for a moment before spinning in lazy circles and sending light in all directions. Answorth stood, holding his arms out, his lips moving faster than an auctioneer's.

"It's a staff," Disha hissed.

A staff. Wasn't that what the administration had claimed had gone missing?

Slowly, I began to notice a pull in my chest. My magic was being sucked out, drained as if Answorth had turned on a large vacuum and was hoovering everything into him. To confirm my suspicions, he began to rise above the forest floor. Hair fluttering in the magical wind and his face lit with wild pulsing light, he looked... different.

He snarled, his mouth changing. His jaw elongated as his teeth flashed in a grimace.

"What the hell?!" Disha exclaimed. "He's... he's a vampire?"

Vampire? Then I noticed the fangs protruding from his open mouth.

Definitely vampire. And not the sparkly, sexy kind. The bite-your-neck-and-leave-you-for-dead kind.

Oh, my God.

I took a step forward to get a better look and it all fell apart. My cloaking spell disintegrated. We flickered into view standing only a few feet from Answorth. He spotted us immediately. Eyes wide, he opened his mouth, bared his fangs and growled.

Turning to my friend, I spurred my wobbly legs into motion.

"Disha, run!"

CHAPTER TWENTY-THREE

SPRING SEMESTER
LATE JANUARY

WE RAN as if our asses were on fire.

Disha sprinted ahead of me, impossibly fast on her damn heels. What the hell? I pressed harder, fists pumping, feet pounding the dirt and fallen leaves.

Behind me, branches cracked, sounding as if they were being run over by a bulldozer.

My cuffs throbbed once, urging me to go faster.

Gee, thanks.

First, they'd gotten me in trouble and now they abandoned me to my own fate.

"Help!" Disha screamed as the edge of the woods came into view.

I dared a glance over my shoulder just to find Answorth flying straight at me. I cried out as he plowed into my body, sending me sprawling to the ground.

We crashed on top of gnarled roots, Answorth's clawed fingers digging into my sides. I cried out again, both from pain and terror. As we rolled over damp loam, he snarled like a mad beast.

We came to a stop with him on top of me. He growled in satisfaction, face upturned heavenwards, the column of his throat pale and throbbing with black veins. His face was horribly distorted. Besides the large fangs, his cheeks were sunken and his skin glowed a sickly white.

Chuckling deep in his throat, he glanced down, his blue irises opalescent and the whites lined with the same dark veins as his neck.

He licked his lips, red tongue flicking between white, pointed fangs.

I fought under him, arms and legs pushing on his rock-like body.

"You want this," he said in a husky voice. "You don't wish to struggle."

The fight went out of me, my body going limp and filling with a strange warmth.

"I want this," my mouth repeated.

My own voice echoed in my ears like a faraway murmur. A part of me fought the stupor, but I felt intoxicated, my eyelids heavy, my muscles weak.

A cruel smile slashed Answorth face. His head dipped—straight, blond hair dangling and brushing my cheek as he angled himself for the kill.

A violent thrill ran through me as his fangs sank into my neck, a wave of desire and pleasure making me throw my head back and moan.

Behind my closed eyelids, images of Rowan's face flashed in quick succession. The weight of his body against mine, molding itself perfectly, two puzzle pieces reunited. I dug my fingernails into his back. An animalistic growl of pleasure reverberated in my ears.

My eyes sprang open.

No, not Rowan. Answorth!

I tried to scream, but my throat was petrified. I tried to push, but my arms and legs were useless. *Why can't I move?*

The answer came to me from my *Supernaturals and Their Lore* textbook. We had studied this. I was enthralled. It was a power vampires possessed.

Suddenly, the pleasure turned to agony as Answorth's fangs dug deeper into my neck and sucked. My veins turned into rivers of pain, cutting paths from every corner of my body straight to my jugular.

Help me! Somebody help me!

The cuffs pulsed, squeezing my wrists, reminding me they were there.

I concentrated on their cool grip on my skin, remembered the way they'd blazed when I healed Rowan. For an instant, I feared the immense heat they'd released that day, the burns and blisters that marred my skin after all was said and done, but that pain was nothing compared to the sure death that awaited if I didn't do something.

"Help me." I managed, hissing the two words through paralyzed lips.

Energy blossomed in my chest, spreading quickly, reviving my useless limbs. Lifting my hands, I clamped them around Answorth's throat and felt him swallowing, relishing in my blood.

"Fit glacies sanguinem in venas."

Unfamiliar words flowed independently past my lips. They were weak, a mere whisper, but determination grew in me as knowledge flooded me. I suddenly knew what the spell would do. It would freeze my blood in Answorth's veins.

"Fit glacies sanguinem in venas," I repeated, this time louder.

Answorth made a choking sound.

"Fit glacies sanguinem in venas." Now, my voice was loud enough that it rang in my ears.

The pull, the tug on my veins, stopped.

"There! By that tree," Disha's alarmed voice broke through the woods, barely reaching me through the trance of my spell.

"Fit glacies sanguinem in venas," I pronounced with authority.

This time, Answorth stiffened, becoming a heavy boulder on top of me.

He had stopped drinking, but the wound in my neck burned like acid while his weight crushed my lungs, making it impossible to breathe. My vision swam. Too late. He had already drained me dry. I was fading fast.

Voices and steps.

"Oh god! Get him off of her."

Disha? She sounded hysterical.

The weight that crushed me disappeared all at once.

"Is she dead?"

Precious air rushed into my lungs. I gasped and coughed.

"Oh, thank you, thank you, God."

Hands smoothed my hair back.

"You'll be alright, sweetie."

My eyes flickered open for an instant and caught sight of a blurry Disha, brown hair draping on either side of her face. She was so pretty. I attempted a smile, but my mouth barely twitched.

She glanced away from me. "She's gonna be okay, right?"

I sensed someone else taking a knee beside me, across from Disha. I attempted to open my eyes again to see who it was, but my eyelids seemed glued shut.

Pressure on the side of my neck... on the bite. Murmured words I couldn't understand.

My skin tingled, then began to itch. There was a wet sound as I felt the wound knitting itself back together.

"Is she going to turn into a vampire?" Disha whined anxiously.

"Fortunately for her, Charlie's spell slowed the poison and I drew out the rest. She'll be fine." A hand slipped behind my head.

"Drink this, Ms. Rivera." It was Dean McIntosh's commanding voice.

I obediently parted my lips and drank whatever she poured into my mouth. It went down like honey, and I hardly needed to swallow as the thick liquid found its own way down my throat.

A lazy sensation spread over my muscles, same as when I first woke up in the morning. I blinked my eyes open. Disha and the dean's worried faces hovered over me.

"Hi," I said, smiling stupidly.

Disha exhaled in relief, her big brown gaze darting to Dean McIntosh's hand. "What was that?"

The dean shrugged one shoulder and slipped a small vial into the front pocket of her slacks.

"Velour Vitae," she said. "I always carry it with me. You'd be surprised how often students need a pick me up. Lots of shoddy spells."

"I have to learn how to brew that," Disha said, her hands still a bit shaky. She examined my face, relief washing over it. Then, she startled, realizing something. "Dean McIntosh... how was Answorth able to perform magic all this time if he's a vampire?" But before the dean had time to answer, Disha snapped her fingers and answered her own question. "The items that have been stolen! He was drawing magic from them."

The dean nodded.

"I always knew he was no good, but I didn't take him for a *vampire*," a voice I recognized said from the side.

I cringed. Not him. Not now.

Dean McIntosh's shoulders swiveled as she glanced back, revealing Macgregor Underwood leaning over Answorth's immobile body. And a step behind his father stood Rowan, his features dark and stern. He stared at the cuffs around my wrists, then at Answorth's frozen form.

The image of his eager, kind face over mine as we kissed in his bedroom disappeared from my mind and was replaced by the desolate expression he now wore. He looked miserable, nothing like the happy Rowan I'd last seen. What had happened.

Now what? What had happened?

My gaze darted to Macgregor.

Fucking dear ol' dad happened, that's what.

Rowan had spent a whole month with Macgregor. Anything could have happened during those long weeks. The man seemed to a have knack for breaking his son's spirit.

Great. Just great! I didn't just almost get killed by a vampire. Rowan was broken again and only God knew exactly why.

CHAPTER TWENTY-FOUR

SPRING SEMESTER
LATE JANUARY

"Drink!"

For the third time, Disha tried to stick a straw into my mouth, while she held up a glass of orange-flavored electrolyte drink.

For the third time, I batted her away. I'd already drunk a full glass, and my stomach was sloshing with it.

"Nurse Taishi said you should drink as much as you can," Disha fussed at me like a brooding hen.

"And I have," I said, my eyes darting to the entrance.

I was lying on a hospital-style bed in the infirmary, a long room with six more beds and dividing curtains between them. I was the only patient and Disha, my only visitor. She sat on a wooden chair next to the bed.

Nurse Taishi had checked me and found my heartbeat and breathing too fast, both signs of dehydration. He'd said that, thanks to Dean McIntosh's Velox Vitae potion, I could do without an IV, but only if I promised to drink plenty of fluids. I hated needles, so I'd promised to chug down whatever they gave me. Though, at the moment, I wasn't counting with Nurse Nightingale and her mighty straw.

"How about a popsicle?" Disha asked.

"Yeah, sure." Anything but the prodding straw.

Disha skipped to a small fridge in one corner of the room where Nurse Taishi kept nourishing supplies for his patients. The light that came through the windows was dimming, letting me know the day was winding down.

"Grape or strawberry?" Disha asked, holding two popsicles in transparent wrap.

"Strawberry."

She handed me the red one, while she took the purple one and sat back down. We removed the packaging and got to work on them, silent for a moment. I glared at the door again.

"*Char*treuse, I warned you about him," Disha said.

"Chartreuse?" I asked. "What? Do you like... use a dictionary to come up with these names?"

"You're avoiding the issue," she said in a singsong tone.

I took a bite of my popsicle and huffed.

"Rowan carries too much baggage, girl," she said. "A lifetime of it, actually. Just imagine Macgregor as your father."

"What the hell did he do to him? He was so happy last time I saw him and now he looked... depressed, lost."

"It's anyone's guess. Macgregor is very hard on Rowan."

"What is wrong with that man?" I asked. "He's worse than Hitler on a bad-mustache day."

Disha giggled.

"Well, I almost died," I said, "Rowan will come and see me. He has to, right?"

Disha shrugged. "I think we're better off unattached. You should do like me and find a *play thing*, instead. Someone easy on the eyes but shallow, by which I mean uncomplicated."

I shook my head. "Not my style."

"Seriously, give it a try. It's quite fun." She licked the popsicle as if it were a lollipop, her eyes growing dreamy and far away as if remembering exactly how much fun "uncomplicated" guys could be.

The door to the infirmary opened. My heart leapt, thinking it had to be Rowan. Instead, Nurse Taishi walked in. He *was* easy on the eyes, with his shiny black hair and ready smile, not to mention the muscular frame inside those blue scrubs, but he was not Rowan. My shoulders sank.

"How is the patient?" he asked, striding in my direction, a stethoscope draped over his neck. "I'm glad to see you're hydrating yourself." He gestured toward the popsicle.

Disha leaned over coquettishly, putting an elbow on the bed and resting her chin on her hand. "She didn't want to, but *I* made her."

Nurse Taishi squirmed on the spot and hid a blush by turning toward the blood pressure machine. What was Disha doing? Hadn't she learned her lesson with Henderson? But what did the Academy expect when they hired such young, good-looking staff?

I waved a hand, *shooing* Disha away and frowning. She rolled her eyes and sat properly while Nurse Taishi checked my vitals.

Ten minutes later, I was headed to my room, walking on my own two feet with Disha by my side. I was wearing a pair of scrubs Nurse Taishi had given me as no one wanted me walking around with a bloody T-shirt, the evidence of another attack on campus.

I could only imagine the amount of damage control Dean McIntosh would have to do after they'd assured everyone the school was safe. But there was no way to avoid it, not when Disha had run all over the place, screaming like a maniac that a vampire was killing her BFF.

Disha and I walked into the Freshman Dorm, discussing what to do for dinner, though I wanted to take a hot shower before going anywhere. However, we came to an abrupt halt as soon as we reached the common area. A gaggle of students had sprung to their feet from the comfortable sofas as soon as they saw us and started firing questions like paparazzi after hot gossip.

"Is it true that Answorth is a vampire?"

"Did he bite you?"

"What was it like?"

"I wouldn't mind him biting me... a little."

"Are you going to turn into one now?"

Seriously?! I pushed past them, ignoring all their questions.

"Guys, we're tired. We need a bath. We need food. If you care for your lives, get out of our way," Disha said, opening a path ahead of me.

A deep voice rose above all others. "Is it true that he escaped?"

I whirled around. "What? Who escaped?" I demanded.

"Answorth," a tall guy with horn-rimmed glasses and a lumber-jack shirt asked. His name was Ian. We had Spells together.

"Where did you hear that?" Disha demanded.

Ian adjusted his glasses. "Dunno. Everyone's talking about it. They're saying he knocked Underwood out and took off."

I exchanged a glance with Disha. My heart clenched as my thoughts immediately went to Rowan. Was he okay? I opened my mouth to ask Ian if he meant father or son, but before I could manage, Disha grabbed me by the elbow and led me away from the gawkers.

Blinking in confusion, I went along. When I realized she was leading us toward Rowan's bedroom, I walked with firmer steps and pulled ahead of her. I practically ran down the hall, passing closed and open doors and ignoring the students who milled about.

I stopped in front of Rowan's door, heart thumping.

He was hurt, and I'd been mad at him for not coming to see me in the infirmary. I'd already convinced myself he'd suffered a worse fate than me when Disha knocked, and Rowan himself opened the door, looking as rosy-cheeked as ever. When he realized it was us, he sighed, walked inside, and sat on the bed.

My heart thudded with anticipation as we entered the room. I glanced around at the bare walls and piles of scattered clothes on the floor.

"Is everything alright?" Disha asked. "We heard Answorth escaped."

He twisted his mouth to one side in an indifferent gesture. "Apparently, he got the best of my mighty father, knocked him over the head and left him unconscious." Rowan seemed rather pleased by this development, judging by his twisted smirk.

"But... you're okay, right?" I asked.

He met my gaze for just an instant, then glanced away. "I'm fine, yes."

Disha and I exchanged a skeptical look. That was a lie if we'd ever hear one.

"The truth is I'm tired," he said. "I'd like to... rest."

"Oh, sure," Disha said, gesturing toward the door for us to go.

"Um, meet you in the cafeteria in an hour?" I asked her.

She nodded and, offering me a *good luck* expression, walked out of the room.

Once Disha had left, I sat next to Rowan. He shifted on the spot and put a few more inches between us. I stared at the floor as my heart broke in two. Did I need any more proof to show me that what had started between us over Christmas break had already crashed and burned?

"It's... good to see you," I said. Yep, apparently I did need more proof. If he still wanted this thing between us to go somewhere, he would take this as an invitation, right?

"It's good to see you, too." The words seemed genuine but not as warm as I would have liked.

"What happened? Where did your father take you?"

He shook his head. "I can't talk about it."

"*Classified*, huh?" I attempted a smile that felt like a grimace.

"Look, Charlie..." he began.

I jumped to my feet. Nothing good could start with those words. I had to get out of here.

"It's good to have you back." I stuffed my hands in my pockets and strolled to the door. "I'd better let you rest. You look tired. Plus, I have to shower and change, then meet Disha for dinner. I'll see you around, okay?"

He nodded, his expression a combination of sadness and relief. I'd just saved ourselves a very hard conversation.

So much for a chance at my first boyfriend. It was over before it began.

CHAPTER TWENTY-FIVE

SPRING SEMESTER
MID FEBRUARY

IT WAS Saint Valentine's Day and I had no boyfriend.

One heated make-out session, it was all my relationship with Rowan had amounted to. That and a very awkward last couple of weeks as we tried to avoid each other at all costs.

"Why are we going through this again?" I asked, glancing at Disha in the backseat of our Uber.

She was dragging me to a party, and a fist-sized knot was already forming in my stomach as we pulled down a long tree-lined driveway. Why had I let her talk me into this? Parties were so... people-y. Lots of chit-chatting with classmates who stared at me and whispered to their friends. I knew rumors were circulating that I had turned into a vampire and was working for Answorth. God, would I ever fit in anywhere?

Disha closed her lighted compact with a snap. "Because you've been avoiding every party all year and the end of the semester is around the corner. I will not, as your best friend and party advocate, allow you to finish freshman year without attending at least one rager. And Kenny said their Valentine's party is going to be killer."

She batted lashes that were so incredibly long she must've used a grow spell on them. Her outfit was impeccable—slinky red dress, chunky heels, and perfect makeup. Her eyelids and lips shimmered red to match her dress, and she'd even gone into town to get a blowout for her hair, something I didn't even know existed until now.

People actually paid to have someone else blow dry their hair for them. Inconceivable.

Me, on the other hand, I'd worn what I normally wore— skinny jeans, Chucks, and one of Disha's red hand-me-down sweaters. Though, I had to admit to putting more time in on my hair and makeup than normal. Disha had mentioned that Rowan would be at the party. Yeah, I was clinging pathetically to some irrational hope.

Thinking of him was like the memory of a bad fall—all pain and bruises that never seemed to heal. After his return from the excursion with dear ol' dad, it was as if our time at his house, in his *bed*, hadn't happened. Now I wished I, at least, knew the reason, but I'd been too chicken to hear him out, fearing the *it's not you, it's me* conversation.

At least, the dean and the staff had managed to keep Answorth's attack as quiet as they could, downplaying my injuries and sending a team to track him down. Plus, they'd beefed up security, buff men and women from Magical Law Enforcement.

They'd had no argument from me. I didn't want the school to close. Honestly, I had no idea what I was going to do at the end of April when the semester ended. But that was two months away. Time enough for me to figure out how to avoid living on the streets again.

The car pulled up to a large farmhouse and let us out. I stood on the curb and took everything in.

The house was rented by several upperclassmen, including Kenny, Disha's new boy toy. Only seniors were trusted to live off campus and this was one of the college's sanctioned houses, situated about ten minutes away in a little, barely populated township called Greenville. The huge ring of sky-high evergreens in every direction was a clue as to why. With no neighbors, the students here couldn't get into too much trouble.

The old farmhouse was enormous, sporting a giant wraparound porch lined with twinkle lights above thrift store couches. Music thumped from the house's interior as bodies moved past the glowing windows. Everyone wore reds and pinks, per the invitation, and paper hearts hung from the tree boughs. There were also recently-sprouted shrubs decorated with red and white roses.

Disha grabbed my hand and pointed. "It's *Alice in Wonderland* themed."

"A *theme* party? Ugh." I rolled my eyes.

"See? This is exactly why I didn't tell you until the Uber guy drove away." She winked at me and then tugged me up the cobblestone walkway.

The house was jammed with bodies and loud music. My eyes did their best to take it all in—a couple already making out on the couch, two DJs in Tweedledum and Tweedledee costumes manning a set of turntables at the far end of the living room, and a counter with treats labeled "Eat me" and cups labeled "Drink me."

As I watched, a girl took a little yellow cake and nibbled. Her body blew up to twice its normal size, head *thunk*ing on the ceiling. She guffawed and handed the cake to a friend. If they all ate those, we'd be in trouble.

God, it was loud. In addition to the music and the chatter, a very drunk girl in a crooked Red Queen wig kept yelling, "Off with their heads."

I wondered how long I would last. I should've paid the Uber

driver to hang around, but then I remembered I had no money.

"Kenny's in the barn," Disha yelled, pulling me away.

Weaving through the house, we stepped into the yard and I sucked in a breath. If I thought the decorations out front were amazing, the backyard could only be described as out-of-this-world.

Giant, bioluminescent mushrooms loomed above our heads, casting dim shadows. Flowers and vines of every color oscillated in time with the music. In the center of a brick patio, a huge table was set for tea with at least fifty cups and saucers. Tucked among them, a stoned guy in a rabbit costume twitched in the center while others sat around, oblivious while they smoked a hookah and blew smoke rings.

I had to hand it to these guys. When they picked a theme, they really dove in.

Disha led us across a stone path to the largest of the three barns. Kenny was waiting out front. He was clearly very excited about his party's chosen theme, dressed in a full Johnny Depp style Mad Hatter costume with a big bowtie, curly red wig and makeup.

He pulled off his top hat and took a bow. Disha ran up, squealing and threw her arms around him.

"You look amazing!" She held his face in her hands. "You even changed your eye color."

Kenny smiled. "Lawrence did it for me. He swears they won't stay this way once the spell wears off, but time will tell. Charlie," he said, addressing me, "what do you think?"

I grinned at him. Kenny was a nice guy, one she'd met in the library, actually studying. Too bad Disha was going to chew him up and spit him out in a few weeks. "This is amazing, Kenny. How'd you guys pull it off?"

He shook his head, casting his gaze around. "Honestly, we didn't attend class all week. Probably a terrible use of our time, but we love it."

Disha leaned into him, batting those bird-wing eyelashes. "He says last year they did *Jurassic World*."

"That got *way* out of hand," Kenny said laughing. "Dinosaurs everywhere. This is way safer and less to clean up."

I tried to picture it, wondering how they kept the lizards all contained and managed not to kill the neighbors.

"Much better choice," I said, pointing at the tea table.

"You haven't seen the best part!" Kenny said, jumping up. Placing his hat back on, he got into character, accent and all. "Behind us, ladies, is the *pièce de résistance*—a maze of sorts that will require cunning, wit and a little magic."

Disha clapped her hands. I raised an eyebrow. Now, this sounded interesting.

"How does it work?" I asked.

"Simple. You go in, walk through the maze, and try to get out. It's not that bad. I've only had to rescue a few people and you girls have a better shot because you're sober, unless..." He gestured to the cooler by his feet.

I shook my head, remembering the witch's brew. I couldn't trust what warlocks offered, even if it was from someone as nice as Kenny.

"Okay, then." He pushed open the barn door, revealing a dark interior.

I took Disha's hand and together, we stepped inside. Darkness enveloped us as soon as Kenny shut the door.

"There better not be any of those pixie minotaurs in here," I said.

"Remind me again why I'm in here with you instead of out there making out with him?" Disha asked as she wove her hands in the air and cast a light spell.

"Because you love me," I answered, peering forward into the barn. It seemed very ordinary—hay, yard tools, and shelves of fertilizer that smelled terrible.

"I don't see any ma—"

My foot, which I thought would land on a solid barn floor, fell into empty space. My body pitched forward. I wheeled my arms, trying to keep from falling in, but there was nothing to grab.

Down I went.

"Charlie!" Disha screamed.

I fell through the rabbit hole, a shout tearing from my throat. My hands clawed at the sides, dislodging dirt and roots, but nothing stopped my fall. I tumbled end over end.

The bottom reared up, and I feared I would splat, but, at the last second, my body hit a pocket of air and hovered a few feet off the floor, before gently landing on the dirt.

I glanced up. Way, way up.

Stupid boys. Stupid theme party.

Dusting myself off, I found the tunnel I was supposed to take, the only one here with torches to light my way.

This was Kenny's game and I'd have to play it. I stared up to see if Disha would follow me, but after a few minutes, it seemed like she'd changed her mind. Whatever. I could do this alone. It'd take my mind off of *other things*.

I trekked down the dirt tunnel and found a room at the end of it. The hollowed-out space was empty, nothing in it but a very tiny door at the far end. I'd seen the movie more than once as a kid and I knew what I had to do, but as I glanced around, I didn't see any "Eat me" or Drink me" items to shrink myself.

"But Alice didn't have these," I said, pushing my sleeves up to reveal my magic cuffs.

Conjuring a shrinking spell was easy. Down, down I went until I was the size of a Pomeranian, small enough to fit through the door. Then, I turned the knob and strode through.

A similar landscape to the farmhouse's backyard lay before me —big mushrooms, glowing plants, a huge Cheshire-Cat-smile in the sky, lighting everything in dim shadows.

The door slammed shut behind me and the knob wouldn't turn when I jiggled it.

Only forward, eh? Okay, Kenny. Forward it is.

I walked through the mushroom forest until I spotted a hand-painted sign reading, "Royal Croquet Game." That had to be where I needed to go.

Approaching, I could hear the crack of croquet balls and the shouts of players. When I walked under a hedge arch, the game came into view. Several students were playing with frozen flamingo mallets. Card soldiers danced around, forming the rings that the balls rolled through.

"Wanna play?" a girl called, holding up a flamingo to me.

I shook my head. I wasn't here to play drunk yard games, and I didn't feel great about using birds as clubs. The sooner I got through the maze and back to Disha, the sooner I could get back to my bed.

"Not your game, eh, Rivera?" a voice said.

When I whirled around, Rowan stepped out from the shadows.

"Rowan." My heart climbed up into my throat as I tried to decide what to do. Every other time we'd met, we'd ignored each other, or Disha was there as a buffer. Here, there was no one but the grinning moon to see what would be a terribly awkward conversation. Even the croquet players were too far away to create a distraction.

"Didn't think you'd be here," I lied, crossing my arms over my chest. "Thought you might be following Daddy around Kingdom Come." I didn't know what made me say that. I guess I was resentful.

Rowan winced, covering it up with a smirk. "Daddy has bigger fish to fry. Mainly Answorth. You don't know where he is, do you?"

"Who? Answorth? Why would I know where he is?"

His eyes lingered on the spot on my neck where two puncture marks would now always be.

"Did it hurt?" he asked.

I nodded. "Like a bitch."

His hooded eyes tightened. Then, as I watched, he put a flask to his lips and took a long pull. The smell of hard liquor was unmistakable. So that's why he was talking to me.

"My father," he said drunkenly, "is back to thinking I'm useless. It's better actually. At least now we have a dynamic I understand."

He took a few steps and sunk onto a downed mushroom cap. Then he took another drink.

Reaching out, I snatched the flask. "I think you've had enough."

"Have I?" he laughed dryly. "Tell me, Charlie. Am I still a disappointment? Hmm? Will my magic return? Will these ever go away?"

At this, he reached down, grabbed the hem of his sweater, and pulled it off over his head.

I expected the sight of his half-naked body to turn on the faucet of my desire, but it was pity that flooded me instead. His chest, arms and neck were covered in dark blue veins again. They had spread like a cancer onto nearly every square inch of his body.

Oh god! The curse was back with a vengeance.

Was this why he'd pushed me away? Had he been alone, suffering, all this time?

"How did this happen? It's worse than before," I said, gasping.

"It just came back, and at an inopportune time, too. My father found about it during our little excursion. All that hiding... Useless. After hunting down all those rabbit trails that lead nowhere, he did take me to the best magical doctor money can buy. And do you know what they said?"

"No," I whispered.

Rowan's teeth flashed. "They said there was no cure. That I would lose magic completely. So my father plans to pull me out at the end of the semester. He wants to set me up as an *accountant*." He said the last word as if it were a curse in itself. I couldn't imagine tasting magic and then losing it all. A life like that would be so... empty.

Falling to my knees before him, I reached out to touch his skin.

Rowan pulled back, hurt playing in all of his features. "Don't. Don't touch me."

A second before, all I'd wanted was to help him, but his attitude angered me.

"So if I can't cure you, I'm nothing then?" Was that time in his room only because I'd taken the curse away? Now that it was back, I was worthless. Tears sprung to my eyes. Oh Jesus, I was going to cry in front of Rowan Underwood. I *could not* let that happen.

Jumping up, I turned to leave, but he was up fast, grabbing my wrist. When I faced him again, he just looked... broken.

"I don't... want to hurt you," he said, one trembling hand cupping my cheek. His touch felt so good, but there were tears in his eyes, too. And I could feel the sickness rolling off him like heat.

"Rowan, let me try to heal you again," I whispered.

He shook his head, letting his hair fall into his eyes. "It's not worth it. I'm not..."

His hand on my wrist found the scars from my first attempt. His thumb brushed over my damaged skin, sending tingles up and down my body. Even in my rage, my fear, I wanted nothing more than for him to pull me into his arms and press his lips on mine.

Instead, he snatched the flask from my hand and drained it. "I'm going to have to do something... drastic."

"Drastic? Rowan?"

He pulled away, staggering off down the path. "Stay away from me, Charlie. You will, if you know what's good for you."

I watched him disappear into the dark.

The irony was, I never did know what was good for me.

CHAPTER TWENTY-SIX

SPRING SEMESTER
MID FEBRUARY

I WANDERED down the mushroom path, the ache widening in my chest. If I still had Rowan's flask I would chug it just to drown out the voices in my head. Rowan was going to do something crazy, but what? We'd already tried everything legal we knew. That left unimaginable, unspeakable things.

I had to stop him.

But his words echoed in my ears. *Stay away from me, Charlie. You will, if you know what's good for you.*

Was I turning into one of those girls who threw their own lives away following after broken men? That couldn't be my fate. I was more than an attachment to some male, no matter how much he'd grown to mean to me. I vowed then and there to help Rowan, but to not let it take me down, too. If he was planning some of the things we'd studied in *Spells* like using blood magic or summoning some demon, I would not get involved.

But still, my heart ached for him. *Ill-fated* was his middle name.

I had to find my way back to Disha and get her advice. She knew more about what Rowan might attempt than I did. Plus, she cared about him. Maybe, between the two of us, we could stage an intervention.

The question was how to get back?

I walked the path, noticing the change in landscape. Here, the mushrooms grew smaller as large gnarly branches took their place. Without the mushroom's glow, the shadow's deepened, making each branch look like gnarled hands ready to snag and catch. A chilly wind made me shiver and shook some wind chimes that jangled off key, only adding to the fear creeping up my spine.

If I was in one of Alice's wonderlands, this had to be the Tim Burton one for sure.

My bracelets throbbed. A bad sign. But when I turned around, the path I'd just traveled on was gone. Behind me, the trees closed in, blocking the way.

"Oh, shit," I whispered.

"Hello, Alice," a voice said, echoing above me.

I spun around, heart pounding. "Show yourself."

"I knew you'd come."

The voice boomed from all directions so that I couldn't get a read on where it was coming from. I spun around, eyes roving over branches and darting past shadows. Was this part of the game? Maybe, but I drew power from my cuffs anyway.

As I watched, the moon floated down toward me, morphing into a set of sharp, glowing teeth. Yellow feline eyes blinked above them.

The Cheshire cat. I should've known. My terror eased off a bit as the cartoon face of a pink and purple cat came into view.

"Alice," it said, hissing the last syllable.

"Hey, how the hell do I get out of this maze?"

Its yellow grin widened to an impossible length. "To get out, you must pay the toll. Hand over something valuable and I will let you pass."

"This isn't part of the movie. And, besides, I don't have anything valuable." I hadn't even brought a purse since Disha always insisted on paying for everything.

The cat's grin morphed into something more hostile. Fangs that once appeared harmless lengthened and sharpened.

"You lie. The bangles on your wrists." Yellow eyes trailed down my arms.

"What? No." I took a step back. On second thought, this really didn't feel like part of the game.

The cat's face began to change. Its eyes and mouth shrank as the fur turned pale and a body took shape. A moment later, the cat was gone and in its place stood a man.

Answorth.

"You." I fisted my hands, drawing as much magic as I could and running through battle spells in my head. There were only a few I knew. Freshmen year focused on defenses, not attack. Quickly, I formed a shield charm and cast it over myself.

The vampire ran a hand over his white-blond hair and laughed. "A shield charm? How quaint. We really should do a better job as teachers. I'll be sure to bring it up with Dean McIntosh."

His right eye twitched, and he seemed to flicker like an image on an old TV. Was he really here? Or was he just a projection? He took a step forward. A leaf crunched under his foot. Yep, he was here, all right. Or maybe the mushroom spores had addled my brain.

He waved his hand dismissively and my defensive charm disintegrated before my eyes like a popped soap bubble. He must have gotten hold of another magical item to be able to perform spells. Hell, he probably had a stash of them somewhere.

"What are you doing here?" I asked, backing up as I tried to stall, but branches closed together behind me, forming an impenetrable wall. Woodsy fingers dug into my clothes and I jumped away.

"There's no use running," he said, flashing his vampire fangs.

They were longer than I remembered. The punctures at my neck tingled, remembering his attack.

"I made sure no one else could come down the rabbit hole," he added.

That's why Disha didn't follow me! No one else could come down. My mind turned to Rowan who might still be nearby. But his magic must be gone, and who knew if he was even still in the game? There were the few other party goers playing croquet, but would they be close enough to hear and sober enough to do any good?

I opened my mouth to scream. Answorth flicked two fingers. My lips clammed up like they'd been zipped shut. My legs locked next. I was frozen in place.

Terror ran riot over my useless body. Would he attack me again? Drain me lifeless for once and for all. I was done for.

As panic coursed through me, another sensation grabbed my attention, my bracelets were growing steadily hotter, making my skin feel as if it would melt. Answorth's eyes locked onto the radiant bands.

"You have no idea what these are. How powerful," he said, moving closer. The light from my bracelets made his pale face almost translucent as he stared, transfixed. "You need to hand them over to someone who knows what they're doing."

He placed his hands over my wrists, closed his eyes, and started muttering. I shuddered with impotence and fear, knowing there was nothing I could do.

Heat burned my flesh where his skin touched mine, as if he were planning to burn my hands off to take the bracelets. When my desperate gaze darted up to his cruel face, I could tell from his muttered spell that was exactly what he intended to do.

There was no growth spell in the world that would replace my hands. Magic would be lost to me, too. A shock went through me as I realized I would rather die.

My skin felt as if an inferno was eating every inch. Pain made my eyes water, but I couldn't cry out. *Rowan!* I thought. My only hope was that he might save me, but then I thought about how drunk he'd been.

No one was coming.

I had to save my damn self.

The image of the Shadow Puppet flashed before my mind's eye. I had been frozen then, but I'd been able to break the spell by conveying all my energy outward in one big blast.

Pushing everything I had in me outward, I thought *Stop!*

There was a blast of power like the shockwave after an explosion. I spilled on the ground as Answorth's spells fell away. On my hands and knees, I sucked in a deep breath.

"What?" he gaped, his face flickering as if it had also been bewitched. It must've been residuals from his Cheshire Cat trick.

I didn't give him time to recuperate. I used the first spell I could think of—a propel defense.

I put my hands on his legs and pushed.

Answorth flew back like someone had turned a firehose on him. Arms wheeling, he crashed into a tree, and fell into the brush.

Staggering up, I found my voice. "Help!"

I didn't wait for the cavalry. I ran.

I tore through the landscape, having no idea where I was going but desperate to get away. Maybe if I could get to the party, Answorth wouldn't risk trying to attack me. There'd be too many witnesses. Plus, Disha would be there.

But the landscape was still a tangled mess. The thorny trees died away, but now giant chess squares dominated the rolling hills. I scanned the horizon, panting. I saw no door, no ladder, no way out.

He would come after me. He had to be right behind me.

Then I heard a familiar baseline. Someone was playing the song *Under Pressure*.

The party!

I ran toward the sound, plowing into a field of flowers and smashing right into a bale of hay.

I spit out dry grass, whirling around. The barn.

"Charlie!"

Disha clomped on her wedges and, like a freight train, barreled into me.

"You're okay! I couldn't get in. Something went wrong. Your hands!" She touched my throbbing mits.

When I glanced down, each wrist had bright red burn marks in the shape of hands. Great. More scars.

"Who did this?" a male voice asked.

Glancing around, I saw a dozen students had gathered inside the barn. More awaited outside.

"It's like I need to put you in a bubble or something," Disha murmured, waving her hands over my burns. I felt them cool under her healing spell. "Seriously, Char. Why does this keep happening to you?" she said a bit hysterically.

I stared down at the golden rings on my wrists. A blessing and a curse.

"It's the cuffs. Answorth wants them and I don't think he'll stop until he gets them."

CHAPTER TWENTY-SEVEN

SPRING BREAK
EARLY MARCH

I PLODDED down the empty corridor of my dorm, the sound of my flip-flops bouncing against the walls. All the doors were closed, no rowdy girls hollering at each other from across the hall, begging to borrow a flat iron or demanding to know who ate their chocolate.

Happy spring break to me, yay!

Coming to a stop in the common area, I kicked at a sofa in frustration.

"Ow!" My fat toe throbbed.

Literally everyone was gone to the beach, to parties I wanted the opportunity to turn down. But no, I was stuck on campus. By myself. Even Disha had abandoned me. Not that I blamed her. Kenny had invited her to Cancun, no less.

Charlie...or Cancun? Charlie...or Cancun?

Yeah, I'm sure she pondered that choice for about two seconds.

I stared through the glass doors to the lawn outside. Sun seeped down from the skylight above. With a sigh, I went out, my book and towel tucked under my arm.

A few moments later, I found a sunny spot close to the Enlightenment Fountain, determined to sunbathe while I enjoyed the sound of rushing water and the steamy words of my novel. If I couldn't get real romance, the hunk in the book would have to do.

Kicking off my flip-flops, I spread my beach towel over the grass and lay down on my stomach, facing the standing turtle. Of the five marble statues in the middle of the fountain, it was the one I found least intimidating. Plus, as water jetted from its mouth, it made a pretty rainbow in the sunlight. Beautiful to say the least.

Since I was the only student on campus, I was breaking all the rules, wearing a pair of cutoffs and a bikini top. Warmth rippled over my bare legs and torso as I made myself comfortable. The sun felt wonderful. The hottie on the cover of my thrift-store novel tempted me with his six-pack. I smiled and began to read.

After only ten minutes, my eyelids began to droop. Well, this wasn't as bad as I'd thought. It was actually very relaxing. I closed the book, rested my cheek on folded arms, and shut my eyes. Soon, the warmth and the sound of rushing water lulled me to sleep.

I woke up sometime later with a weird tingling sensation on my back. I shot up to a sitting position and glanced around, certain that someone was watching me. I spun around. A distance away, in front of the Humanities Building, someone stood, partly hidden by a column.

Rowan?

According to Disha who'd heard it from Kenny who'd heard it from Counselor McIntosh who'd heard it from Macgregor, Rowan was supposed to be out of town, enjoying the break with family in

Savannah. I narrowed my eyes. The figure was too far away to tell, but it seemed the right height, the right hair color. Looking down for an instant, I pushed to my feet and, when I glanced back up, he was gone.

Damn!

Had I imagined it? No. Someone had been there, but was it Rowan? Was Answorth back to drain me of all my blood and possessions? I shook my head. I was getting carried away. For all I knew, it was a creepy janitor, getting his kicks by watching me sunbathe. My skin crawled with disgust.

Great, Charlie! Way to ruin the fun.

With a huff, I snatched my towel and book and marched back toward my dorm, my thoughts inevitably back on Rowan. God, I was so tired of trying to keep him out of my mind. It was work, worse than all the history essays Mrs. Middleton loved to assign us.

I'd been fighting his presence in my mind since Christmas break, and his drunken threat to do something *drastic* had made things harder still. He was constantly in my thoughts. I fretted over what he might do, even though Disha told me not to worry since Macgregor wouldn't let anything bad happen to his son now that he knew about the curse.

She assured me that the trip to Savannah was another attempt on Macgregor's part to cure Rowan. The Underwoods had powerful relatives in the coastal city, including a great uncle by the name of Everett Underwood who was supposed to have renowned healing powers. Apparently, the old man hated Macgregor which was the reason they hadn't gone to him sooner and why Rowan had gone to see him on his own.

"There is hope," Disha had insisted plenty of times. "Don't despair, Charmander. And maybe once he's cured, you two can finally get your freak on because, I swear, all the sexual tension between you two is killing me."

Killing her? Yeah, right. Killing *me*!

Rowan and I hardly said *hello* in class or when we inevitably ran into each other around campus, but every glance we exchanged seemed charged with electricity, which made things so much harder for me. I'd even tried a few spells to help take my mind off him. They'd been weak, little charms that lasted only a few minutes and left me feeling worse. I didn't dare try anything stronger, for fear of forgetting him altogether.

God! I was pathetic.

Back in my room, I flung my towel and book on the bed and paced the length of the room, silently praying Rowan's great uncle could come up with a permanent cure.

Rowan. Rowan. Rowan.

Here I was, thinking of him again, even as a more pressing matter loomed over me, the reason why I was stuck here on campus while everyone else partied their eyeballs out.

"What is wrong with you, Charlie?! You're about to lose Aradia's Cuffs and all you can do is worry about Rowan who, by the way, is not worried about you. Get a grip."

Awesome. Now, I was talking to myself. Not that it was much different from talking to Trey's urn.

I stared down at the cuffs. They flashed for an instant as if to reassure me, as if saying, *No matter what Macgregor or the dean try, we're not going anywhere.*

And maybe that's why I wasn't worried. Macgregor was still hell-bent on taking the cuffs from me and restoring them back to the museum. Apparently, he'd found some kind of spell that would do just that. The only caveat... it had to be performed during the vernal equinox, which happened to be right in the middle of spring break. Joy, joy.

Macgregor didn't give a damn I was now excelling in my classes or that the cuffs had chosen me. He just wanted to get his way, even if he didn't gain anything from restoring the artifacts back to their glass boxes.

Maybe he's only trying to keep the cuffs from falling into the wrong hands, a backstabbing voice echoed inside my head. *Answorth had tried to kill you for them, after all. Macgregor might be trying to save your life.*

It wasn't the first time I'd had that thought, or the first time I'd pushed it away, because the Aradia Cuffs had chosen *me.* Not Georgia. Or Macgregor. Or Answorth.

They'd chosen ME. Charlotte Sofia Rivera.

Eat your heart out, Macgregor "Douchenoggin" Underwood.

I needed these cuffs to stay alive because, if nobody else had noticed, magical things tried to kill me on a regular basis and, without them, I was a sitting duck. These cuffs weren't going anywhere. Equinox spell or not.

I passed the next couple of days in the same fashion: sunbathing and reading, then feeling as if someone were watching me. As I meandered around campus passing time between sacked meals from the student cafeteria, I cast around for Rowan, hoping to see him at every corner. He was not there. It was just my wishful thinking.

On the fourth day, there was a knock at my door, bright and early. I'd barely finished taking a shower and getting dressed, and they'd already come for me more than three hours early. I figured they weren't leaving anything to chance, or waiting till the next equinox.

When I opened the door, I was surprised to find Counselor McIntosh beaming at me, her fat ferret draped around her neck. Irmagard was wearing a pair of drawstring shorts in a psychedelic pattern, leather Jesus sandals, and a bright yellow tank top. A multicolored band the width of my thumb circled her head and beads and feathers adorned her necklace.

"Hi," I said.

"Hello," she responded, holding up two fingers in the peace sign and marching into my room. She glanced around with a frown as if she didn't approve of my organizational skills, but hello... I'd seen her office, and my humble mess had nothing on hers. She turned her blue eyes on me once more. "My sister had to attend other matters, so she put me in charge of things today." She glanced down at my wrists.

"In charge..." I echoed doubtfully, trying not to sound rude. It seemed to me the one in charge of my "cuff situation" was Macgregor and no one else.

She seemed to catch my meaning and winked. "In charge of making sure you make it out in one piece."

I swallowed. "You mean... the spell is dangerous."

"Oh, no." She clucked her tongue and made a dismissive gesture with her hand. "The spell is harmless. It's Macgregor we're worried about."

I blinked. Well, that was reassuring.

The ferret climbed down her torso and started digging in her shorts pocket. I stared at the animal, but Irmagard went on unfazed.

"I need to get you ready, then make sure you're on time," she said. "The vernal equinox is exactly at eleven fifteen AM, and Macgregor must speak the last word of the spell not a second past that time. If he fails to do that because we're late or any other reason, there'll be hell to pay, I assure you. So let's make sure that doesn't happen." She winked again and walked out of the room.

I trotted after her, closing the door behind me.

"What do you mean get me ready?" I asked.

"Nothing much, just cleanse you from all possible hexes that might interfere with the spell. Students hex each other for all kinds of silly reasons. The other day I had to help a boy whose ex-girlfriend was trying to teach him not to cheat." She held a finger up, then let it go flaccid.

"Oh," I said, catching her meaning, surprised that she would recount such a story. I stifled a laugh, imagining how embarrassing that must have been for the poor guy to admit.

"The word *cleansing* doesn't sound fun," I said, wondering if she'd tried to give me a laxative or something.

She petted her ferret and, giving a careless shrug, said, "Nothing to worry about, it's a piece of cake."

It turned out that "cleansing" was indeed a piece of cake, but it was also ridiculous. While in her office, Irmagard smoked a pipe and blew the smoke straight at my nose, ran raven feathers from the top of my head to the tip of my toes, let her ferret sniff inside my ears, rubbed a chicken egg against my forehead then cracked it over a bowl and, finally, when none of the crazy rituals revealed any hexes, prepared a cup of Angelica root and fennel tea for me to drink.

The brew looked and probably tasted like ferret pee, but Irmagard made sure I drained the cup to its last drop. When that craziness was done, she guided me outside and led me toward the hedge maze.

"We're not going in there, are we?" I asked, panicked as I remembered the water nymph that nearly drowned Rowan.

"No, dear, we're going by the sundial," she said, veering off to the right.

Good. I'd been past the sundial. It was harmless, or it had seemed so until I saw Macgregor Underwood standing next to it, dressed in a black suit as if he were going to a funeral.

My funeral, he was secretly wishing, I was sure.

"Underwood," Irmagard said, nodding in his direction.

"McIntosh." He inclined his head back, then glanced at me... or, should I say, at the cuffs. I was worth less than the dirt under his Berluti shoes, a ridiculous brand I hadn't known existed until I came to the Academy.

The sundial—a large copper plate with time markings in Roman numerals and a metal wedge to cast a shadow—sat between us, its patinaed surface making it appear aquamarine under the noon sunlight.

Underwood checked his wristwatch, a golden monstrosity almost as wide as my cuffs. He pressed a button on the side, his eyebrows furrowing slightly.

"Step aside, please." He gestured toward Irmagard. "It's nearly time."

My stomach contracted with nerves, worry suddenly unleashing from wherever I'd kept it corralled. What if Macgregor succeeded and removed the cuffs? What if I went back to being a mediocre student and I lost my scholarship? What if—

I should run, I thought, bolt as far away from Underwood as possible. That would at least buy me some time until the next equinox. They couldn't kick me out as long as I wore Aradia's Cuffs, right?

I took a step back. Macgregor's eyes widened as he comprehended my intention. His right hand went up, fingers clenching. I froze on the spot.

"No, Ms. Rivera," he chastised. "Bad idea. This is for your own good, whether or not you choose to believe it."

Holding me in place, he checked the time again, without taking his eyes off the dial. My heart raced. The cuffs throbbed as if in protest. I gathered my magic and tried to push outward like I'd done with Answorth, but nothing happened. Underwood was too strong for me, too practiced.

After a few interminable seconds, he gave a barely perceptible nod, then glanced at the sundial. Satisfied, he began the incantation in a flat tone that revealed no emotion.

"Accipere clavi fons et accipere sua potentia," he said succinctly.

I waited, teeth clenched, for something to happen.

Nothing.

I exchanged a glance with Irmagard. She shrugged, cocking her head to one side. Still frozen, I waited for Macgregor to repeat the spell. Instead, I witnessed a major, wizardry tantrum.

"Damn it all to hell!" he exclaimed, throwing his arms up in the air and releasing me from his magical grip.

He stared down at me with ill-restrained anger, then, in the most undignified way I'd seen from him, he stomped away, though not before pointing a finger at my face and saying, "I'm not done with you, Rivera."

Irmagard and I watched him leave.

"Oh boy, that man is *intense*," she said once he was out of earshot.

I frowned at her. She'd made the word "intense" sound rather suggestive.

"Oh, don't look at me that way, young lady," she said. "It's not like you are immune to the many charms the Underwoods have to offer."

My mouth fell open. How did she...?

Irmagard tapped her nose and smiled. "Nothing escapes my notice, Ms. Rivera. You'd do well to remember that."

Then she strolled away, leaving me staring at the cuffs and wondering why Underwood was so bent on getting them back. It wasn't as if they didn't have hundreds or even thousands of similar artifacts in the museum. It wasn't as if Answorth hadn't burned who knows how many of them while he pretended to be fae.

Something more than Macgregor was letting on was going on here, and I was going to find out what.

CHAPTER TWENTY-EIGHT

SPRING BREAK
EARLY MARCH

LATER THAT NIGHT, I was sleeping in my bed, having my recurring dream of Rowan and I kissing, his body molding against mine in a deliciously intimate way, when suddenly, I was on the floor, butt up in the air, the bed bucking like a wild horse.

No, correction: the entire room bucking like a wild horse.

What the hell?

The lamp rattled on the night table until it crashed to the floor, so did the alarm clock, which read half past two. My desk slid from side to side as if on skates. The sheer curtains danced like ghosts in front of the window. My textbooks on the built-in shelves *thumped* to the floor one by one—all while I huddled on the spot, arms over my head, raw screams tearing from my throat as if I were on a roller coaster from hell.

Shit!

I'd never heard of earthquakes in Georgia. No, scratch that...

mega earthquake in Georgia because this had to be in the scramble-your-brains-into-next-week scale.

Except something told me I wasn't in the middle of an ordinary earthquake.

An instant later, my suspicions were confirmed as a wave of kaleidoscopic light broke through the window and swept across the room like some sort of visible sound wave, then everything went still.

For a long moment, I stayed on the floor, tightened into a frightened snail, fearing that aliens or at least a battalion of Supernaturals would smash through the window like a *Mission Impossible* SWAT team.

They didn't.

Only stillness and silence followed.

Warily, I rose to my feet and glanced around. My room was a disaster area, with all the furniture clustered by the door. It was as if someone had picked up the building and tipped it to one side before setting it down. What the hell had happened?

Trey!

I ran to my desk and breathed a sigh of relief when I spotted his urn at the very edge of the desk but safe.

Fearing another shake-up, I decided to get out of Dodge. Taking the urn, I climbed over the bed and, setting my feet against the wall, pushed it away from my only exit. I opened the door and peered into the hall. The emergency lights were flashing but, other than that, everything appeared normal, though deserted.

Crap! Was I the only one who'd witness this mess? I certainly hoped not. Maybe there was a staff member somewhere who could explain.

Barefoot, wearing only a pair of skimpy shorts and a tee, I stepped into the corridor and ran on tiptoes toward the common area where I found the framed pictures hanging askew on the walls, and the sofas and chairs packed against the back of the room. Everything was deathly quiet, and only the hum of the emergency lights filled the air.

My breaths came in short spasms as I slowly stalked toward the double glass doors that served as the dorm's entrance. I was desperate to get out in the open, worried about being buried alive or attacked by shadow puppets, vampires, werewolves or whatever creatures had decided to come and get me this time. Could it be Answorth back for more?

When I was close enough to see my own reflection on the glass door, something appeared to move behind me. I whirled, my free hand raised, cuffs flaring with power. The common area was empty.

There's no one here, Charlie, I reassured myself.

As I began to lower my guard, a violent rapping shook the glass door.

I screamed and whirled back, hand at the ready once more.

Macgregor Underwood stood on the other side of the glass, his door-rapping fist paralyzed in midair, his wide eyes fixed on my glowing cuffs.

"Are you alright?" he asked, cautiously taking a step back and holding his palms up. His voice was muffled by the glass, but I could still hear him. He glanced at the urn with a frown.

I swallowed and lowered my hand. My heart slowed. The glow around my wrists dimmed.

"I'm... I'm okay," I said.

He nodded, then walked closer and tested the door. It didn't budge. It was properly locked as it should be. All residents had an access card, and security engaged automatically after the door swung shut.

Tension apparent in his movements, Macgregor held his hands toward the building and, after a few seconds, nodded approvingly.

"The *spells* held," he announced.

Spells? Something about the way he said the word made me

think he was talking about more than just the normal spells that protected the entire school.

Had he placed extra spells on my dorm to protect the freaking cuffs?

I bet my panties he did.

Anger flared in my gut. I didn't care if the extra spells had likely saved my life. I was tired of this. Someone needed to explain what was the deal with the freaking cuffs.

I opened my mouth to say something but realized Macgregor was moving away from the door.

"Wait! Where are you going?" I demanded.

"Stay put," he said. "The building is protected. You'll be safe in there." He rushed away.

"Hey, hey!" I went for the door handle. A jolt of electricity hit me. It snaked up my arm and sent me careening backwards.

"Shit shit shit." I shook my hand, air hissing through my clenched teeth. It hurt like hell.

When the pain passed, I stared at the door, fuming. He'd locked me in. The nerve.

But no freaking way I was staying in here. Macgregor's spells might have survived the first attack, but a second one could easily bring the building down on my head.

With a deep breath, I focused on the door and aimed my hand at the handle. Magic tingled across my body, marching its way into my chest, gathering into a dense ball that grew and grew. My ribs expanded until I felt like an overblown balloon, then the cuffs throbbed, letting me know it was time to let go.

I did.

A current of power blasted from my fingers, hitting the metal handle then spreading over the glass, forming what resembled an iridescent spider web. It flickered for a moment, then slowly disappeared.

Huh? Had it worked?

I inched closer to the door, anticipating another jolt. For a tense instant, my hand hovered hesitantly over the handle, then, donning my courage, I touched it with one finger.

No electric jolt came.

At once, I pushed the handle. The door opened, which was all the excuse I needed to go after Macgregor but not before carefully setting the urn on the sidewalk.

Dewy grass met my feet as I ran across the lawns that fronted the student dorms. The overhead lights that normally illuminated campus at night were out. Buildings loomed at either side, their shadow-filled windows staring like huge, vacant eyes.

Looking straight ahead, I kept on, ignoring the voice in my head that said I should turn back.

A flash of movement several yards ahead caught my attention. *Macgregor.*

I veered left, squinting into the darkness. He was headed toward the center of campus, toward the fountain. I thought of calling out to him, but I never had time to make up my mind because the ground shook, and I spilled sideways, landing on top of a bush.

A mighty explosion rocked the world. The earth rumbled. The night sky turned white. Radiant light, like a supernova's, blinded me. I cried out, threw my hands over my face and buried deeper into the bush, its branches tearing at my naked legs and arms.

I waited for death to wrap its arms around me and take me to Trey. I would miss Disha, and Rowan, but I would see Trey again, at least.

Except death didn't come, only quiet and a sharp branch that poked my butt with the ferocity of a hunter's spear.

"Ow!" I scrambled out of the bush, fighting to keep my shorts on as the depraved branch tried to steal them.

Blinking, I let my eyes adjust. White stars winked in my retinas for a long moment before I was able to make out my surroundings again. When I finally did, the orange glow of large leaping flames drew my attention.

"Shit!"

I ran toward the fire. Smoke rose into the air, painting serpentine streaks against the black backdrop of the night sky.

Something was on fire, but what?

As I got nearer, the answer appeared before my eyes: a pyre of flames, coiling and swirling around the Enlightenment Fountain like a merry-go-round on steroids.

Enthralled by the mesmerizing fire, I gradually came to a stop and gawked. Heat radiated from the conflagration, lapping at my skin like a cat's tongue. I shrank a bit, but couldn't tear myself away from the savage spectacle.

"What are you doing here? Get back!" Macgregor came out of nowhere and pushed me backward just as a huge whip-like flame pulled away from the inferno and lashed at us.

We went sprawling over the grass and rolled away from each other. A small crater smoldered in the spot where I'd been standing.

"Run!" Macgregor said, springing to his feet faster than any man his age should be able to do.

I didn't hesitate and obeyed him this time. He joined me as I ran, casting a shimmering shield around us. I peered back just as another lash of fire struck at us. It hit the shield, making it flicker. Red and orange embers rained around us, sliding down the dome of our protection.

We ran and ran, leaving the angry fire-beast behind.

Macgregor only stopped when we got back to the dorm area. There, he turned and stared back the way we'd come.

"What was that?" I said between sharp intakes of breath.

"I don't know," he responded. "Though I might have been able to find out had you stayed where *I left you*." He said the last words through clenched teeth.

Shame flared in my cheeks. "Sorry," I mumbled.

He faced me, carefully scrutinizing me from head to toe.

"Are you hurt?" he asked, real concern in his expression. To his credit, he didn't even glance toward my wrists.

I nodded, having the bothersome impression that maybe he wasn't as bad as I thought.

"Good. Now, go and stay inside your dorm until I come back." He jostled me along. "And stay there!"

"I will," I promised as I ran back with Trey's urn hugged closely to me.

Once I was safe inside the Freshman Dorm, he took off again, headed back toward the fountain.

Damn it, Charlie, you idiot! You almost got yourself and Rowan's father killed.

I whirled away from the door, angry at myself, which is when I noticed the trail of blood leading from the door to the back of the common area.

A foreboding feeling nestled at the pit of my stomach. I followed the trail as it snaked around an overturned loveseat.

Behind it—shirtless and pressed against the wall—was Rowan, sitting in a puddle of his own blood.

CHAPTER TWENTY-NINE

SPRING SEMESTER
EARLY MARCH

"Oh, my God, Rowan." I fell to my knees beside his bloody shape and set Trey's urn to the side. One jagged gash cut across Rowan's chest from his right pec to his abdomen. My brain going a million miles a minute, I grabbed the closest thing I could find, a couch throw pillow, and pressed it to his chest to try to stop the bleeding.

"Just... hang on. Oh god. How did this happen?"

He ignored my question, waving a weak hand. "The healing spell... from Henderson's class."

Oh, shit. Of course. What was I thinking?

I pulled the bloodstained pillow away and channeled my magic. The glow of my cuffs lit up his face, highlighting just how bad off he was. Sweat dappled his forehead and darkened his hair and his eyelids drooped heavily as if he were battling for consciousness. Pale and hollow-cheeked, he seemed to be suffering not just from blood loss but from the horrible curse that had now spread to his hands and neck. His skin was choked with veins.

I thought that was what his spring break trip had been about, getting a cure from his great uncle. Apparently, it too had been a failure.

Tossing those thoughts aside, I forced my scattered brain to focus on the wound. Muttering the spell was easy, but taming my energy was not. I watched the spell stitch the wound in a jagged line. It would help stop the bleeding, but it was far from perfect.

Rowan winced in pain.

"Sorry!" Lord, I was botching this.

"My... pocket." He pointed to his jeans.

Ignoring how awkward this situation was, I dug into his pants' pockets. A smooth object grazed my fingertips and I latched on. When I pulled it out, I found a glass vial with dark blue liquid sloshing inside.

He held out a wavering hand. I uncorked it and gave it to him. He drained the liquid in one gulp. As I watched, the pain drifted from his features and his posture relaxed. This time, when he stared up at me, his eyes were able to focus.

"Thank you," he finally said.

I bit my lip. "How did this happen? The ground was shaking and there was a fire outside. Your father and I..."

"My father's still out there?" His eyes darted behind me toward the dark windows. The glow of the fire could be seen in the distance.

I put my hand up as if to stop him from running off, though it didn't seem like he could even manage to stand. "Rowan, you are in no shape to go out there."

His brow furrowed. "My magic's gone, anyway. I couldn't even lift a finger to stop whoever was trying to take the portal."

"Take the portal?"

A tense expression passed over his face that made me realize he'd just revealed something without meaning to.

"Rowan, the fountain, is that the portal?"

His answer came out slowly. "I'm not supposed to tell anyone."

"Okay, but let's just say I figured it out on my own. I just saw it ringed in fire, for Pete's sake. And, when I touched it that day, it made me see things."

He nodded, swallowing thickly. "It's the epicenter of magical power for the Academy, primal magic that runs on its own fuel and feeds every Supernatural being. Plus, it also connects us to the network of portals all over the world. But, you can't just access it. Unless, you've been granted special access by the High Council, it takes a very special item, a sort of key, to be able to travel through the network."

"A key," I said, slowly putting all the pieces of the puzzle together. "Is that... is that why Answorth is after my cuffs?"

Rowan nodded.

Thoughts swirled in my brain. So these bangles on my wrists were more than just high-powered magical batteries? And I'd been wearing a key that could unlock world travel and vast amounts of magic?

The places I could go. The things I could see and do.

That also explained why Macgregor wanted them back so badly.

"But why would Answorth want to travel between portals?"

"Some of the world's most powerful magical items are stored in guarded places with the only access being a portal. They have to be or any magical creature would snatch them up. If Answorth can get the portal to work, he can steal those items and become unstoppable."

"It's always about power," I murmured.

"Yeah," Rowan said as he sat up a little, wincing at the effort. "Also, he could shut our portal down, leaving the Academy basically without magic. It could cripple everyone here, knock down all the school's defenses. Think of anything bad that could happen, you name it, and Answorth accessing that portal will make it happen."

"That's why he was willing to cut my hands off to take the cuffs." I stared down at them, realizing that the items on my wrists had to be among the most wanted, most dangerous in the world. That was why Macgregor was desperate to get them off me. Maybe he did have my best interests at heart, after all.

Rowan tenderly touched the giant scar on his chest, then gazed out the window. "If my father doesn't come back in five minutes, I'm going out there."

"No, you're not. He made me promise to stay here and the same goes for his gravely injured son. I'm sure he's fine." I glanced over my shoulder, too. The firelight had diminished, giving me hope, but why was it taking Macgregor so long?

"Answorth deserves to rot in hell for what he's done," Rowan said.

"You saw him at the fountain?"

He shook his head. "But we know it's him. After what he did to you..." his eyes traveled from his chest to the faint burn scars on my wrists.

I gripped my scars self-consciously. "It's nothing compared to what you're going through." My gaze traveled the length of his curse-ravaged body. "What did your great uncle say?"

Rowan dropped his gaze. "Nothing good. How I got lucky enough to be the recipient of an unbreakable curse, I'll never know. He did give me that potion. Helps with the pain. Most days." He stared at the empty vial in his hand.

So the curse not only sapped his magic but left him in pain. No wonder he'd been so hard to deal with. And the alcohol at the party had to be self-medication.

I reached out, touching the back of his wrist with my finger-tips ever so gently. "We'll figure something out. Maybe, if your dad can get these cuffs off, we can give them to you. They're pretty powerful."

The expression on his face was so tortured it hurt me just to witness it. He flipped his hand over, lacing his fingers through mine. The feel of his skin sent chills down my body.

"Charlie, I still meant what I said about staying away from me. Either I'm going to be cursed forever, or..." He trailed off.

"Rowan, whatever crazy thing you're thinking of doing, you don't have to do it alone. I get that you're trying to protect me, but honestly, have you seen the stuff I've managed to stumble into all on my own? I think protecting me is an unrealistic goal at this point."

I laughed a little at this, but Rowan didn't. Concern played on his features as his thumb traveled the length of my hand. "If I had magic, I could help you. I could help a lot of people. Like this... I can't be normal, Charlie. I'd rather die."

I winced, but how could I blame him? I'd felt the same thing when I'd thought I might lose my hands.

When my eyes trailed up, Rowan was still staring at me, the intensity in his gaze like a magnetic force drawing me closer. My lips tingled at the thought of his mouth on mine. I didn't care if the world burned down around us. I *needed* Rowan right now.

Frantic footsteps outside made us pull apart. Macgregor Underwood thundered up to the door and through it.

"Rowan?"

I felt his hand slip away from mine. His eyelids drooped, revealing how much staying conscious cost him.

Macgregor ran over and stooped over his son. "What's all this? You're bleeding!"

"He got hurt," I mumbled, standing up.

Useless and impotent, I watched as Macgregor levitated his son and whisked him out of the room. Snapping out of it, I went after them.

Macgregor gave me a sideways glance that said I wasn't

welcome, wherever they were going. I opened my mouth to say I wanted to be with Rowan, but Macgregor beat me to it.

"You've done enough, Ms. Rivera." He gestured toward Rowan's jagged scar. "He needs special care right now."

Heart shrinking with the harshness of his words, I stopped and watched them leave. When they were gone, I stood alone with Trey's urn in my arms, feeling as if the weight of the world might crash down on me at any moment.

CHAPTER THIRTY

SPRING SEMESTER
EARLY MARCH

AFTER THE ATTACK, the Enlightenment Fountain was left a charred mess.

I saw it the morning after the explosion. The lion had lost its head. The turtle was scattered in pieces across the blackened lawn. The other three statues managed to remain in one piece, though they were cracked and stained with soot.

There had been no happy gurgling of water, no little rainbows sparkling in the sunlight. The water was gone, evaporated in the inferno, and the bottom of the fountain was filled with nothing but broken pieces of marble and ash.

But by the time classes resumed, no one could have suspected what happened. Dean McIntosh had come back from wherever she'd gone and, together with Macgregor, magically restored the fountain and the lawn to its previous grandeur.

I'd watched them from a distance, sitting on the steps that led to the library, while the cuffs vibrated lightly against my skin as if happy the portal's facade was being set to rights.

As I'd observed their progress, my mind whirled. I knew where the Academy's portal was. Few people possessed that information. Should I be worried I'd joined their ranks? Would this new knowledge be my undoing?

During my two remaining days of spring break, I hadn't sunbathed again and my thrift store novel completely lost its charm. I could do little else but think of the portal, the cuffs, and, most importantly, Rowan. I hadn't seen him since Macgregor had levitated him out of the dorm, and no one had bothered to let me know how he was doing.

Finally, the afternoon before the recommencement of class, I lost it and marched into Macgregor's office, determined to find out what I could.

After I burst through the door, the all-mighty Dean of Admissions glanced up from his paperwork and fixed me with his cold, blue stare.

"Let this be the last time you barge into my office, Ms. Rivera," he said.

For once, I held his gaze. "Where is Rowan?" I demanded.

He set his pen down and assessed me for a long moment. Finally, he said, "You really care about him, don't you?"

No shit, Sherlock.

I almost mocked him out loud, but I managed to bite my tongue. I wanted to see Rowan, and antagonizing his father wouldn't accomplish that.

He rose, wearily pushing away from the desk, and came around. As he stood in front of me, I could see the huge circles under his eyes, the rumpled state of his shirt under the black jacket, and the way the graying hair at his temples stood on end as if he'd been running his fingers through it over and over.

"Follow me," he said and walked out of the office.

I stood frozen for a moment, before whirling around and

rushing after him. He led me toward the infirmary. I frowned. I'd already gone there, the only logical place for a sick person on campus, but the place had been empty. I'd concluded that Macgregor had taken him elsewhere, home most likely. Apparently, I'd been wrong.

As we entered the empty infirmary, I glanced around the vacant beds, wondering if Macgregor was playing a mean joke on me. I was about to ask him just that when he whirled his hands toward the ceiling and a large, circular section dislodged from it.

Gaping, I watched a cylindrical structure detach from the ceiling and silently descend toward the floor. Soon, there was a spiral staircase in the center of the room. When Macgregor climbed the first step, I realized it was an old flight of stairs made of stone and wood with an intricately carved handrail.

Halfway to the top, Macgregor peered down, giving me a raised eyebrow. I snapped out of it and climbed after him, wondering how many more such secrets the Academy hid in its many corners.

Holding my breath, I took the last step and emerged in a room as big as the one below, except much different. Here, the walls weren't sterile white, but made of polished wood. Instead of harsh fluorescent fixtures overhead, there were metal lamps that hung from the ceiling, bathing the space with a warm, gentle light. Where the room below had windows, this one was closed in, its far stone wall fronted by a massive, wall-to-wall set of shelves and worktable.

A myriad of jars, canisters, candles, tinctures, amulets, and mortars and pestles occupied the shelves. Thick tomes rested on the worktable and on the floor. They were stacked waist-high, many cracked open, their yellowed pages brimming with words and illustrations from another time and place.

Of course, there was a second infirmary. Not one for feverish or dehydrated students, but for terminally cursed ones.

My eyes wavered with tears as I finally allowed them to drift toward the farthest bed in the room. A canopy of thick fabric hung over it, glowing from within.

Macgregor approached the bed and gently pushed the canopy aside.

The tears that had pooled in my eyes spilled at the sight of Rowan's paralyzed, floating shape. He was hovering a few inches off the bed, wearing only a pair of white, linen pants. His skin glowed as if it were bioluminescent, making the dark veins that trellised his skin stand out even more. The scar on his chest was almost gone, and only a faint mark remained.

"What... ? Is he... ?" I didn't know what to ask—not that my constricted throat would allow me to form the right words.

"I'm forcing him to rest, buying him a bit more time," Macgregor said as he regarded his son, fists tight at his sides, impotence painted clearly on his features. "He's a hardheaded, proud boy. He should have told me about this earlier. If he had, he wouldn't be in this shape. We would have had more time to find a cure."

Even as he said the word *cure*, I felt his hopelessness, as if he believed it was already too late for that.

"There has to be something that can help him," I said. "Maybe... the portal. It's all-powerful, isn't it?"

Macgregor regarded me with narrowed eyes. I tried to look innocent, like a person who didn't know she was wearing the key to one of the most powerful magical portals in the world. I must have done a good job because he glanced away, sighing and shaking his head.

"Nothing is *all powerful*, Ms. Rivera," he said. "This curse is incurable."

I shook my head. That couldn't be true. Rowan thought there was a way to cure it, didn't he? But what if he believed that only out of desperation? What if he was truly condemned?

"I can keep him this way for another couple of days," he said, closing the canopy again. "You will see him again, Ms. Rivera, if only to tell him goodbye."

Macgregor turned sharply away from the bed and headed toward the staircase.

My heart took a tumble. Tell him goodbye?

No. No. No. Rowan couldn't die. He couldn't. Losing Trey was all I could bear. I wouldn't let anything happen to Rowan. I would find a way, even if his own father had given up on him.

"Please," Macgregor said from the top of the stairs, "Let's let him rest."

After my short visit, I went straight to my room and lay on my bed, fighting the urge to cry. Even though I hadn't bothered to clean up, the furniture was back in its place as if nothing had happened. Someone had taken care to hide the mess from the returning students.

So many lies. So many secrets. Why was it so hard for people to trust?

Classes picked back up the next day, and campus filled with the hustle and bustle of excited students who couldn't help but recount their spring break adventures ad nauseam.

To my dismay, Disha was full of the same exasperating excitement, and, despite my best efforts, I resented her for it. She had gotten back to school sometime during the night and had found me in the cafeteria this morning.

As soon as she sat, she began rambling about Cancun, and all I'd heard for the last thirty minutes was Kenny this and Kenny that—just like it had been with Henderson. She hadn't taken one breath to ask about Rowan, and not even the blank stares I threw her way seemed to faze her.

She stopped her story, about an overzealous dolphin that had tried to steal her bikini bottom, to take a sip of coffee, and finally seemed to notice my irritation.

"Um... so how was *your* break?" She smiled sheepishly.

I rolled my eyes, rose, and picked up my tray.

Disha followed. "That bad, huh?"

God, she had no idea. How could anyone be so self-centered?

I practically threw the tray on top of the conveyor belt as Disha did her best to keep up.

"What am I missing here, Charlie?" She caught up with me outside the cafeteria as I made my way to our Spells 201 class.

"Nothing," I snapped back, "just that Rowan is dying."

I hurried along, leaving her behind. Apparently, I stunned her enough to freeze her on the spot. Minutes later, she slid into the seat next to mine. I ignored her and stared at the cave ceiling, remembering the day I'd levitated myself into the light fixture. Rowan's curse had been torturing him that day. If I'd only known then...

"Charlie——" Disha started.

"Henderson is here," I said, pointing toward the lectern and opening my notebook.

I knew I was being unfair, but I couldn't help all the emotions warring inside my chest. Disha just happened to be the only one on whom I could take out my frustration. I'd make it up to her later.

"Welcome back, class," Dr. Henderson said, a cheery smile on his lips. He had the looks of someone who had also enjoyed the break. "We will start with a new topic today. Teleportation. We'll talk about this extremely hard skill and how, for some, portals will be the only way to ever travel instantly from one spot to another."

My ears perked up at the word *portal* and, of its own accord, my hand went up in the air.

Henderson blinked. "Yes, Ms. Rivera?"

"Um, is that all portals are good for?" I blurted out. "Don't they do other things?" It was a stupid question. Everyone knew they did other things, but I just wanted to get him talking about the topic to see what I could learn.

Henderson laughed. "They certainly do. None of us would be able to perform magic without portals. As a matter of fact, there would be no supernaturals without them. They are called portals not only because they are doors that allow travel to other places, but because they are doors to power itself. Though, no one really understands everything about them, or what may be accomplished by someone strong enough to channel their energy. Some actually think portals hold all the secrets to the universe, all we need to know about the world we live in, why we're here, why we die. Many supernaturals have sought them in pursuit of eternal life, a healing spell, wisdom, you name it. Does that answer your question, Ms. Rivera?"

A healing spell.

My mind raced with the possibilities.

A healing spell!

The words tolled inside my head like giant bells. "Yes, Dr. Henderson. That answers my question. Thank you."

CHAPTER THIRTY-ONE

SPRING SEMESTER
MID MARCH

THE OLD DIGITAL alarm clock buzzed gently from my nightstand, but I didn't need it. I had lain awake in bed for hours, watching the numbers tick towards two AM. Campus was always bustling with late-night hangout and study sessions, but I figured most of the staff would be asleep at this ungodly hour.

A good cloaking spell and lots of luck would hopefully see me through to what I was about to do.

Thoughts multiplied like horny rabbits in my head as I pulled on my boots. Could I get expelled for this? Most certainly. Would it even work? I had no idea. Should I get Disha involved? No, not if expulsion and possibly death were on the docket.

Was it worth it?

Yes. Yes, it was.

Dressed in all black, I did the cloaking spell without giving it much thought. My bracelets hummed in quiet anticipation as if they knew we were about to do something big. Maybe they'd gotten a clue from my sudden intense reading on everything I could find related to portals. Maybe they had tapped into my emotions somehow. Either way, I needed them tonight. This would be the ultimate test of their power.

Slipping out of my room and the dorm was easy. A few night owls were in the common room studying, but they didn't even glance up as I walked by. Outside, the campus grounds were equally deserted. Exams were a few weeks away so people were either studying or getting much needed rest after break.

A three-quarters moon hung overhead as I cut across the manicured lawns. The night was warm and still, a sign that sweltering days were about to descend on campus once again. That meant the end of the semester, and I still had no idea what would happen to me, but that no longer mattered. I could make it out there if I got expelled. Rowan wouldn't make it a week if I didn't do something *drastic,* just like he'd said.

As I approached, the infirmary stood tall and proud in the moonlight. I surveyed the windows, seeing no movement. No patients. People were too tired from their week spent partying to try out love potions or body enhancement spells. As far as I could tell, Rowan was Nurse Taishi's only patient and he was in a magical coma, so hopefully, that meant he was getting minimal attention right now. I'd practiced a knock-out spell I'd learned in a Defensive Studies book, but I really didn't want to use it. Nurse Taishi was cool and attacking teachers did not seem like a great idea. One I certainly wanted to avoid.

I crept up the first set of stairs to the main infirmary, praying I wouldn't run into anyone. All the beds on either side were empty, but, as I walked closer to the hidden staircase Macgregor had shown me, I heard voices, one male and one female, coming from down the hall.

Shitballs.

I debated about what to do so they didn't catch me opening

the staircase. I could try to cast a cloaking spell on it, too, but I had never attempted one on anything but myself.

Tip-toeing toward the voices, I realized they were coming from Nurse Taishi's office. The male voice definitely belonged to him, but the female voice sounded very familiar.

Scooting along the outside wall, I slid myself over until I could peer in one of the office windows.

Nurse Taishi was doctoring something on a young female ankle. At first, all I could see was smooth, brown skin on someone's shapely foot until the owner flipped her hair back and exposed her face.

Disha!

"Thank you so much for seeing me right away," she said more anxious than I'd normally heard her. "I was worried these bumps would spread into something unfortunate." Long eyelashes fluttered as she watched Taishi apply a cream to the skin above her ankle.

Was she attempting to seduce another teacher? No, she seemed honestly concerned about some rash that would mar her perfect skin. To Taishi's credit, he seemed to be keeping it very professional, despite the smooth, young female leg in front of him. And Disha's legs were legendary.

Then I realized that, without knowing it, Disha was giving me the exact distraction I needed. I hurried back to the hidden stairwell and opened it just as Macgregor had.

Luckily, it descended silently just as before. Once the last step was in place, I practically flew to the top step, then ran straight to Rowan.

He still hovered above the bed in his magical coma, looking just as terminally ill. My heart wrenched, but I focused my thoughts. Gathering my power, I disintegrated the spell that held him in place. I didn't know exactly how I did it, but the cuffs certainly did. His body floated down to the bed, and I hurriedly applied the levitation spell and cloaking spell around his body.

"Hang on, Rowan," I said brushing hair tenderly off his forehead.

Then, with him in tow, I booked it to the stairwell.

Needless to say, getting a floating person down a spiral staircase was up there with the things I'd like to never do again.

I was down the bottom step and navigating Rowan around the last turn when footsteps approached from the back office.

"What's this?!" Taishi's voice said behind me as he saw the staircase open.

I was trying to run, pulling Rowan with me, when I felt the blast of magic from behind. My cloaking spell disintegrated like wet paper.

When I glanced around, Disha and Nurse Taishi were staring at me in disbelief.

"Charlie?" Disha asked. "What are you doing here?"

"I could ask you both the same thing," I said, stuttering, stalling. Rowan hovered beside me.

Taishi stepped forward, hands out. I could feel him readying his magic.

"Look, Charlie, I know you care about Rowan, which is exactly why he needs to stay here. Whatever you think you can do for him, it cannot possibly be better than what his father has set up for him upstairs. Macgregor has consulted the best minds in magical medicine. Please, let's not do anything we'll regret."

I stared at Nurse Taishi, letting his words fall over me. Macgregor might have tried most things, but he was also a proud man, and someone who worried about what others thought of him. He wouldn't risk his reputation by damaging the school's magic portal to save his son.

But, luckily, my reputation was trash and I definitely would risk it.

"I'm leaving here with Rowan," I said as forcefully as I could muster. "It's better for everyone if you don't try to stop me. Once we're gone, you can do whatever you need to do."

My heart pounded in my ears as I drew magic from my bracelets, letting Taishi know I meant every word.

He retained his defensive posture, too. "I can't just let you walk out of here with my patient." His eyes were steady, his hands fisted.

We faced each other, magic gathering like storm clouds between us.

Suddenly, Disha jumped on top of Taishi, dragging him back. As they flailed, she yelled, "Go, Charlie!"

God love her. I grabbed Rowan and ran.

Sprinting out of the infirmary, I tore towards the fountain with Rowan in tow. Luckily, the portal was close because I was sure Taishi was sounding the alarm. With little time, I jumped into the water and pulled Rowan in with me. He hovered above the surface, body motionless. In the moonlight, his curse-ravaged body seemed like a hollow shell, as if his soul had already departed.

"This has to work," I murmured to myself and to my cuffs. Slowly, I lowered them into the water. Cool liquid closed over my hands and arms as I waited for... something.

Nothing happened.

Shouts cut through the night behind me. Lights flared on in windows in the surrounding buildings. Taishi had woken up the whole school, it seemed, and the fountain was doing *nothing!*

"Come on," I shouted, splashing my cuffs in the water. I lowered Rowan until his body touched the surface. I placed my hands on his chest and murmured the few healing spells I'd memorized, but my magic seemed useless.

This was worse than failure. This was *me* putting Rowan in jeopardy for no reason.

"Work, dammit!" I punched the water, tears springing to my eyes. "Do as I command!"

At the last word, a pulse of magic shook everything. The fountain trembled. The water sloshed like someone had just done a giant cannonball. Magic flooded in, hitting me in the chest and nearly taking me under. I stumbled, reaching for Rowan who still hovered over it all, a little wetter, but still okay.

Suddenly, water shot up around us. Walls of it blasted to the sky, going up as high as the eye could see, ringing us in. A water barrier surrounded us... like a cage.

This wasn't my magic. It felt nothing like it. My cuffs pulsed a warning, letting me know it wasn't them either.

A laugh from above cut through the rush of water crackling with awful glee. "I just love teenage girls. So impressionable."

Fear radiating through me, I turned toward the voice.

There, standing on top of the fountain's ring of animals, stood Professor Answorth.

CHAPTER THIRTY-TWO

SPRING SEMESTER
MID MARCH

My eyes darted from the foaming wall of water to Rowan's body to Answorth's awful smile. His fangs seemed impossibly long in the dim light.

What had I done?

I tried to draw my power from the bracelets, but they sputtered and died as if something was draining their energy.

"Don't bother," he said, jumping down from the statues and splashing water in all directions. "I've mastered the art of blocking other's magic. It's amazing the spells they have these days." He smirked, licking one fang.

My body coiling with fear and anticipation, I positioned myself in front of Rowan protectively. "I don't know what you think you're doing. The entire campus knows we're in here. They'll be here in seconds."

"They're already here, though they're having a hell of a time with my water spell. I tried fire last time. I figured water was the next logical step. Now... for those cuffs."

He reached for me, but I lurched back and splashed water in his eyes at the same time. Grabbing Rowan, I dragged him away, running around the fountain, though I knew there was nowhere to go. Still, I had to hope that if I bought the staff some time, they would break through and rescue us.

Someone would come. They had to.

But as I tore around to the back of the fountain, a figure loomed in front of me.

It was Professor Answorth, only... he was wearing different clothing and he appeared as if he'd been ravaged by some disease in the seconds since I'd last saw him.

Shocked, I sloshed to a stop, staring at his awful transformation.

Then another Answorth jogged up behind me. What the hell?! *Two* Answorths? I felt as though my brain was melting.

"So you woke up?" the fresher-looking Answorth said to his twin. "I wondered how thin I could spread my magic, and I thought this might happen. That's why I kept you near, so you would come here to take the blame for me." He laughed.

The feeble Answorth stumbled forth, waving at me. "Get behind me, child. Rowan, too."

I froze, unsure what to do. One Answorth offered to protect us and the other wanted to attack us. Turning my gaze to the latter, I ran through it all in my mind. He had to have used so many advanced spells to set this all up. Spells only one man, a magical prodigy, would be powerful enough to accomplish.

"Henderson," I said accusingly.

He waved his hand in front of his face, and Professor Henderson stood before me in Answorth's clothing. It *was* him. It had always been him, disguising himself as Answorth, taking advantage of the vampire's need for magical objects.

"Clever," he said. "Though, it won't matter now. I know how

to get those cuffs off your wrists, Charlie. My apologies if the spell won't bode well for you. After that, my power will strengthen, and I'll be able to spread my magic far and wide."

"You'll never get away with it," Answorth slurred, his speech as weak as his body.

"Answorth, old chap, you served me well. When you confided in me about your... affliction, I knew you would make the perfect scapegoat. No one likes a vampire." He laughed once more, amused with his own cleverness.

"Charlie?" a hoarse voice said.

I blinked and glanced down at Rowan. He was trying to sit up, his gaze darting all around. He shook his head, waking up to a nightmare rather than a nice, warm bed, and it was all my fault.

"Professor Henderson?" Rowan said as I helped him to his feet. "What is happening?"

"Oh, Rowan. I'm sorry you got messed up in all of this, but since you've seen me..." he clucked his tongue and shrugged in mock regret. "It'll be a mercy, really. That curse you've stumbled into... I wouldn't wish it on my worst enemy."

"You..." I said as more pieces of the convoluted puzzle randomly fell into place inside my head, "you killed Georgia."

He didn't deny it, his expression portraying annoyance instead of guilt. "You need to break a few eggs to make an omelet and college girls are *so* breakable."

"But Disha?" I sputtered.

Henderson's mouth curled up. "Disha was my first prospect to steal the cuffs, but her will is strong. Instead, she proved to be a nice distraction from my lofty goals."

Disha would be crushed if she knew, but then, none of us might make it out alive to tell her.

"Enough talk!" he yelled, extending his hands. "This ends now."

I felt the magic gathering as Henderson turned toward me. Whirling his hands and grunting with the effort, he formed a spell and heaved it forward. A bright ball of energy zoomed in my direction.

I held up my hands, invoking my power, but it was still blocked.

A shape dove across my line of vision, catching the spell in the chest and falling into the water. Horror stealing over me, I watched Rowan's lifeless form sink to the bottom of the fountain.

"No!" I screamed.

I dove in for him just as Answorth charged towards Henderson.

"Rowan!" I exclaimed, slipping my hands under his arms and tugging him back to the surface.

As Answorth and Henderson wrestled, throwing water everywhere, I leaned over Rowan in a panic. His breathing was shallow and his pulse weak. If we didn't get help now, he'd die. I had to stop Henderson and get him to take down the water wall so that Rowan could be healed.

Fear and anger throbbing through my body, I laid Rowan safely on the raised platform in the fountain's center and turned toward the fight. Answorth was weakening. Henderson had him pinned and was attempting to push him under the water.

I wondered, fleetingly, why Henderson didn't just zap him with a spell, but then I remembered what he'd said about his magic growing thin. It must've taken all his power to keep the wall of water up and block everyone's magic. That spell he'd thrown at me was what was left in his arsenal.

So it was down to a physical fight. I could deal with that.

I remembered the time Trey and I took on two thugs in a back alley as they tried to steal our shoes. I remembered all those days fighting just to stay alive.

Answorth's head plunged under the water, and Henderson growled with deep satisfaction. His face, which I had once thought of as handsome, twisted in ugly triumph.

I hated him.

Without thinking, I ran over and punched him in the head as hard as I could.

Stunned, Henderson lurched back and splashed into the water.

I shook my hand, wincing at the pain and feeling triumphant. I had knocked him out with one punch.

Then he gripped the fountain's outer wall and began to drag himself up. No, it wouldn't be that easy.

Answorth jumped up, sputtering.

I pointed toward the fountain's center. "Help Rowan!"

Then I went after Henderson again.

He reared up, blowing water out of his mouth and glaring at me.

I held up my fists in a boxer's stance. Sure, Henderson had eighty pounds on me, but I could hold him off while Answorth tended to Rowan.

"Come on!" I shouted.

He hit me like a freight train. One blow crashed into my head and then another jabbed at my stomach, cutting off my air. He shoved me hard, and I tumbled into the water.

My air gone and my head spinning, I thrashed in the foamy waves, trying to get up, but Henderson pushed me down. Strong hands held my shoulders as I fought. My lungs screamed for air. I clawed at his arms, but he was unwavering. His face hovered over me, a faint outline in the churning liquid as he watched me die.

Limbs growing weaker, I fought for life, but it was ebbing. The world grayed. I went limp. The need to breathe was all consuming.

A bright light appeared. The light at the end of the tunnel. I was dying. I hoped Trey would be there to meet me.

But the light grew brighter. It wasn't a tunnel. It was coming from my wrists.

My bracelets. My power was back.

I used my last bit of consciousness to use a spell to propel Henderson away.

Go!

His hands flew from my body as his shape disappeared.

I was free. I lurched up, spitting water and gasping in sweet, sweet air.

Staring around in wonder, I took everything in.

Henderson was gone. It seemed that I had propelled him far, far away. His wall of water splashed to the ground, soaking the crowd of people who had gathered around the fountain. My eyes skipped past the faces of my classmates and teachers, all soaking wet and staring like they had no idea what they'd just witnessed.

They stared at me and the glowing aura that burst from my bracelets and lit up the night like a lighthouse. The water around me glowed, pulsing and trembling in time with my cuffs.

My magic was back in full force. The ring of wet teachers around the fountain probably had something to do with that, but the fight wasn't over.

Rowan.

Maybe my healing spell would work now.

Turning in the direction where I'd left him, I found Answorth folded over Rowan's lifeless body. At first, I thought Answorth was doctoring his wounds, but then I realized, to my horror, that Answorth's mouth was latched around Rowan's neck.

"No!" I screamed lurching forward, but suddenly I had no power over my legs. When I glanced down, I couldn't see them below the water's surface. It was as if my legs were... disintegrating.

Within seconds, the effect traveled up the rest of my body, each inch of me disappearing into golden shimmery dust. I stared at my hand as it blew away, and then I felt nothing at all.

CHAPTER THIRTY-THREE

SPRING SEMESTER
MID MARCH

PANICKED, I patted my legs, my arms, my face. They were all there. I hadn't really disintegrated. Oh, thank god!

But my eyes weren't working.

They were in their sockets, all right, but I couldn't see.

Hugging myself, I took a step back and ran into something hard. I startled, leapt away, just to confirm a moment later—fingers touching the thing gingerly—that the surface behind me was a damp wall.

A dank smell filled my nostrils, reminding me of the abandoned building Trey and I had shared.

Where the hell am I?

I feared I'd died and gone to hell, but the devil wouldn't let me keep the cuffs in his domain, would he? I could feel their still-warm grip on my wrists, but I was afraid to use them to make a light, afraid to see where I was.

My breath came out in broken wisps. A chill crawled up my arms, raising goose bumps. I could see nothing past a couple of yards, but I had the distinct feeling the space I was in was small.

Slowly, as my eyes adjusted, my surroundings began to take shape. I could see little more than shadows, but it was better than nothing. Something big and rectangular sat in front of me. Above, about ten feet up, a round window, no bigger than a dinner plate, provided the glimpse of a black-blue sky and a tree branch, cutting through.

Just as I started to get the courage to use my bracelets to light my surroundings, I became aware of a slight throbbing all around me. I felt it through the soles of my wet tennis shoes first, then in the air. I laid a hand on the wall and felt it there, too. I realized the slight pulse had been there all along. I'd just been too scared to notice it.

The soft pulsing picked up to a steady beat, making me feel like I was inside a giant heart. I stared out of the small window. The tree branch seemed to move farther away, then nearer as the walls beat their still-increasing rhythm.

Shit!

At this rate the room was going to blow with me in it. I had to do something, figure out how to get out.

I gathered a bit of magic and released it in a trickle, afraid to use more than that. The cuffs began to glow like a flashlight with low batteries. I raised my hands and slowly turned in a circle. In small strokes, the room took shape inside my mind.

A large stone structure stood right in the middle of the room, its sides carved intricately with interlaced fleurs-de-lis and winged cherubs. The walls on two sides were checkered with marble slabs —some with names and dates carved in them, others empty. To the back, two stone statues—robed figures with heads bowed and hands pressed together in prayer—occupied each corner. To the front, a metal door. And, like garlands, thick spider webs lined every corner.

My blood ran cold. I was in a mausoleum. But not just any mausoleum, one that was throbbing and seemed about to blow up.

But where? How?!

My thoughts ran in different directions, looking for an explanation. The answer quickly came to me, though it didn't make my situation any easier to digest.

I had teleported.

Rowan had said the fountain connected the academy to a network of portals all over the world. I could be anywhere.

Hoping to gain some information that might hint at my whereabouts, I lifted a hand to one of the stacked graves to my left and read the nameplate.

Mellette LeRoux
Je T'aime Toujours
4 Février 1826 - 19 Mars 1871

OH, my god. I was in France.

The room throbbed again, but I ignored it and kept reading, shining the light on the other graves. The dates went up, moving from the nineteenth century to the twentieth century. They were all in French at first, but they gradually changed to English, making me wonder if I was truly in France or somewhere else.

Larry "Butch" LeRoux
Beloved Son
March 23 1979 - August 7 2002

WHERE THE HELL WAS THIS?

The walls throbbed once more. This time, the door groaned, arching inward, then outward.

Double Shit!

I ran to the back of the mausoleum, hid behind one of the robed statues, and doused my light.

The room gave another huge inhale and exhale. Metal moaned, twisting, grating, until it broke with a deafening crash, the sound of collapsing stone following close behind.

The room trembled. The statue in front of me teetered for a moment, then settled back down. My heart pounded against my chest so hard I thought it might pop through my ribs and skitter across the stone floor. I pressed deeper into the shadows, panic clawing its way up my throat.

Silence followed. Then steps. Someone, or several someones, had entered the mausoleum. I listened intently, holding my breath.

"Well, where the fuck is he?" a contralto female voice asked. So they spoke English here, though with a different accent than what I was used to.

More silence and, a moment later, a frustrated sigh.

"He better hurry up," the same voice said.

"What if... he failed?" a nasally, vibrating voice that I would never forget asked.

Anger descended over me like a falling curtain in a tragic play. That voice. It had to be.

"If he failed, I will kill him," the woman said.

Teeth clenched and fighting to contain my magic as it threatened to burst to the surface, I peeked around the statue to confirm with my eyes what my ears had told me.

Standing shoulder-to-shoulder in front of the stone coffin, waiting impatiently for someone to appear the same way that I had, stood two people: a tall woman with flowing hair and long legs clad in leather, and a man with three missing fingers, his face indistinct, not only because of the poor light, but because he was *vibrating*.

I was right. It was Trey's murderer. Smudge Face.

I wouldn't miss this chance.

Cuffs blazing, I stepped out of my hiding place.

Smudge Face and the woman took a step back, hands lifting to their brows to protect their eyes from the intense light.

"We were starting to think you'd screwed things up again," the woman said with contemptuous mockery.

I pushed a hand in her direction and sent her flying out of the broken door. She probably deserved worse than that given the company she kept, but my beef was with Smudge Face.

"What the hell, Thad?" Smudge Face asked.

"I'm not Thad. My name is Charlie," I said. "Did you even know that? Did you even care?"

I lowered my hands a fraction, dimming the brilliant light so Smudge Face could see me before I took my revenge.

"You?" he said, his face twisting with fearful surprise.

"Yes, me. You killed my friend, and now you will pay for it." I aimed my hands at his chest and released the energy I'd been holding back.

It smashed into him like a white laser, lifting him a few inches off the ground. Feet dangling, his body hung like a marionette's, limbs jerking, head lashing back and forth.

I was killing a man, zapping the life out of him, and I felt no regret.

Before I could finish Smudge Face, a blast of wind hit me. I slid back, my feet uselessly dragging across the floor as I went. I hit the wall with a bone-cracking impact. Air *whooshed* out of my lungs. I collapsed to the stone floor right after Smudge Face did.

The woman stepped back into the mausoleum, her long, dark hair in disarray, one of her hands pointed at me as it swirled with a glowing ball of what looked like wind and water.

She walked closer, heels clicking against stone, and loomed

over me. Her magic shone between us. Her dark eyes scrutinized my face as I scrutinized hers. She was Asian. Chinese, perhaps. Her long, black hair hung over her shoulders and reached past her breasts. She wore heavy makeup, red lipstick and smoky eye shadow. She was as beautiful as any supermodel I'd ever seen on TV or magazines.

"Who the hell are you?" she demanded. "And where is Thadeus?

"Thadeus is dead," I said. "I killed him."

I had no idea what I'd done to Henderson, but watching the way the woman's face crumpled at the news made me wish he was truly dead. If she was with Smudge Face and Henderson, I was sure she deserved all the pain I could dish out.

"Then you won't live to tell another soul," she said, casting her ball of magic right at my face.

I had no time to think of how to defend myself, and I probably would have died, twisting in agony, if not for Aradia's Cuffs. They came to life as soon as the threat materialized and, just as I'd done at the fountain moments ago, I dissolved into nothingness.

———

I STUMBLED FORWARD, sloshing water up my arms as I tried to orient myself. I'd just been in the mausoleum being attacked by Smudge Face and that woman. Now I was hip deep in ice cold water. The sounds of screaming flooded my ears and bright lights dazzled my eyes. Shading them, I tried to get my bearings.

The fountain's statues reared up in front of me, the stone turtle's face staring down as if in disapproval that I'd messed up, leaving Rowan just when he'd needed me most. But I had no control. My bracelets had teleported me away, just as they'd brought me here in time to save me from that witch's spell. Had they done that on purpose? Taken me there to show me Trey's murderer?

I was back, but much had changed. Glowing balls hovered like stadium lights in the night sky, creating strange shadows. Outside the fountain, on the lawn, people were everywhere—running, casting spells, and holding off crowds of students who wore pajamas and gawked at the spectacle.

Stunned and probably in shock, my first clear thought was Rowan. I'd last seen him being attacked by Answorth, which made no sense since he'd been the one to help us with Henderson.

Panic replacing confusion, I lurched through the water.

"Rowan. Rowan!"

Halfway around the fountain, I spotted a commotion that had drawn quite a crowd. People were wrestling with each other and shouting. Was that Macgregor and Dean McIntosh? Henderson must still be alive. Jumping out, I ran over, readying my cuffs.

Nurse Taishi held Macgregor Underwood's arms as he fought like a madman. His normally aloof demeanor had transformed into absolute fury as he tried to free himself from Taishi's grasp.

"I'll kill you, you vile monster! How could you?" He foamed, lashing back and forth as he tried to get his hands on Professor Answorth.

Answorth stood behind Dean McIntosh who was casting a protective spell between them and shouting back at Macgregor. "Now, let's all just calm down. We need clear heads to think this all through. Macgregor, stop."

Answorth looked as though he might pass out at any second. "I'm so sorry. He asked me to. He was dying," he muttered, wringing his hands and glancing down. My eyes followed his gaze and spotted a body on the ground.

Rowan!

I ran around Dean McIntosh's protective shield and slid to my knees beside Rowan's still form. Placing my hand on his chest, a jolt of fear rushed through me. He was ice cold.

Tears in my eyes, I pulled him onto my lap, trying to access my magic through my terror. But as I scanned his body for wounds, I realized his pale skin was blemish free. The cursed blue veins were completely gone.

Then I spotted the bite marks on his throat, still dribbling blood.

Answorth leaned down over us, looking pitiful and sunken. "He asked me to, Charlie. It was the only way to reverse the spell, and he knew it. If I hadn't, he would have died. Henderson hit him right in the chest with a suffocation spell."

"What did you do?" I asked, trembling with fear and rage.

Answorth clutched his hands together as he stared down at Rowan with pity in his bloodshot eyes.

"It's a curse of a different kind. To be shunned. Hated. Always having to hide. That's why I pretended to be fae, you know. They never would have accepted me. He'll have to leave the Academy, but at least he's not dead. You have to give me that. I saved his life. He would have died."

"What did you do?!" I screamed.

"I turned him, Charlie," Answorth said. "I turned him into a vampire."

TO BE CONTINUED IN BOOK TWO, SOPHOMORE
WITCH, COMING MAY 21st.
PREORDER IT NOW.

SNEAK PEEK OF SOPHOMORE WITCH

CHAPTER 1

FALL SEMESTER, EARLY SEPTEMBER

I HELD ROWAN'S COLD, lifeless body in my arms as the tears streamed down my face.

There had to be some magic that could reverse what had just happened. I couldn't believe he would now and forever be...

A vampire.

Cursed. Hated. Shunned.

Answorth hovered over me, wringing his hands as the chaos continued around us. People shrieked and called out. The fountain trickled in the background, the smell of its treated water stuck in my nose. Macgregor was still shouting at Dean McIntosh, while the magic lights burned in the night sky. Crowds of my stunned classmates looked on, horrified.

Standing hunched over and looking like he might faint at any second, Answorth's eyes darted from father to son. He spoke, more to himself than to me.

"It was the only way, I swear. He would've died."

Answorth appeared near dead himself, having only just escaped Henderson's control. What that sinister spell master put Answorth through, I could only guess. But then, Answorth was a vampire. No heart beat in his chest. Could he feel pain like the rest of us?

Was Rowan doomed to the same fate? His body was the same ice-cold temperature of the fountain water and his chest didn't rise and fall with struggling breaths. Was that normal for vampires? I didn't know anything.

God, this was all my fault. If I hadn't taken him out of the infirmary... If I'd just listened to Nurse Taishi... Henderson had tricked me, used me. What a fool I was. How could I live with myself if Rowan...

I cradled him in my arms as my wet hair dripped onto his life-less face.

"Rowan, please, please wake up," I said. "Please be okay."

As if he'd heard me, his eyelids fluttered. Chocolate-brown eyes focused on my face. Oh, God. He's awake! Relief soothed my aching heart flooded my body like a salve.

"Charlie," he said weakly. Then he winced, arching his back. "It burns!"

"What? What burns?"

My eyes scanned his body for wounds, but his skin appeared pristine. The dark blue veins, the visible markers of the unbreak-able curse he'd been afflicted with, were gone. The spot where Henderson's magic struck his chest—that deadly attack that had been intended for me, but had been blocked by Rowan as he acted like a human shield—was only a faded red splotch.

Still, Rowan writhed against me like his very blood was boil-ing. He gripped my arm, his eyes pleading. "Charlie, help... me."

Oh, God. What could I do? I urged my cuffs to help, but they wouldn't respond to my call for magic. I had nothing.

I grabbed Answorth's pant leg and shook it. "He's in pain. Do something!"

He stared down in pity. "There's nothing to be done, I'm afraid. The change is very painful. At least, he's not dead." He gave a half shrug that made me want to punch him in his pale face.

Rowan's mouth twisted up in a look of pure torment. It gutted me. I pushed damp hair off his head, feeling useless.

"Hang on, Rowan." I turned to Answorth. "How long does it last?"

"Only twenty-four to thirty-six hours."

"Thirty-six hours?!" Now I really was going to punch him.

Someone stormed over, blocking out the light spells that illuminated this whole mess. In an instant, Macgregor Underwood was there, waving his hands. In another, he and Rowan were gone.

I stared down at my empty lap in shock. "Where did he go?"

Dean McIntosh was the one to appear beside me and answer my question. She looked as exhausted as I felt.

"Macgregor took him, Charlie. They went home."

"But I... I..."

"I know you're concerned, but I assure you, Dean Underwood will take good care of his son. Now, please. We should get you looked at."

"But... no. I need to be there. I can help." I stood, trying to charge my cuffs, but nothing happened.

However, very powerful magic did ignite beside me. Dean McIntosh's hands glowed a shimmery purple as she stared me down with a no nonsense expression on her face.

"Now, I really must insist that you head with Nurse Taishi to the infirmary to be checked out. You've suffered greatly tonight and there's no telling what kind of damage has been done, both physically and mentally. I'll also be sending my sister to you as soon as she is located."

Another counseling session and an unwelcomed happy spell from Irmagard? No, this was not how it was going to go down. I opened my mouth to protest, but realized I had no idea what I was dealing with. Dean McIntosh's magic felt hella strong and my cuffs didn't seem to be pumping out the juice they normally did.

I lowered my hands, but didn't budge. "Where is Henderson?"

"You flung him halfway across campus. He hit a fence and is dead." Her face was still, but not emotionless. I could tell this information pained her, though I wasn't exactly sure why.

"Good," I said, venom in my voice. "He killed Georgia. He almost killed Rowan and me. He kept Answorth prisoner. And there's probably more."

Dean McIntosh nodded, her tired eyes dipping down in what seemed to be sadness. "It's a shame he made such horrible choices. He was a very talented young man."

Talented young man? She sounded like she was on his side.

"There's more," I said. "When I disappeared, the fountain took me somewhere. A mausoleum. Two people were waiting for Henderson. He's part of a bigger plot."

Dean McIntosh's brow wrinkled. "I suspected as much, but I'd like to hear every detail of what you saw when you are up to it. Now, if you'll proceed to the infirmary." She held out a firm arm as if she were no longer playing around and meant business. Even in her robe and slippers, she was formidable.

"Fine," I said, pouting like a little child. "But I want Disha to go with me." I had scanned the crowd for my friend and didn't see her.

"She's already there, waiting for you," Dean McIntosh replied. This woman thought of everything.

Fatigue settling in my bones, I gave the fountain, and the spot where Rowan had been, another glance before turning away.

***

The memory spell faded and I came to in my dorm room, yet I could still feel the raw emotion of it. Clutching my chest, I fell back on the bare mattress of my new dorm room in Sophomore Hall.

This room was a bit smaller than the last, the bed and dresser a bit more battered, but it wasn't a homeless shelter, so it was perfect for me. Plus, I still barely owned anything, despite Disha and the Dean's best efforts, so all my items fit perfectly in the tiny closet and small pine dresser.

Still, it was hard to be back on campus with all the memories flooding back. During my first few minutes in my room, I hadn't even taken the time to unpack and was already torturing myself with visions of my last day at the Academy.

The last time I saw Rowan Underwood.

That night, after Nurse Taishi checked me over and pronounced me good to go, Counselor McIntosh had arrived in striped pajamas and a matching nightcap, a quaint outfit straight out of a Charles Dickens movie. She'd fretted over me for a bit, then proceeded to dose me with one of her good-time spells where nothing mattered and all I could feel was joy. Just what I had feared.

While I was in that fantastic mood, she'd informed me that, right that minute, she was whisking me away to her beet farm in Idaho. That I would continue my studies with her and finish my semester that way. She assured meThat a little one-on-one tutoring would do me good.

And who was I to argue?

The rest had been a whirlwind of transportation spells and a old ramshackle farmhouse with crops as far as the eye could see. I spent all summer pulling weeds and asking when I'd be allowed to leave, but, surprise, surprise, they'd all decided it was unsafe to allow me and my magic cuffs to roam free.

They'd plotted it all out and trapped me in the middle of nowhere with a crazy lady whose idea of baths was rubbing patchouli oil around in her armpits.

And, also unsurprisingly, my cuffs didn't work. Something

about the beets, Irmagard had murmured before lathering herself with suntan oil, tucking her ferret under her chin and splaying herself across an old rattan lounge chair in the weedy yard. For my part, I suspected the entire farm had some powerful blocking spell on it, though I never found out the truth.

So, beets, dusty magic books, and Irmagard, who I'd gotten to know very well. In fact, I'd seen enough of her fluffy, gray armpit hair this summer to fill two lifetimes.

Yeah, not exactly the summer break I'd been picturing.

I had spoken to Disha a few times a week on Irmagard's ancient rotary phone. She'd kept me informed on the goings-on, letting me know that it was pretty clear to everyone that I was being punished for my part in the fountain incident. She'd gotten in a heap of trouble with her parents, too, when they'd been informed she'd "attacked a teacher." Luckily for everyone, Taishi hadn't been hurt.

Rowan, of course, had been.

No one knew where he was, not even Disha's well-connected father. No one had seen Rowan or Macgregor all summer. Disha's father had confirmed, however, that the school's bylaws forbid vampires from attending the Academy. Apparently, they'd done some terrible things in the 1900s and had been banned as a species forever, along with other Lessers, for good measure.

Answorth had been stripped of his professorship, even though it was proven he'd only stolen that one magical item the same day we'd found him in the forest. And he'd only attacked me out of sheer desperation since he'd not fed in sometime.

So, weeds, ferrets, and sporadic phone calls had been my summer. What a difference a year made. I'd gone from homeless kid to witch to prisoner to—

Knuckles pounded on wood, drawing me out of the swirling vortex that was my thoughts.

I strode across my barren room and opened the door.

Disha practically fell on me, twirled around, and slammed the door behind her.

"What the hell?" I asked.

"She's coming. Shh. Don't say a word." She gripped the door handle and pressed her ear to the crack.

"Well, hello to you, too," I said. "Who is 'she'? And why are we hiding?"

"Bridget and shh." She put a finger over her ruby-red lips.

"Who's Bridget?" I whispered, putting my ear to the door beside her.

Disha gave me a bug-eyed stare. "Bridget is my roommate."

"Your what?" I replied loudly.

Last year, Disha had occupied a single room, paid and royally furnished by dear old daddy who had big bucks. I couldn't imagine what had happened between then and now. Was campus that full that everyone was doubling up? Whoever ended up with me would have a rude awakening since my room was barely bigger than a broom closet.

"Disha, how did you end up with a roommate?"

A moment later, a fist pounded on the door, startling both of us.

"Deela? Is that you?" a shrill female voice called.

"Shit," Disha whispered, darting to my closet. "Tell her I'm not here."

"Deela?" I asked. "Does she not know your name?"

Disha waved a hand at me. "She's a transfer student. Now, shh." She ducked into my tiny the closet and pulled the curtain closed.

Lord, just what I needed, to deceive the new girl on the first day.

Carefully, I constructed my lie and a confused expression, then opened the door.

A flurry of curly, red hair and waving hands greeted me as a girl pushed past. "Are you Charlie? Boy, I've heard a lot about you. Where's Deela?"

I stared at her, taken aback. What exactly had she heard about me on her first day? Were rumors already that rampant? Students knew I'd killed Henderson, though the exact reason was left untold, which was probably why rumors had grown and spread like a fungus. Disha had heard rumors consisting of anything from my allegiance to a vampire coven, to a secret sex cult gone awry.

I fake smiled at the new girl. "Bridget, is it? Disha is not here, but she told me to tell you to head to the cafeteria without her. She's got a bad case of the green apple quick step, if you know what I mean."

Disha would kill me for telling Bridget that, but it was payback for making me the bad guy.

Bridget barraged me with questions as I gently guided her to the door. I managed to dodge all of them except the one about me being in league with the water nymphs, which I laughed at and denied.

Then I "helped" her out of my room.

"Thanks for coming. Nice to meet you. See you soon," I said, trying to shut the door, but I stopped short as my eyes traveled over her shoulder to the figure walking down the hallway. My heart stuttered in my chest as I took in those deep brown eyes.

Rowan was back.

ORDER NOW.

LUMINOUS: A DRAGON'S CREED SERIES

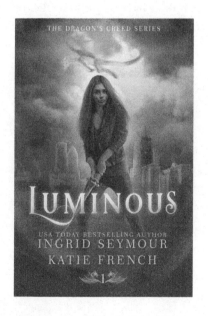

I used to see dragons.

That was before they killed my mother, and people stamped the "crazy" label on my forehead.

These days, I have no time for that. I just want to graduate and get out of Summers Lake.

But when a group of my classmates vanishes without a trace, I'm sucked back into a supernatural whirlwind. Desperate, I enlist my forever-crush and two of his friends who seem to know more than they let on, except they won't tell me anything.

They're sexy and infuriatingly charming, but that's not going to stop me from figuring out what happened.

Soon, I get the truth out of them, and it's not pretty. They're dragon shifters and have answers about my past, and my role in their hidden world. It turns out it's my duty to protect humans from evil dragons, whether I like it or not.

And when my classmates start turning up dead, the race against the clock is on. I have to find the killer or bare the guilt of my friends' death on my conscience for the rest of my life.

READ NOW.

ABOUT THE AUTHOR - KATIE FRENCH

Katie French is an author of Young Adult sci fi romance. Her book, The Breeders, has had over 100,000 downloads and counting and was a semi-finalist in the 2014 Kindle Book Awards. She also has a kids series starting with Portia Parrots and the Great Kitten Rescue for ages 5-9.

She works as a high school English teacher. In her free time, she writes manically, reads great books, and takes care of her three beautiful and crazy children. She aspires to spend as much time in yoga pants as possible.

You can join her mailing list at www.katiefrenchbooks.com and receive TWO FREE full-length novels.

Contact her at katie@katiefrenchbooks.com.

KATIE FRENCH

THE BREEDERS
BOOK ONE IN THE BREEDERS SERIES

THE BREEDERS SEVEN PART COMPLETE SERIES:

FIND THEM ALL HERE AT
WWW.KATIEFRENCHBOOKS.COM.

ABOUT THE AUTHOR - INGRID SEYMOUR

Ingrid Seymour is a USA Today Bestselling young adult author. When she's not writing books, she spends her time working as a software engineer, cooking exotic recipes, hanging out with her family and working out. She writes young adult in a variety of genres, including Sci-Fi, urban fantasy, romance, paranormal and horror.

Her favorite outings involve a trip to the library or bookstore where she immediately gravitates toward the YA section. She's an avid reader and fangirl of many amazing books. Potterhead, anyone? She is a dreamer and a fighter who believes perseverance and hard work can make dreams come true.

Visit her online and get a free book at:
http://www.ingriseymour.com

ALSO BY INGRID SEYMOUR

Djinn Empire

One Wish Away

Two Hearts Asunder

Three Words Promised

[The Discounted Box Set]

The Morphid Chronicles

Keeper

Ripper

The Jeweled Goddess

Godmaker

Made in the USA
Monee, IL
24 June 2020

34583712R00173